Hard Lessons Tri

CW00549570

This story was supposed to be a writing challenge on a Fetish web
The characters took on life of their own and became one of my favourite writings. I hope you enjoy these three stories.

I hope to return to their lives sometime in the future as I am sure there is a lot more to tell.

Hard Lessons
(Book one: The tuition of Rebecca)
By M Alex Wyllie

Foreword:

For Lady Penelope x

The inspiration for this story was a lovely lady and model who did a rather racy photoshoot where she played a rather provocative St Trinian's schoolgirl. In one photo she was sitting leg wide, flashing a pair of traditional white panties. This got me quite aroused and led to me writing a short story about a girl flirting (outrageously) with her teacher. Initially, it was only a few chapters, but the journey of Rebecca and Mr Wyles took on a life of its own. This is part of that story.

All characters are imaginary and of legal age. Any resemblance to real events or people is just a coincidence.

Hard Lessons
The tuition of Rebecca

Prologue: Rebecca's Crush.

Today, like pretty much every day, I am sitting at the back of the class, and as usual, I am bored! Bored, bored! bored… School is so bloody boring. Today is no different and as usual, I am checking my phone, finding far more interesting things to read about on my phone than this dry old book that sir is making us read. Sir is talking to the class as he is walking up the aisles. He is always pacing up and down. Seeing him coming my way, I quickly slip my phone away and pretend to be reading the book.

He stops at my desk, looking down at me. I don't look up, avoiding his eyes. He has this way of looking at you that makes you feel like he knows what you are thinking….

Sir is still standing next to me! I wonder what he wants but I don't look up, then he taps the book… I look at the book, this time I actually look at the book in my hand and notice it is upside down.

Flushed with embarrassment, I turn the book up the right way and he walks away, back down the aisle to speak with another student. My face is burning! That was so embarrassing, but I also feel something else, a strange tingling in the pit of my stomach.

It's odd, I feel weird that he made me feel that he was disappointed with me without saying a word, and now I'm feeling bad for disappointing him. Usually, I don't care about the class, the teachers or the coursework. Never really expected to do well in the exams, never have been that interested in school, or anything outside of gossip, fashion and TikTok.

1

My friend Nicole does not have to go to school anymore! She had a baby last year and now has her own place. I wonder if I should do the same. It has to be a better life than school or working in some lame shop. My mother did. She never finished school. She had me before she finished school! So why should I be any different, can't be that hard to get pregnant?

I have had sex a few times; it was disappointing though, with lots of grunting and prodding. They try but they don't know how to make me cum! I get more satisfaction from touching myself while in the bath. Boys just feel as if they poke away enough. They are good, and I should be happy they spent time with me! Boys...

As for being good company, honestly, I can't stand talking to them at all, so boring, all they want to talk about is cars, Call of Duty, and football, *Yawn*.

Watching Mr Wyles as he is walking away, I think to myself; I bet he does not talk about football all the time. I wonder what he is like out of school. Is he married? Does he have children?

He has a good butt! The thought just pops into my head while looking at him standing over another student. OMG, what!! What am I thinking? Staring at sir's bum!

Picking up my book, this time to read, but I realise I am looking up now and then to see if he is coming back towards me. Did I want him to come back! Do I like Mr Wyles? But he was old, like fifty or something. Ancient... There's that weird feeling again, a tingle in the pit of my stomach every time I think of him looking at me or coming over to speak to me.

Seeing him walking back towards my row, I put my book down and pick up my phone and pretend to be reading from it, but I am not... I am waiting for him to see me, notice that I am not working. OMG, I really do want him to tell me off!

"Miss Lawson!" sir says, his voice has this disappointed tone to it.

I look up; he is standing over me; he is very tall; a lot taller than me. His hand is out. I know what he wants; he wants the phone. I close the app and lock the phone, handing it over.

"Sorry, sir!" I say blushing, but that tingling grows in the pit of my stomach but now I feel it down between my legs! I do like him! I must be mad; he is like old enough to be my dad!!!

I pick up the book again and he walks back down the line of tables and I watch as he puts the phone on his desk; it is not the only one there. Some teachers don't care if you use your phone in class, but Mr Wyles always confiscates them, should he catch you looking at them, keeping them until the end of class.

Class ends, and I hang back, waiting until everyone has left the room before approaching Mr Wyles's desk. Standing waiting for him to notice me, while he marked papers and made me wait. Or maybe he has not even noticed me standing here. This makes me feel weird again, but not the tingle from earlier, something else. I don't like it whatever it is.

I shuffle my feet a bit; hoping he will hear me or notice the movement, notice me. Please notice me! I think to myself; why do I want him to notice me? It is weird, it's not just that I want my phone back, I want him to look at me and notice me, notice I exist!

"Ahh yes, Miss Lawson, your phone, of course."
Without looking up, he picks up the phone and holds it out.

Still, without looking at me, he says, "You really should apply yourself more, Miss Lawson." Then he finally looks up at me, but his eyes speak of disappointment (that feeling again, hollow,

queasy feeling in the pit of my stomach and my knees want to buckle).

"Final exams are not that far away, you know?"

"Yes, sir, I know, I'm sorry, sir."
I reply, taking my phone and heading out of the class (I wonder if he watches me leave; or if he noticed the extra wiggle, I put into my walk for him).

Later that day:

Arriving home. My mind is racing, so instead of watching some TV, I go straight to my room and throw myself onto my bed. As usual, mum is not in. She probably won't be back until after midnight.

Sprawled across my bed, hugging my bear, I am replaying the day again and again in my head, thinking about that lesson and my reaction to Mr Wyles telling me off! Wondering why I can't stop thinking about him.

Later, making myself a little to eat, as mum has left nothing out for me again! Cereal for dinner again, I suppose. Later that night, I run myself a bath. I love soaking in a hot bath. Often, while I have a soak, I like to play with myself a little; especially if mom is home. The bathroom is the only place I can be sure to get any privacy and with the door locked, I can explore myself without her walking in on me. She has been a nosy mare all her life, and even more so since I started getting attention from boys. (Like she can talk!)

Relaxing in the scorching water (I like it hot) steam rising from the bath like a thickly scented fog, I relaxed in the scorching water. Laying there, thinking about Mr Wyles, how he made me

feel earlier. There's that tingling feeling again, and this time I feel it between my legs. Feeling it in my special place.

Touching myself, fingers slowly circling, probing, and rubbing against my clit, the feeling became more intense, as I fantasised about Mr Wyles. Cumming two or three times during the bath, as I imagined Mr Wyles looming over me, watching me with disappointment in his eyes! I wanted to please him, so he never looks at me that way again.

Then I imagine myself sitting on his knee, my arms draped about his neck. He no longer looks disappointed. He calls me a good girl, as he kisses me, slowly sliding his thick cock into me. It hurts a little as he slid it in but hurt in a good way!

I feel happy that I am with Mr Wyles, happy that he thinks I'm his good girl. Looking up, I almost scream as I realised, we are in class, and I am naked! Everyone is watching, and sir is fucking me, as he continued to teach the class…

I woke; with a splash, I had dozed off in the bath! But OMG, I really do like Mr Wyles, but why would I imagine him fucking me in front of the class? Though being watched is a bit of a turn on, but that is going too far!

Later that night, I Google Mr Wyles; I get his first name (Alexander) from his school profile, then Google his name. Looking for FB (Facebook) IG (Instagram) and tumbler profiles. He has an IG account, but that seems to be private. (I wonder what he is hiding.)

His FB is open though, so I check him out on there. No relationships at all, no family or children listed. I check through his photos; he has lots of his doggos. Gosh, they are ever so cute. A few of him dressed up in suits, very nice he looks too, one of them is of him on the beach, he looks to be nude!!

(There's that feeling again.) He definitely has a good arse, though; he must work out.

He has only a handful of female friends listed, so I check them out. Most seem to be younger than him, the mid-30s mostly, so he likes them younger than him it seems. Good to know, I think to myself, a please smile on my face, as I consider that thought...

A lot of them have uploaded images of themselves at parties or weekends away. I start checking them out, their likes, groups and follows, searching through their posts.

While nosing through their profiles and follows, I notice quite a few seem to be into wearing rubber dresses and fetish clothing. Some of the outfits are very hot (I'm kind of jealous, I want one). There are also pictures of the girls bound up in rope! That's some Fifty Shades of Grey stuff.

I had watched Fifty Shades of Grey at Lucy's house and we both had played at being the girl, Anna, something. I recall also the video from Rhianna I had watched on YouTube, that had a lot of rubber and kinky stuff (S&M). Lucy and I had taken turns spanking each other's bottoms. That had been a laugh and I had felt a little turned on by it.

But then her mum come in and told us off, and insisted the movie was not appropriate for little girls. She could talk! As it was her video. I bet she did not mind being spanked by Lucy's dad! Ever since that night, Lucy's dad watches me closely when I'm there. I bet he wishes he had caught me being spanked, instead of by Lucy's mum.

Checking through their images, I spotted Mr Wyles was in a few of them. In one of the photos, he is holding the rope! Like he was the one that tied her up!! He has also commented on the

image, thanking her for a fun weekend and promising next time he will show her his dungeon, and give her a good spanking!

OMG Mr Wyles is a perv! He ties girls up and likes to spank them! Also, he has a dungeon! This reminds me again of the playroom in Fifty Shades of Grey, I wonder if that is what his dungeon looks like and imagine him showing me his secret room. This makes my belly flip, and the tingly feeling returns between my legs...

Lying in my bed as I played with myself again, imagining Mr Wyles as Christian Grey and me as the Anna girl. He is disappointed with me, telling me I displeased him, and he has to punish me. Imagining feeling the hot sting of his hand as he spanks my pantied covered bottom over a desk. Shivering as I climax again and again, while I am picturing him looming over me, his strong rough hands touching my special places.

Wondering how I can get Mr Wyles to notice me? Maybe get him to spank me! I can't seem to get the image or thought of his hand on my bottom, out of my head! But would he like to spank me? I have a nice bottom and I am younger and prettier than those women on his profile.

We can't date obviously since I am a student, but it has happened in the past. One girl I know at school claims she slept with the gym teacher. He left soon after; I think she had his baby, not sure though it might just be a rumour...

The boys are always bragging that they banged their teachers, especially Miss Rousseau, the art teacher; she is kind of hot; I have to admit... But don't believe them, or the teachers would be sacked. I don't want Mr Wyles to be sacked. I just want him to notice me.

The next day I put a lot of effort into my makeup, also deciding to wear a dark bra under my white school blouse. Black bras

show through the material of our shirts and are not supposed to be worn. Then, before entering Mr Wyles's class, I undo a button so he might see down my top when he walks past.

Every time he came up the aisle, I pushed out my chest, just a little, not too much. But I was certain that if he looked down at my desk, he would see down my top. Maybe see the bra and tell me off for breaking school rules, or maybe he will notice that I have nice breasts. Better than those girls in his profile have, I bet.

Maybe it is my imagination, but it seems like he is avoiding coming up this aisle as much today, though earlier he had stopped to check my book. I had asked him to explain a sentence to me. He must have seen my breasts then. He stood right over me, but he has not been back this way since. It's not working, he is not noticing me!

Again, I hang back until last and walk down the aisle slowly swinging my hips from side to side, but he is not looking, just working on the papers on his desk. I stomp out of the room, annoyed with him for not noticing me…

Feeling frustrated, why won't he notice me? Men always notice me; mum's boyfriends always do. Sometimes I tease them, lying on the floor in the front room, watching TV in my nighty. Knowing that they can see my bottom. I kind of like the feeling of being watched and giving them little teasing flashes turns me on a little. Mum is always telling me off for wandering about in my undies when they are there. Cock tease, she calls me. I bet they have fucked her thinking about me more than once, though.

That's it, I realise; if I let sir see my panties, he will notice me. He is a man, after all. Maybe if he sees me in a sexual way, he will want me the same as the boys all do. I was certain this would work; it worked on the boys all the time and I enjoyed

8

teasing them, but I don't want to tease sir. I want sir to see me as a woman, not a girl.

When I got home, I sat on the end of my bed and practised in the mirror, lifting my skirt little by little until I could see my panties, then spreading my legs to see what sir will be able to see from his desk. This will work, I was sure of it… *Hmm* I better trim my hair back a little tonight.

The next morning, I decide to wear a white thong. Knowing the material barely covered my pussy, the thin cotton will reveal the outline of my vagina. Arriving early, waiting outside the door at class, so I can take the seat at the front, right in sir's eyeline. He won't be able to ignore me now, I thought to myself.

Sir enters the room, takes the register, and sits down. I hitch my skirt a little and part my legs waiting while he gives out the work for today's lesson. Sir is working on papers at his desk and does not seem to notice that I am at the front of the class, nor has he looked my way. (I may be pouting right now.) Notice me!

I decide to get his attention by asking a question, so raising my hand, I call out,
"Please, sir?"

Mr Wyles looks up, noticing me. (Butterflies are dancing in my stomach now.)
"Yes, Miss Lawson?"

I was sure his eyes flashed for a second. I ask my question and as he answered I parted my legs a little more (God I feel like such a slut, but it is exhilarating as well).

He answers and returns to his papers; I keep watching to see if he notices me; if he is looking, but I don't see him look. Panicking now, I have risked expulsion by doing this. The least

he can do is notice me! Deciding to go all in, I open my legs as wide as I can, so he can't miss the obvious show.

Watching him, instead of working or reading the book that I was supposed to study, I saw as he glanced up once but then return to his papers. Then I realise something odd. He has not walked up the aisles today, as he usually does, but stayed at his desk... That's really odd, but all I really care about is that he is not looking my way at all. (And yes, I am pouting now.)

Then the bell goes signalling the end of class and still, he has not looked at me (really pouting now; I want to cry). As I am about to leave; I hear sir's voice; he is talking to me!

"Miss Lawson, please wait..."
His voice is quiet, but I hear him clearly.

I start panicking inside, wondering how much trouble I am in.

Hard Lessons
The tuition of Rebecca

Chapter 1: After Class.

The bell rings, signalling the end of the lesson time; as it was lunchtime now, the students will be in a rush to get to the food halls and beat the inevitable queues.

As they headed to the door, I call out,
"Miss Lawson, please wait for me!"

The girl halted, said something to her friends, and returned to her seat. Her seat was directly in front of mine today! This was unusual. As she would normally sit at the back of the room and try to avoid being noticed. Today had been rather a different affair, to say the least.

I wait as the room empties the class door is left open of course. This is a rule in the school. No teacher could risk being alone with a student with the door closed. More than their job was worth these days.

Looking up at the girl, a young woman really, now in her final year and last few months of school. Soon, many would go off to college or find work if they were lucky. She would be eighteen now, I guessed, a young woman really, yet still she wore her hair long and straight, like many of the younger girls did these days.

Not an overly high achiever and I feared that like so many girls these days, she would be pregnant more than once before she hit twenty-one. (We had a few girls at the school who already had or were currently carrying a child.) Still, she was rather attractive in a fresh-faced sort of way and still a little coltish of limb, with almost an athlete's build.

11

"Come here girl," I order her, in what I hope is a calm voice. I did not want the girl to worry herself too much, well, not yet anyway!

She slowly walked over and stood by the desk; head bowed. I suspected she knew full well why I had requested she stay behind. In fact, I was certain this request had come as no surprise at all.

"Well, Miss Lawson, I can see that your uniform skirt is regulation length. So please explain to me how it is possible, then, that your panties were exposed to the class, throughout the entirety of the lesson?"

My eyes not leaving her face, waiting to see if she would look me in the eye. I waited a moment before continuing,
"Well Miss Lawson, I am waiting!" a touch of annoyance creeping into my voice now.

"Should we take this to the Headmaster, or a call to your parents. Maybe that will that loosen your tongue, girl!"
Yes, there it is! That got a reaction.

She looked up, a worried look on her face.
"No sir, I'm sorry sir," she muttered.

Good, I thought, a small inner smile. Though careful not to let it show on my stern facade, I looked over to the door, making sure her friends had not hung back to wait for her. The hall was clear; the classroom being on the third floor, and food halls on the ground, we should be undisturbed for a while, though someone might still walk by and teachers would still be about.

"Take your seat again, girl…" Said in a tone that made it more of an order than a request.

She sat, I noted. Her skirt covered her knees as it should have done. I looked at her coldly, taking a chance that I had read this situation correctly.

"Now show me that white thong again, and yes, I had a good enough view that I could tell it was a thong. Were that for my benefit, girl?"
My eyes locked on hers now, daring her to look away.

For almost forty-five minutes, whilst I sat behind my desk; I had a clear view of her inner thighs, her crotch, and her panties. It had been dammed distracting! I had tried not to look. I was a teacher, and I knew better than to take notice of these little silly games students sometimes play.

But I am a man still, and it has been a while since I had such a pretty view. I sneaked a look while marking papers, hoping she would not notice me glancing up. But I was certain that she had noticed the overt glances at least once. She had even spread her knees for the last part of the lesson. I would normally walk up and down the aisles, but not today, and even now I dared not rise from my seat.

I watch as she stood, adjusting her skirt, hitching the band up her waist, and as she sat hitched up the skirt further, I could glimpse the inner thigh, and a slight flash of white, she looked up then, no coyness now, and opened her legs even wider than she had dared to do so earlier, during class.

I could see a slight discolouration now in the crotch area, a wetness to the material. I looked up and her reaching into my pocket and withdrew my phone. Keeping my eyes on her, never dropping my view, I lifted my phone, pointed it at her, and took a picture. She smiled and put a finger to her lips as I took another. Clearly, this girl was a natural exhibitionist and did not care that I was taking photos of her! I had to wonder why.

"I now have photo evidence of your misbehaviour in my class, Miss Lawson! I really should take this to the Headmaster and call your parents. This will mean a suspension, at the very least, or expelling. Do you understand what I am saying, Miss Lawson?"

"Please sir, don't sir, I am sorry, sir. I won't do it again, sir," her voice panic and broken with stutters.

That's more like it a bit of fear in her voice now. I decide to relieve some of the fear she might be feeling.

So, I tell her,
"Well girl, I suppose detention and lines would be punishment enough! But let me be clear, never sit that way in my class again. You were lucky today, lucky that no one else noticed, or my hands would be tied, and I would have to inform the headmaster."

"Now before you go to lunch, Miss Lawson, tell me why?"

"Sir, I wanted you to notice me!" she replies, looking at me expectantly, a nervous smile on her face.

Gods, that girl is going to get me fired, I thought. My cock was so hard that I was in danger of breaking through my trousers.

"Well, you have your wish, Miss Lawson, I noticed... I could hardly miss such an overt display!"

Pausing to look into her eyes once more,
"My office after school. I will decide what punishment fits this action, Miss Lawson."

"Rebecca sir..." She said her name, shyly, as if telling me was a great secret.

I snapped at her.
"After school, Miss Lawson!"

She left the room, adjusting her skirt again, and now looking just like any other of the female students.

I sat there, waiting for the aching stiffness to subside, thinking to myself, well what are we going to do with her... A lesson needed teaching, but I was also thinking that it had been years since a student offered me such an interesting opportunity.

I was no young teacher, not hip or considered cool, and I no longer risked over-familiarity with the students the way I did in my early days. It was frowned upon these days. Many careers have been ruined by idle chatter in the lounge and among students. Still, I had to wonder at the sheer audacity of this girl's approach. Flashing me in class! Well, at least she had worn panties I suppose, and on that thought my cock sprang back to full erection.

I had two lessons and lunch to ponder this, handled right, this could be a lot of fun, lots and lots of fun. I smiled to myself and reached down to adjust my again aching prick. Yes, I thought, she wanted my attention, and now she would get my full attention.

Hard Lessons
The tuition of Rebecca

Chapter 2: After School.

At 4:05 PM, I was in my office, my door closed, waiting. Waiting rather nervously, to be honest with myself. This was a big risk. One I really should not be taking at this point in my career.

Spotting a shadow as it pauses before the frosted glass of the door, then a gentle, hesitant knocking at the door; rising from my chair, walking over, and poking my head out; I spot Miss Lawson.

"Please take a seat. I will be with you shortly."

I returned to my seat and started marking papers, needing it to be a bit later in the hour before I could risk having a student in my office with the door closed. I did not want another student or teacher to notice this breaking of rules. And I was in no doubt I was about to break a very big rule.

4:30, I poked my head out and beckoned her in. Checking the corridor was empty before closing the door behind her.

"Stand in front of my desk… And wait." I told her. My voice, cold, stern, emotionless.

I had moved the chair aside, so she had no choice but to stand there. I returned to my seat, picked up a file and showed it to her.

"I have here, Miss Lawson, your academic record! And I must say it does not make pleasant reading. You are scraping by!!" A long pause, a little bit of dramatic effect never hurts.

16

My voice was calm all business, the same voice I always used for these reviews.

"Add a few week's suspension and I think you will fall so far behind that you will fail all your classes."

"So, I am left with a quandary. Do the right thing but ruin your future by informing the Headmaster of your actions, thus getting you at the very least suspended for a few weeks…"

"Or do we work out another way to punish this behaviour?"
I looked her up and down, then looked her directly in the eyes.

Tears now, running down her cheeks. Stirring up a warm and familiar feeling in my loins. My body betraying me. Such a shameful lack of control. A man of my years should have more self-control, I thought. But damn me if this girl was not making me feel like a teenager again.

"Well, girl, what do you have to say?" I said, reaching for my phone.
(A bluff, the door was closed; I was in as much trouble, if not more than she now.)

"Sorry sir, please sir don't…" Tears flowing freely now.

"Please sir, I will do anything, sir, don't let my parents know, they will send me away!"
Such a forlorn look, and big wet sparkling eyes. (Damn it, man).

She looked down then,
"I will do whatever sir says, whatever sir wants, just don't call the Headmaster, please, sir."

My loins all but broke free at this statement. The way she said this, the sultriness of her voice, a few more years to perfect that, and she would have men eating out of the palms of her hands.

I smiled, though. I had read this situation correctly, and I was sure I had her now (or she had me). She had wanted my attention and now she had delivered herself to me, given me ammunition and an opening. Play this right, and things could be very interesting (that or I take early retirement).

"Ok, Rebecca." Using her first name now.
"I am an old-fashioned teacher. You have been a naughty girl, and for such behaviour, punishment is called for."

Waiting for her to look up, then once she looked up, I continued speaking,
"In my day we caned pupils for such behaviour, but alas the days of caning students have long since passed…" Another short pause.
"But I think the ruler will suffice for today…"

A small smile crossed my face as I reached over and picked up my ruler, a fifteen-inch, hardwood rule, my old school ruler from my childhood schooldays.
"Are you sure you don't prefer the suspension, Miss Lawson?" I asked, waving the rule at her...

"Yes sir, I mean no sir, I will take my punishment, sir."
Her voice was a little broken, but she looked me right in the eye as she spoke.

I could see she was fighting back tears now (I hoped they would be more of those later). A girl's tears always got to me, either touched my heart or made me hard, depending on the circumstances, quite often at times both.

Standing, I walked slowly behind her, before I said to her, my voice firm.

"Bend over my desk, Rebecca," Using her first name to put her more at ease, then pausing for effect "and hitch up your skirt…"

"You have demonstrated that you know how to do that."
My voice became icy cold. I did not let a touch of the lust that would be very evident, should she see my crotch…

She took the position and lifted her skirt and exposed her pale bottom. I could see the string of her thong disappearing into the crack of her arse! She then spread her legs a little, and I got a good view of the stained crotch of her panties…
(Fuck me, I thought. Control mister, control, keep to the plan.)

"Usually Miss Lawson, I would have you remove those panties, but seeing as the thong does not cover any of that bottom, I think you can keep them on." Said calmly, betraying none of the excitement I was feeling inside.

I stopped to press the Bluetooth camera record button in my pocket; I had set this up earlier and would have a video recording to enjoy afterwards.

"Six strokes per cheek, I think. Is that ok Rebecca?"

"Yes," she said.

"Yes, Sir!" I said, emphasizing the Sir, and waited.

She stuttered out a nervous "Yes, Sir."
Seems she got it.

I brought the ruler down on her pale flesh, for the first of the dozen strokes she was to receive.

I watched her reactions as the first strike landed; she shivered but did not try to move away.

I could see the outline of a red welt forming on her pale skin immediately. Virgin flesh, I thought, almost salivating.

"Good, Miss Lawson…"

(Pausing for effect.) "Rebecca, this will soon be over."

Five more times, I struck her cheek, moving the ruler down her bottom to the top of her leg as I did so. I was not overly hard, though I doubt she knew that.

"Good Girl…" I said, as I went to the other side of her and readied for another six strokes.

I could hear her sniffling and knew that tears would be running down that pretty face. Shame I did not have a camera set up on that side. It would have been nice to capture her reaction and her tears.

Again, I struck her, and saw the rewarding red outline of the ruler, repeating the pattern from the other side. I worked my way to the top of her thigh and delivered the last stroke firmly. Ok, that one was with force, a habit. (The last one is always a bitch.) Leaving the ruler in place while I watched her shudder and compose herself.

Stepping back behind my desk and telling her to stand up, I got a good look at her face, tears rolling down her cheeks, lips pouting, breath slightly halted as she sobbed quietly.

She could see me clearly now though, and I did not hide my bulging manhood, covered only by the thin material of my trousers. My arousal was obvious for her to see.

I waited whilst she looked, waited for that look I wanted to see, yes a smile, she had my attention now, that is what she wanted

and she could see that her plan had worked, though I was certain she probably did not see the ruler coming.

"Well Rebecca, I shall call you that in private now. Miss Lawson will be for lessons only." Pausing to smile at her.
"You wanted me to notice you. I have."

"Yes sir, I wanted that Sir," she said, the coyness returning to her voice.
The tears drying up now.

"Well, I think I should see what it was that you wanted to show me… Don't you think, Rebecca?" Pausing again to look her up and down. "Those panties are small, but they also cover you efficiently…"

"They are also quite wet, I notice. Give them here… Now Girl." I said this last part in a firm tone, an order.

She looked at me, face paling again, this had probably not worked out how she imagined, flirting with a teacher, is not unheard of, and I knew of a few that had banged a pupil or two in the past, risky, always a risk, one I had avoided for many years, since my younger days at least.

She slipped her hand up her skirt, wiggled a little, and they dropped to the floor, she turned and bent over and removed the panties, turning again to face me, a smile wide across her face… (The tease, she would pay for that sometime.)

I took them from her, feeling the very noticeable wetness of them before placing them on my desk.

"Now show me, show me what you were hiding behind those!" Gesturing at the damp tiny piece of white material on my desktop (her panties).

"Show me what you wanted me to notice, wanted me to be thinking about during the lesson! A lesson where I should have been educating your mind, not have you putting thoughts into mine!" I said this with a voice that was warm and friendly and probably betrayed a tincture of lust.

I took up the camera, placed it on my desk to record this as well. She noticed the camera, now that it was in front of her. If this alarmed her, I could not tell. Nor did it stop her from following my instructions. Definitely an exhibitionist, I thought.

She lifted her skirt, gathering up the hem, and exposed her little hairy cunt to me, not too hairy, and the curtains matched the drapes, I noted happily. Trimmed, I thought so that it would not stick out of the side of those little panties she had worn.

I sat and viewed this gift for a few minutes, looking up at her occasionally, watching her shake while she was exposed to me.

"Down…" I said finally.

"Rebecca, from now on, you will behave in my class… No flashing of knickers or cleavage! Yes, I had noticed!" I said before continuing,
"Is that understood?"

"Yes, Sir."
She remembered to emphasise the Sir; good, she is a fast learner.

"You have my attention now. Are you sure you want this, Rebecca? You are not a child. You know what might happen, yes?"

"Yes, Sir, I know what Sir will do with me, Sir…"
She had that coy look again, almost like she could not wait or knew something I did not.

"Good, we cannot risk this at school, so I am going to offer you private tuition. This will be to get you through your exams with passable grades. These lessons, Miss Lawson, will be held at my house on Saturdays. I shall write to your parents, telling them that you have offered to babysit my dogs. Geri and Freki, in return, I will give you free tuition to get you through the upcoming examinations."

"I will send instructions to your mobile. Please leave your number on the pad in front of you."
I watched as you picked up a pen and wrote her number down.

I walked over to her, picking up her panties from the desk, then as she watched, I sniffed them, emitting a deep sigh, as they released their scent, filling my nostrils. Taking her hand, I placed it upon my bulging cock. Pleased as I felt her fingers tighten about its shaft. Even more pleased by the look on her face, her eyes, I could read the lust in them.

"This will be your reward, but you have felt the price today. I will expect you to be willing to pay this price. There will be other punishments for failing your duties, failing lessons, but there will be rewards too."

"Now off with you, girl, before your parents wonder where you are."

She turned and left the room; I was still holding her panties. I also had a massive grin on my face, ohh what fun I was going to have.

Returning to my desk, I set about writing the letter to her parents. My thoughts, though, were on watching that video later, when I could enjoy it properly.

Roll on Saturday, I thought.

Hard Lessons
The tuition of Rebecca

Chapter 3: Tuition.

I wrote a text message to Miss Lawson, keeping in mind that her parents might read her messages.

The message:

Miss Lawson as agreed, Saturday tuition will commence at 11 am sharp. Please do not be tardy. I will supply appropriate revision resources as well as paper, pens and equipment.
There will be three hours of tuition in Maths and English Literature. Afterwards, I shall introduce you to the dogs, and we can walk them together, so they become accustomed to you.

I shall drop you back home for about 6 PM.

If your parent's wish to meet with me or call me, please give them my number.

Earlier that week:

I had called Miss Lawson to my office. (Door left open this time.)

We had discussed the message I would send. She had said her mother would be ok with her babysitting the dogs and was happy that she was getting extra tuition as payment. She had also insisted her mother would never read her messages.

But I am not such a fool as to write anything untoward down. She may be of legal age, but I would certainly be dismissed and

likely struck off! Should it become public knowledge that I was involved with one of the students?

I also instructed her on what to wear for this visit, and that I would give her guidance on what to wear each time she visited.

"Are you still sure you wish for my personal tuition, Rebecca?" I asked in a friendly tone.

"You are aware of what might happen. You have had a taster of what I like?"
She nodded at this.

"There will be punishments, but there will also be fun. We shall talk more about this at the weekend. This is not the place for such conversations."

"Yes Sir, I understand, and I look forward to meeting your doggies as well." She smiled at me as she said this, such a sweet smile, pretty mouth, I thought. (I could not wait to have those lips around my cock.)

"Good, await my text and I shall see you as planned on Saturday."

Saturday:

My house is situated on the outskirts of town, in a small cul-de-sac, the house is detached with a double garage between the houses. So, they are not too close to each other giving us quite a bit of privacy.

The house is large, probably too large for a single fellow, but it is comfortable, and I have room for my hobbies. It also comes with a good-sized garden with several trees encircled by large, well-kept hedgerows. Meaning the garden was private, private enough that I did not worry about sunbathing naked. The garden

also has a rear gate that leads out to the fields behind my property. Across from the field is woodland which has a small, cobbled stream running through it, perfect for walking the dogs.

I set up the desk in the living room as the sun is coming through the front windows at this time of day. My back will be to the window, and I will be sitting on the sofa. From there I shall be able to watch her while she studies. I sat and tried the seat and the view, yes that will do, I thought.

My watch beeped, telling me it was 11 am. Glancing out of the window, it pleasantly surprised me to see her walking down my drive. On time, I thought, good girl.

I went to the door, and greeted her, looking her up and down to ensure she was dressed as I had instructed, sensible shoes for walking, a summer dress, not so short that her mother would think it odd to wear, to see her teacher but short enough that it showed plenty of leg.

"Come in, Miss Lawson…"
"Rebecca!" I corrected myself,
"I think we will get straight on with the lesson, then a tour of the house before meeting the dogs," my tone was friendly, as I knew that she would be nervous.

Showing her to the living room and directing her to the desk and the seat, I had set out the desk, pens, calculators, and workbooks. I had picked up some tuition books from WHSmith's that covered the subjects I wanted her to improve.

"I have marked the relevant pages for you, highlighted a few paragraphs that will assist you in the tests I have set out for today. Please read through. You may ask questions if you do not understand anything you read, but I believe the books cover the subjects quite adequately…"
I used my usual teacher's voice for this.

"You have thirty minutes to read, then twenty minutes for the test."

"And Rebecca, there will be a penalty for any question you get wrong, is that clear, Miss Lawson?" I asked this in a much sterner voice.

She looked up and quietly replied,
"Yes, Sir."
Too quiet, really, but I let that slide.

"The punishment, Miss Lawson, will be a bare bottom spanking, one minute for every wrong answer." My tone was serious, underlining that I meant what I had said.

Waiting a moment to allow that information to sink in before I continued.
"I am pleased with your choice of dress; now did you remember to wear the white panties as I instructed?"

As to answer, she lifted her skirt to show me, and yes, white cotton briefs! A snug fit, maybe a size too small, but that meant the material was stretched thinly across her little cunt. That sight alone made my cock spring to life. (Dirty old sod, I thought.)

"Good Girl, I shall supply you with a packet of spare panties to keep at home, as I am afraid, they will probably not last long in my house Rebecca," I tell her this with a warm smile and probably a rather lascivious look upon my face.
I was indeed picturing them being ripped and shredded by my own hands.

She laughed a little.
"Thank you, Sir." Still nervous, I thought.

She pulled out the chair, a wooden straight-backed number, with two holes in the seat, she looked at the holes, I could tell she was wondering.

"Those will not come into play yet, Miss Lawson, you have to earn those!"
I did not expand. Let her mind work on that.

"Please sit, I shall be over there monitoring and raise your hand should you have any questions."

I then went and sat in the window. From this vantage point, I had a good view of under the table and up her short dress. Watching as she seated herself, opened the book, then she looked up at me, realising why I had seated myself there. She opened her legs, not a subtle tease as she did in the classroom. This time just put her hands on her legs, lifted the hem of her skirt and spread them wide, placing a foot behind each chair leg.

Good Girl, I thought. I sat back a little more, eyes not leaving the erotic vision before me. I could make out the lines of her vagina through the thin material of the panties, and already see that there was a little staining from her pussy juices. nervous she might be, but she was also turned on.

I was looking forward to tasting her soon, though maybe not today, today was for acclimatization, an introduction to my world! I had to be sure she really understood what it was she was getting into, flashing her privates, and a little spanking was only a taster of what I had in store for her.

I sat watching. My own pants were struggling to contain my cock. I thought of releasing it from its confines but maybe later. She needed the tuition, and I would be a poor teacher if I did not help her get through the final examinations. I checked my watch and let her know the revision time was over and to start the maths tests.

28

"There are twenty questions, and you have twenty minutes to answer them. As I mentioned earlier, one minute of spanking for each wrong answer. Also, I should be clear that includes unanswered questions as well…"

"You may begin…"
I started my stopwatch and continued my perving.

The damp patch had grown to cover her pussy area, the material becoming almost transparent with the wetness. I could just make out the outline of her lips through the material now. I looked forward to removing them after the lesson… I pondered on whether or not I should put them in her mouth to stifle her cries? Yes, good idea, I told myself.

The time ticked away; I watched her work on the test. She looked up now and then, checking that I was still paying attention, that my eyes were fixed on her. After all, this is how she had gotten my attention in the first case, and she knew now that I enjoyed looking at her panty covered pussy. (I did rather enjoy the view, truth be told.)

She never tried closing her legs, though she had slumped down on the chair a little so I could get a better view. This also caused the panties to pull tighter against her crotch. This pleased me and I had smiled. I was pretty sure she had seen that smile.

"Time's up. Please put down your pencil and bring the paper here."
I was not in any state to walk over to her without some serious adjustment to my trousers.

She got up and picked up the paper, came over to hand it to me.

I watched, then said,
"Stop. Hold it with both hands, please."

Watching her, as she adjusted her hold on the test paper.
"Yes, that it, now bring it here girl!"
I waited while she came around the table and stopped in front of me.

Not taking the proffered paper from her,
"In this house, when we are alone, you will kneel before me and await my attention…"
I looked up at her then repeated the word.
"Kneel."

She knelt, then held out the paper for me again. I waited, not taking the paper for a mental count of sixty. Finally, count completed, I took the paper, telling her to stay there and to place her hands on her thighs and not move or look up at me until spoken to.

Sitting back, I proceeded to mark the first paper of the day.

"Not too bad, Miss Lawson. You clearly understand the subject, with only two incorrect answers and one unanswered question. I think we will save the chastisement until after the English Literature test."

I smiled down at her, still kneeling there in front of me, perfect I thought.
 "Please stand and then remove those panties. I will keep them safe until after the next test."

She replied with a quick,
"Yes, Sir."
As she stood and lifted her dress to remove her panties!

This time not turning away from me nor dropping her dress to cover herself… Giving me a good view of her privates while she

was doing this. I could see clearly that she was wet. The small strip of hair she still had was noticeably moist.

Handing them to me, she watched me as lifted them to my mouth and nose and sniffed them like a perfumed handkerchief, savouring the musky smell of her cunt.

"Hmmm, you have a lovely scent, Rebecca."
A warm smile spread across my face as I informed her of this.

"Thank you, Sir."
She replied, smiling and obviously happy with the praise.

Off with you girl, same as before, thirty minutes' revision followed by a test. After the test we shall settle up, Miss Lawson. Is that clear?"

"Yes, Sir, thank you, Sir."
With I noted the proper deference to my position. I wondered if she had watched some of those films; Fifty shades, was it? Total rubbish but seems to be popular with those new to the scene.

Again, I called time at the thirty-minute mark and watched as she did the test, my eyes ever glued to her pussy. She slunk down low on her chair. I would fix that soon; the holes would keep her fixed in position. (Yes, I had an evil grin on my face thinking about that.) She had spread her legs in what could not be a comfortable position, giving me a very good view of her vagina. (Good girl again, I thought, also flexible.)

Her vagina was slightly open due to the way she had slunk down on the chair spreading her legs. The position also proffered me quite a view of her little pink, rosy arsehole. I spent the last fifteen minutes imagining myself balls deep in that tight little hole and wondered what else I could stuff in there.

31

I called time and this time without being told. She came over holding the test answers in the way I had told her to previously, stopping before me, lowering her eyes and kneeling, arms out, waiting for me to remove the piece of paper from her hands.

Again, I mentally counted, though this time to a hundred before taking the proffered test paper.

"Hmm, again, you seem to have a good grasp of this subject. I wonder why you do not perform so well in the class?"

I pondered on this for a few seconds (being all dramatic). "Maybe you should sit in front from now on, away from your friends, so you do not get distracted."

I paused as if calculating her test score.
"Three unanswered questions and one wrong answer."
"Really, this is quite good, acceptable even…"

"In class though, Miss Lawson! here there is a price to pay..." I said firmly.

She had done better than I thought she would, only earning herself seven minutes of bare bottom spanking. (I was a little disappointed that she had not earned more, but seven minutes would get her bottom nice and warm, I was sure).

"You have earned seven minutes of spanking, Miss Lawson. You have a choice, over the desk or across the knee. Choose now…"

"Knee sir!" she replied, not a second's hesitation, almost as if this is what she wanted all along.

Good, I thought, she will feel my hardness against her as well… I was sure she would like to know how the little show she had put on for me had made me rock hard.

Hard Lessons
The tuition of Rebecca

Chapter 4: Introductions.

Sitting up straight, I instructed her first to stand then to lie over my knees. I then adjusted her position, so she was balanced, and I could feel my cock pressing into her midriff. (I hope she liked that feeling. I know I did.)

Then lifting her dress, pulling it up so it would not interfere with the strokes or my view. (I thought as I view her naked bottom. What a fucking lovely arse! Pert and with the firmness that comes only with fitness or youth.)

Caressing her bottom, a little enjoying the feel of such young, firm flesh. Removing my watch and setting it to stopwatch mode, I set the countdown to seven minutes, then handed it to the girl.

"Press start, when you feel the first strike of my hand; ohh and please open your mouth, girl."
I told her, taking her panties from my pocket and pressing them into her mouth and told her, "Do not spit them out."

Again, taking the time to get a good feel for the curve of her arse. As I lifted my hand in readiness, before bringing it down in a rather gentle stroke. I spanked each cheek in turn, increasing the firmness of the stroke gradually as I went. Until I felt her squirming as the stinging sensation of each spank reverberated through her body. I stopped occasionally to gauge the warmth of her bottom, and also to slide a finger down between her legs, feeling the wetness of her pussy.

"You are getting warm, Rebecca, and you are wet. Are you are enjoying your punishment, Miss Lawson?"

34

I did not expect an answer. She had a mouth full of panties, after all.

Returning to the spanking. I again built up the firmness of each stroke until I was hitting her as hard as I possibly could! My hand stinging with each strike. Still, I did not let up. My other hand now was pressed firmly into the small of her back, comforting but also controlling her movements. She would learn not to move so much in the future, but I would make some allowances for her being untrained.

Continuing to spank her, I occasionally paused to feel the warmth and of her bottom and wetness between her legs. At one point, not just touching but slipping a finger into her wet cunt! Raising it to my lips, licking the finger, tasting her. I was rather enjoying this. I thought to myself that I could have easily continued the spanking all day… But alas, she raised the watch up, trying to say time! Muffled by her panties, though, it was hard to make out.

I pulled her up to sit on my lap. (Let her feel that now, I thought as her arse settled on my engorged cock.) I removed the panties and used them to wipe the tears from her eyes. Her mascara had run, so she was a little panda eyed.

I held her to me, comforting her and told her she was a good girl, that she had made Sir happy. She had done well on the tests and taken her punishment so well. I felt her adjust her bottom a little, guessing she could feel my cock and was moving it into a more pleasurable position.

"Now, Rebecca, you can feel that I am pleased with you, and if you are good, maybe you can have a little treat later. The purpose of today is introductions and so we will take things slowly for now and I will try not to get carried away." I smiled as I said that to show that I was very pleased with her.

35

"I will explain what I expect from you, on top of your school tuition. I will tutor you in the ways I expect a submissive in my service to behave!"

I held her like that for a while, a little aftercare. It was also a pleasant sensation for me to hold someone in my arms like this, so I rather enjoyed the aftercare myself. (I rather also wanted to just ram my cock in her, but that was not how things were done.) If she was to become my submissive, then I had to do this the right way, she had to consent and be fully cognizant of what was involved in being not only a submissive but my submissive.

After about ten minutes of holding her, her head nuzzled against my neck, her pussy parted by my trouser constrained manhood, I decided that enough time had passed, and it was time for the tour. (Aftercare is important, but one must not let them milk it.)

I showed her about the house, the library, the media room, then the kitchen, giving her a bottle of chilled water to drink while we were there. I lead her up the stairs, showing her the master bathroom,"

"This is my room. You will only enter at my invite or instruction. Are you clear on that rule?"

"Yes, Sir!"
Her face was a little saddened by this rule.

I showed her the master bathroom and walk-in closet. Again, you may not enter unless invited or instructed. This is the guest room and ensuite. This will be your room should you stay over at any time. Though often I might invite you to stay in the master bedroom from time to time. I told her as I then showed her upstairs.

As I showed her up to the loft room, this loft space was large with exposed beams, to which I had affixed several mooring

rings and yoga straps. There was also a king-sized bed, with large wooden posts; these all had mooring rings attached, one to each of the four corner posts.

There was a dog cage, not that the dogs were allowed up here. A horse bench and a device called the Spanish donkey. (Look it up, it is quite evil.) A lot of rope hung from hooks on one side of the room, and a bamboo pole was hung from a beam near the window.

The attic opened on to double doors and a veranda that overlooked the garden and views beyond; this had enclosed sides to protect from the wind but also effectively made the space invisible from all sides but the field.

She looked about the room in wonder; I had fairy lights wired about the room and I thumbed several buttons, changing the lighting scheme. She felt the rope and hung from one of the poles, testing their strength, I guessed. Then going out onto the veranda and checking the view. I informed her that is very pleasant in the summer. I often sat out there naked and enjoying the cool night air.

Leading her back inside, showing her the rigging kit and explaining about the rope, the beams and the rings. Explaining that I had been a fan of rope play for many years and that I love to dangle pretty little things from the poles, the art form is called bondage or Shibari, I further expanded, though I did not expect her to understand the difference yet.

"I have seen some of your work Sir, it is incredibly beautiful!"

I raised an eyebrow at that, and she continued to explain about finding some images on one of my FB friends' profiles. Well, that explained a lot, really! (Mental note to set my profiles to private.)

Continuing to explain to her the ins and outs of bondage, Shibari and Kinbaku, expanding only a little only on the differences (I could go into more later, should she be interested).

"If you please me today, I may show you some rope later,"
I told her as an enticement. I could see she was interested and had taken an interest in a few pictures I had hung on the wall; of women, I had tied in the past.

I then showed her the cage.
"This is where you will wait or sleep depending on my mood…You will only sleep in the big bed If I invite you, other times, once I am done playing with you, I may send you to the sleep or wait in the cage, especially if you have displeased me."

"Is that clear, Rebecca?"

"Yes, Sir; wait or sleep in the cage until Sir lets me out, I understand."
She looked a bit crestfallen by the thought. Though I knew full well that I only used the cage a few times, much preferring my guests to keep me company through the night.

"OK, now for the best room!"
Taking her by the hand, I guided her back down the stairs to the kitchen; she looked confused, having seen the kitchen already. But I lead her over to what looked to be a larder cabinet door.

Reaching on top, I flipped a hidden leaver, releasing the catch that held the cabinet in place. Opening the door, I gripped the shelf and pulled the unit towards me; the cabinet slid on the rollers that allowed it to smoothly and gently slide away from the wall, exposing stairs that led down to the basement.

"This leads to the basement, or as I like to call it, the dungeon…"

I told her, smiling. I had installed the cabinet to hide the entrance away,

"Adds a little mystery, don't you think Rebecca?"

She was too dumbfounded or shocked to say anything about this secret doorway.

I led her down; the stairs were lit by LED strip lights, and the room was lit by both black lights and a couple of strip lights on the ceiling. The floor had LED lights around the edge so I could adjust the lighting at a whim to suit the mood.

I started explaining the room and all the toys that she could see. A massage bed, not only for massaging, but the cross against the wall is also for leaning on while being flogged or restrained.

"Please do feel free to try it, touch and feel anything you want," I told her.

There was a hobbyhorse with straps, and in another corner was a cabinet painted black with holes in the sides - she went inside, and I put my hand in to touch her, telling her this was a grope box and glory hole, she laughed at that; I guess she knew what that meant. Confirming my suspicion, I noticed her mouth and a protruding tongue in one of the lower holes. (Tempting I thought.)

She fingered the wall of floggers, several types and sizes and a couple of paired floggers I used for florentining she looked confused by that description, so I demoed the process, spinning them about in the air, a lot easier than when hitting someone, but it did look kind of cool.

I showed her some other impact toys and some sexual play toys, including electrical stimulation toys that she seemed rather worried about.

"Don't worry, I will show you how each of these works and explain their function fully before using any of them on you."

She then found the cane rack. This had various canes of different thicknesses and flexibility, as well as a few differing materials.

"These are not for you yet! I can hardly send you home, let alone to school, where the marks from these would raise some awkward questions!"

I saw a slightly disappointed look cross her face (damn me, I thought, I could feel the old familiar stirring in my loins and the thought of this little lady under my cane).

In what I hoped was a reassuring tone, I told her.
"Don't worry, there will be plenty of time for these later, hopefully."

I led her over to the hobby horse, pressing on her back; she seemed to get the gist, and she laid down on the horse.

"I think, Miss Lawson, it is time you saw what I eventually expect from you."
"I am going to play a short video. Please watch and when I return, you can tell me if you still wish to be tutored!"

I fixed the strap about her so she could not move, adjusted the horse so she was facing the screen, and turned on the video. It was a twenty five-minute video of me administering a brief scene with one of the local ladies. There was a little warm-up, spanking, flogging, a caning followed up with a rather rough throat fucking! Finishing up with me pinning her to the ground, as I pile drove my cock into her well-rounded arse... When I had done, she had knelt before me, sucked, and licked my cock clean and thanked me for my time.

I waited until the video showed me fucking the poor lady's arse mercilessly. Before I came up silently behind Rebecca, then dipping down between her legs, gently blowing on her moist exposed cunt. Letting her know I was there. She could not see me, nor could she stop me should I want to take her.

"You can say no, by calling red at any time, please confirm you understand this."

"Yes, Sir, I can call red to stop anything I don't like."

"Good girl." I said, as I leaned in and kissed her, tasting that most delicious of forbidden fruits.

She was so wet, so juicy and so sweet, forbidden fruit for me really, but one I had dreamt about for many days. I slipped my tongue in and while the video played in the background I set about biting, licking, and sucking illicitly upon that most tender of fruits. Sliding my tongue about her clit and up to her arse, then back again...

Teasing her, feeling her press back at each pass of that little hole, clearly wanting to feel my tongue's press as I explored her sweet little cunt. Finally, not being able to resist, I spread her cheeks with my hands, opening her arse up to my tongue and pressed in as hard and deep as I could.

Hearing her gasps was all the answer I needed to confirm that given time, she would become a proper anal slut. (Lucky Sir, I thought).

The video ended. I stopped my probing, resisting again the urge I had to fuck this little rose. Undoing the binding straps, I released her, telling her to kneel again before me.

"Miss Lawson, Rebecca, you saw on that video what I will eventually expect from you," pausing to look at her before continuing.

"It will not all be beatings and sex and humiliations though!!"

I proceeded to run off a list:
· Rope, lots, and lots of rope play.
· Wax play.
· UV play with paint and wax.
· Bath and shower times.
· Dressing up and costumes.
· I will supply clothing for you to wear when we go out, or you will be naked if I so desire.

"That's a few of the fun things," I told her, before continuing the list.

Sex-wise:
- Cock worship.
- I do not allow spitting.
- Sex will be whenever and wherever I demand it.
- Anal sex is a must. You should be always clean and ready.
- You will not play with yourself unless I give permission.
- You will not orgasm unless I give permission.
- You will not have sexual relations with anyone other than those I grant permission.
- Body care, clean and shaven or at least trimmed at all times.
- Club events, you will behave and not speak with anyone unless I give permission.

"Remember always you are a reflection of me, disappoint me, and there will be consequences."

I continued to list the following.

Funishments vs Punishments:
- You will submit to funishments and punishments, whatever they might be.
- I will decide on the severity and on the implements to be used unless I tell you to choose.
- You will call red without fear of reprisal. I shall be more disappointed if you don't.
- Punishments, you will be expected to submit and not call red if it is a punishment. Calling red will stop all play until we have had a thorough conversation on what the issues are.

"This list is not exhaustive and will be updated as we grow."

I further explained.
"You may also, once you are settled, negotiate any of the above and add to the lists those things you wish to be part of our dynamic."

I pause to give her an appraising look, judging her sincerity, gauging if she had really understood the gravity of this situation.

"This is important as the relationship is not one-sided, even if it has the appearance of being so to outsiders."
"Do you understand that, Rebecca?"

"Yes, Sir, I understand I can negotiate. I will think on what Sir has said, though I really liked the sound of most of it, Sir…"

That's smile again, Ye gods, to have met this girl twenty years ago.

Hard Lessons
The tuition of Rebecca

Chapter 5: Playtime.

Leading the now flushed young lady back up the stairs and into the kitchen, telling her to wait in the corner.

"Go stand in the corner, face the wall, hands clasping elbows, and await my return."

Firmly instructing her, then waiting while she complied with the instructions. I then concealed the entrance to the basement/dungeon. My secret, hidden away once again.

"I need to change for the walk. I shall not be too long Rebecca." By using her familiar name, I hoped to put her at ease. I was sure this was a lot to take in, and I did not want to overwhelm her.

Quickly, I changed into more suitable summer walking attire. I take a few minutes to compose myself, reminding myself that this is an introduction day and that I should not fuck this lovely young lady until she is ready to become my submissive.

Calmed once more, I grab my backpack, which contained treats for the dogs, water, and some fruit. (Must enquire about the girls' preferences for the future, I hoped she was not another vegan.)

Selecting a few hanks of coconut rope as well; always liked to have some rope in my bag. The coconut rope is water-resistant, did not shrink when wet, so I need not worry about getting it wet or dirty. Adding my phone stand to the bag as an afterthought, as I might get a few pictures and maybe a video to enjoy later.

Returning to the kitchen, I was happy to find her still in the position I had left her in. (Good girl, she learns fast.) I donned the backpack and told her to follow me, whilst grabbing the dog's leashes from the hooks by the back door.

"Time to meet the family. Do you remember their names?"

"Yes, Sir, you told me in your office that evening after school, Sir."
A pause, before she continued to name them both,
"Freki and Geri, I think Sir, is that correct Sir?"
Repeating the unfamiliar names.

Probably dredging up the unfamiliar names from that clever little mind. I had no doubt she was clever, unfocused like so many young people, but that mind was sharp. I was certain of it.

Smiling happily, a smile that confirmed that she was indeed right, that she was very clever to have remembered such unusual names. Opening the door to the garden. As expected, they were sitting patiently waiting for me. (Though their tails were wagging a million miles per hour…)

The dogs: Geri, the bitch and the boss is a mixed breed that looks much like a Bearded Collie, stands about knee height and is very friendly. Freki is the boy, and very boisterous boy to boot, a Jack Russell, about half the size of Geri and she makes sure he behaves. Well, most of the time. Geri is a hairy little beast, whereas Freki is short-haired, but both are white and tan.
As usual, they waited, tails wagging but seated, ready to have their lead clipped on. They only needed the leads until we reached the woods, where I would let them off the leash and let them have a good run about.

They spotted Rebecca, who had followed me out; she greeted them by letting them both smell her hand; I figured that she has or had had a dog at some time. They sniffed but did not bounce

up at her; I had trained well them and knew they would wait until she called them.

She dipped down onto her knees and called each in turn, holding out her hand. Each, in turn, placed a paw into her to shake (such good doggo's). She then petted them, scratching them and their bellies when offered.

"They seem to like you," I said, happy that this was going so well.

"I love doggies, Sir. We only have a cat now and I miss having a fur faced friend…"

She was laughing a little and seemed really pleased that the dogs both like her.

Handing her the leash to Freki, Freki being the smallest and though a feisty mutt, I figured she could control him without any issues. Maybe she could have Geri or both on the return trip.

Guiding her down the garden, showing her the trees often used for hammocking and lazing in the sun, letting her know that the garden was not overlooked so she could sunbathe naked here should she wish.

Leading her down the garden (or is that up) to the gate that leads to the fields and woodland beyond. Unlocking and opening the gate, then ushering her out ahead of me, following closely behind. Admiring her from the rear. The little dress she was wearing gave me a lovely view of her shapely little behind as she walked.

We trekked across the field, reaching the woodland in about five minutes; leading us to a small path that the dogs and I knew very well. There were no other dog owners on the cul-de-sac and even on a sunny day like today, we were likely to have the

woodland to ourselves. The woods belonged to the forestry commission, so were technically not public land nor was there a public right of way through them, but that never stopped me from exploring as a kid and I was certainly not going to change my ways, especially with them so conveniently close by.

Telling her to let Freki off the leash, as I unhooked Geri to let them run and explore. They loved the woods and knew them well from our previous walks. Running off in search of fresh scents, and I expect to leave a few of their own. Occasionally bounding back onto the path to make sure we were still there.

Upon reaching the stream, we followed it as it wove deeper into the woods; crossing at a crossing point, bridged by a fallen tree. Before following the stream on the other side. The dogs running in and out of the stream, excitedly enjoying the water and chasing each other about.

Reaching a point that I thought secluded enough, 15 minutes into the woods, suggesting that she dip her toes.

"I would like to take a few pictures if you don't mind Rebecca?" Pausing, then adding,
"In the dress, paddling at first, please. Then if you are happy to do some nude modelling, you can go naked."

"You will look like a beautiful water nymph," I said, imagining her dancing naked in the water with her long hair flailing in the summer breeze. (Ohh my.)

"I would love to pose for you, Sir! Do you really think I am really beautiful?" She asked as she was slipping off her shoes and socks.

"Yes, you are very pretty. You are a beautiful young lady!" It does not hurt to flatter one so young, I thought to myself.

She splashed into the water while I clicked away; she played with the dogs when they came to see their new water buddy. Once I had a few dozen good images, happy I had some nice photos, I changed to video mode and took a short film of her. Then asking her to remove her dress, so we can get some water nymphet like shots.

She did so immediately, almost as if she had wanted to do this all along. Naked, splashing and dancing in the water, I admired her youthful beauty while taking many pictures and a short video recording. Then I just sat back on the bank and watched her for a while. Taking in the beauty of this creature who had come into my life. So youthful, so beautiful, tall athletic build, coltish, they called it in my day…

I called her over after a bit, telling her to kneel by some flowers so I could take a few more photos. She seemed to be a natural at modelling and after a while knew without being told to lie down in the grass and flowers, flipping on her side then back and then hands and knees, in a pose that could only be taken to be an offering. (Again, the temptation was there, but I wanted to take my time, needed her to be begging for me to take her, before giving in to that need). Grabbing my bag and rummaging about until finding what I sought, extracting the rope, then telling her to stand before me.

I said to her,
"I think we should try a little rope."

Whilst stepping behind her and running the rope down her arm then across her body and up to her neck, where I grabbed the other end of the rope and pulled back against her, strangling her just a little reinforcing my dominance and control over her, reminding her of her place.

Releasing the hold, unfurling the rope fully before I tied her into a simple TK chest harness. Nothing too tight but it did allow me

to saw the rough rope across her flesh and against her perky nipples. (The cold water had made her all goose-bumpy and her nipples like little bullets.) Once tied, I told her to go kneel in the stream again, so I could get some images of her tied in the water.

Getting a few good shots, and a few when the dogs came to visit her before calling them both over and tolling them to sit and stay. Removing my boots and setting up my phone stand, selecting and setting the video function running, then I stepped into the water myself.

I waded into the ankle-deep water, sidling up to her, then with two fingers, I lifted her head until she could look at me directly as I looked down upon her.

"You have pleased me today, Rebecca. You have done well, learned fast and have made me feel quite youthful again, whilst doing so. Earlier you saw the sort of play that I have with my play partners and submissive. I would like for you to become my submissive in time…"
Continuing to explain what this would involve.

"This will not happen overnight. In fact, until you finish school, we shall keep things on a more playful level. Easing you into the scene as it were."

"I rather hope that once you finish school, we can move on to the next progression and you can become my full time submissive, but this is not a given…"

"I will teach you what is required; but in the choice will be yours to make, I will not pressure you, only can make that decision. Alternatively, I may decide that you do not fulfil my requirements, though that will be a reflection of me and not you, as I am the one guiding you on this journey!"
I looked down at her as I said this, watching her reaction.

"I want to Sir; I want to learn. I want to be Sirs submissive! Very much want to be Sirs. Just like that woman in the video." She replied, with no hesitation at all.
(Gods, what a gift.)

Letting go of her head, I allowed it to drop, noting that she eyed the obvious bulge in my trousers! Watching her, as she watched my hands as they released the fly and dug out my cock.

The look on her face as she saw the size of my fully erect member was priceless, wishing I had the camera focused on her face at that point. It's not that big, maybe a little above average length, but good and girthy.

"This is your reward. I think you will not have to work hard to get me to cum, but you will get me to cum! Show me what you know and do not worry about being good or bad. Just remember to not swallow! Until I instructed you to…"

Looking at her sternly now before I continued to say,
"And Rebecca, DO NOT SPIT!"

Pressing my cock up against her partially open mouth; she opened wider to accommodate the full girth of my manhood. Her eyes looked up at me, big and green and very wide, as she accepted my cock. I had no idea if she had even done this before, though I had an inkling that she may have.

"Good… That's it, take it in, suck on it, show me what you know, show me what you can do, show me how you worship a man's cock…"

She sucked away, not a great action and a bit wet and sloppy, I thought, but that can be corrected. Pressing forward and then grabbing her hair pulled her towards me so that she would take more of my cock into her mouth.

I pressed until feeling her gag. So not able to deep throat yet! But again, that skill can be trained. Fucking her mouth while using the handful of hair to control her movements. Then after a little while I released her hair, giving her back control. She got the point though and was now pressing the cock to the back of her throat, trying to swallow as much of my cock as she could.

Feeling the build-up; hours my cock had been aching for this girl and now I was going to release, hoping it would be a flood. Sometimes it was, and I hoped this would be one of those.

"Good girl; now remember, do not spit. I am about to cum, I may make some noise, but do not worry."
I told her, as I felt myself losing control.

And like a good little slut she sucked harder, bobbing more ferociously and just as I came, she stopped the sucking and I felt her tongue lapping at the end of my cock, while she held it between her lips.

Withdrawing, I ordered her to show me. Watching as she opened up her mouth, her mouth widened, eyes sparkling with pride... Showing me the spunk that had been released into her pretty little mouth. Taking my cock in hand, milking the last few drops into her mouth, making sure none went to waste.

"Stay there, do not swallow, I want a photo of this, as this is our first time."

A little mean I know, but it would show that she was willing to follow orders, even if a little gross.

I fastened up my trousers and went and retrieved my camera phone. Returning, setting the camera to record again, and told her to roll her tongue, then to swallow...

She rolled her tongue, making the cum ripple and roll, before she pulled back her tongue and with a gulp, she swallowed it all, then showed me her opened mouth. She had the biggest smile on her face, and I watched as her tongue flickered out to get the last drops from her lips.

"That was very good, Rebecca, room for improvement, but very good all the same."
I helped her up and led her to the bank. Untying her then, handing her the bottle of water, I left her to dry off in the sun for a while and I played fetch with the dogs, so they would leave her be.

Coiling up the rope, a thought popped into my head. She had been very good but not perfect, a punishment to let her know to do better, I thought. Yes, it's justified.

So, walking over to her, and saying,
"Miss Lawson, you did well, but you did not manage to get all my cock in your mouth! I expect you to practice until you can deep throat my cock! I wish to fuck your throat as I would any other hole in your body."

"So, Rebecca, I am afraid a small punishment is in order. Please go stand facing that tree, you may hold on to it if you wish."
I was again in teacher mode, my voice firm, brooking no argument.

She stood naked and hugged the tree, awaiting her punishment (I would not be harsh, but a little lesson is still worth teaching. Folding the rope into a flogger, proceeding to flog her back and buttocks; not too hard, as the coarseness of the rope would be too much for her still. Laying on the rope flogger more of a caress than punishment, I was sure she would train herself to please now, and the toy I would give her to take home would help. (A seven-inch suction-cupped cock shaped dildo that she can affix to a mirror and practise her skill.)

"Get dressed. We must return home and return you to your mother."

"Before you leave, I will give you a training aid. You will practice each night until you can accommodate the toy all the way down your throat!" I told her, my mind picturing her in her uniform after school each night sucking down the rubber willy.

She replied by nodding her head, followed by,
"Yes, Sir!" As she remembered herself.

Calling out to the dogs and not waiting for her, set off back towards the house. I was sure she would catch up soon enough. She caught up after a little while and we retraced our steps back to the field. Upon reaching the field, I told her to leash the dogs and hold them there while I return to the house.

"You can see my gate over there; I want you to hold the dogs here while I cross the field. Do not lose control and do not follow until I reach the gate."

Setting off not looking back leaving her to master the dogs, sure in the knowledge they would be whining to follow but if she was to take care of them as per our cover story, then she had to learn to control them.

Upon reaching the gate, turning back to check on them, I was happy to see that she was still waiting by the woodland path. I watched as she led the fur faced troublemakers across the field. She had them under control and they walked beside her like they had been doing this for years. This please me as the dogs were family to me.

I greeted the dogs, giving them a reward and a belly rub, before unleashing them and letting them off into the garden. Letting her know she had done well. They seemed to like you and they

clearly followed you just then so I think you will be able to handle them in the future. A few more walks with me along and we can let you try alone.

"Ok, off to the house, get tidied up and put on some panties, girl!"
Smiling as I said those words, letting her know I was in a good mood.

When she came down, I handed her the gift, new in the packet and unused of course, explained again what I wanted her to practice, and she was not to use it on any other part of her body unless given permission to do so.

"Next week I think we shall try some more rope, maybe a small suspension, though only if you do well on your test, otherwise a timeout in the cage is all you will receive."

I returned her home at 5:59 pm (I do not believe in being late) stopping by to say hello to her mother and give her a report on her tests today. Informing her that I thought Rebecca was a smart girl and with a little application, she will do well in the upcoming exams. Telling her that she and the dogs got on well and I hoped that she would be ok with her looking after them in a month's time while I was away for a weekend.

Bidding them good evening and returned to the car; I had a bit of a skip in my step; I was happy; the day had gone exceedingly well, and I looked forward to the coming weeks and months.

Selecting something pretty I had ordered for her online, a matching set of retro lingerie made up of a black lace bra, waspie and suspenders outfit and a pair of heels. I had also purchased some makeup for her from Kat Von D and collected that up as well.

I returned to the hall, happy to see her standing there, not trying to hide or cover her nakedness in any way, seemingly happy to be standing there exposed like that. I took a good long look, my cock stiffening as I soaked in the beauty of this young lady. I then handed her the outfit and makeup. (Really is a natural exhibitionist, this girl, I thought once more.)

"I will be in the other room waiting. The lesson begins in fifteen minutes. Make yourself look pretty, Rebecca!" I said, before leaving her to go and get dressed.

I readied the room, setting up the video camera so it would be looking under the table. I planned on getting a recording of her during today's lesson. I checked the remote for the wand; it was working and was rewarded with the sound of buzzing against the wood.

Happy that all was in order, I sat in my window chair and waited for her to get ready. Hearing her coming first, heels clicking as she came down the stairs. She stood in the doorway, unusually looking a bit shy. I guessed that she had never worn anything this provocative, this overtly sexual before.

She looked amazing, and I told her so. I picked up my camera and took a picture and told her to go to the table and pose a little for me. She was getting better at posing, much better than last week, I noted.

"That's it, lean back on the table a little, now over the table, and yes, sit on it, lean back and cross those legs, you little tease!"

I ran her through a few more poses and then she seemed to get the idea of moving about and showing her body and the outfit off.

"That's great, Rebecca, you are a natural…" I told her with a big grin.

"Thank you, Sir, and thank you for the outfit. It is beautiful!" She said, looking so happy I think she was about to burst into tears.

"There will be more, and prettier outfits. Such a beautiful girl should be adorned in suitable attire," I told her. Again, a big happy smile on my face.

(I am such a lucky old pervert.)

"Now take your seat, Miss Lawson, you will see the wand is now in place on the chair. Please sit with your legs on either side of it and that sweet little pussy, pressing gently up against it!" I was now back in teacher mode.

"I shall turn it on in a moment, but first get comfortable and we shall talk about today's lessons."

I waited while she seated and adjusted herself into position.

"Good, today will be revision, followed by a test."

"The wand will be set to the lowest speed while you revise Miss Lawson. You have thirty minutes of revision, and twenty questions will follow."

"For each wrong answer, I will increase the speed by one notch. Also, for each wrong answer, you will stay sat for an extra ten minutes."

I paused to look at her.

"Is that clear, Miss Lawson?" I finished.

"Yes, Sir." Her eyes were wide, biting her lip in a way that would destroy the resolve of a lesser man.

"Your revision time starts now!" Switching on the wand to its lowest setting and I enjoyed the look on her face as the mild vibrations started to rumble through her little cunt.

I sat back, started the video recording, and watched her. Her legs were spread, her pantie covered crotch pressed against the vibrating head of the wand. She stayed sat upright this lesson, not able to slouch down on the chair. I could not see if she was wet, the black panties not giving that secret away, but I would bet my pension that her little snatch was more than a little moist right now.

I sat and watched her as she studied; watching as she began squirming a little, and she seemed to have a little sweat going on; I wondered if she is going to cum while I watch. Yes, she is. I watch her as she gripped the desk edges and tried to control herself. My dick was again rock hard watching this little cock tease, who had wanted my attention so bad that she exposed herself in my classroom, well she had it now.

She came twice during the revision section; I wonder how that affected her memory; I guess I will see soon enough.

I ran through the twenty questions (I won't bore you with them) but the result was not surprising fifteen out of twenty, so I guess the vibrations distracted the poor little dear.

I now set the wand to five. The rumbling on the wood increased, becoming rather loud now, and I could see her shuddering under its assault.

"Five wrong answers equal fifty minutes, Miss Lawson. Please revise and try to do better this time."
"I will ask those five again after the fifty minutes are up."

"There will be a further punishment if you get any wrong…" I said coldly, belying the lust that I was trying to hide with feigned disappointment.

I set my watch and left the room, happy that the camera will catch all her reactions. I expected that she would be sitting in a pool of her own cum by the time I returned.

Fifty minutes later, I was not disappointed; in fact, the floor could have been described as being awash with fluids! She had orgasmed and if I am not mistaken, squirted from the state of the floor. I kind of wished I had seen her face when she did that and wondered if that was her first time.

I repeated the five incorrect questions and was pleasantly surprised that she got them all right.

"Well done, Miss Lawson."
Smiling, as I looked down at the floor.

"That seems to be a lot of cum! Did you squirt Rebecca?" I asked.
(Hoping the answer was yes.)

"Um, I think so Sir, I never felt that before. I thought I had wet myself, but it happened a second time and I realised what it was…"

"I did not know I could do that Sir. Sorry." Remembering herself, she added "Sir!"
She was blushing (how cute) a very vibrant shade of red.

"Lord girl do not apologise for that. I am more than pleased that you can squirt, my good girl. I hope that you do so many, many times in the future…" I said, smiling as warmly and reassuringly as I could.

I walked over to the desk and placed a collar and leash on there for her, telling her to stand. I went behind her and removed her sodden panties and placed them in her mouth. I removed a fresh pair and put them on her, trying my hardest not to linger and give in to my temptation to eat that fine-looking arse as I pulled them up.

Picking up the collar, I fastened it about her neck and then attached the leash. Putting a hand on her shoulder, I pressed down, and she picked up on my meaning by this gesture and dropped down to her hands and knees. I then led her out to the garden.

The dogs greeted us and her with a bit of a sniff but left us alone when ordered to their cages. I led her over and showed her the cages and she watched as I latch the dog's cage closed, then led her to the new cage that I had recently installed. I then attached her collar to the hook in the cage and commanded her to stay.

"I will return in one hour. There is food and water in the bowl and as you can see you are on camera, and I will be recording your behaviour for later viewing."

She looked up, spotting the camera, trying to smile, even though her mouth was stuffed with her sodden panties still.

"Afterwards, you can dress, and we will walk the dogs in the woods again, and we can do a little rope suspension as a reward for doing so well today."

I went off and fixed us some lunch and packed my rigging kit up, ready for some fun later.
An hour later, I let her out of the cage, then handed her a coverall and shoes to wear until we were in the woodlands.

"Put this on for now. You can change back when we get into the woodlands."
Waiting while she complied, then letting the dogs out so she could leash them both, ready for their walk.

We left via the back gate again, crossing the field and entering the woodlands using the same path we used last time. I watched as she got both the dogs to sit and wait before she released them to run and explore. Happy that they seemed to have bonded already. (I'm sure they enjoyed having her as a kennel buddy for the last hour.)

"Now remove the coverall but leave the shoes. I do not want you breaking an ankle today."

The dogs ran, chasing each other about and enjoying their freedom. Meanwhile, Miss Lawson was on her lead, walking behind me, keeping pace as I pulled her leash when she fell behind. Feeling I was missing out on a lovely view, I told her to lead the way and let her walk ahead, dressed only in the black lace lingerie. (It was quite a lovely sight, I might add.)

We reached the river spot we had visited the previous week, and I instructed her to play with the dogs while I set up the rigging ring on the tree. I threw a climbing strap over a branch and connected a ring, so it was just about my head height. I laid out some rope and gave her back her shoes, instructing her to put them on.

I did not want to bundle her up too much as she looked so hot in that outfit, so I decided on tying a dragonfly chest harness and simple butt harness. I connected the down rope to her chest, lifting her onto her toes. Then pulled on the line connected to the butt harness and pulled until she was level with the ground. Tying off the lines and attaching another line and throwing that over the branch so her legs were now level with the rest of her.

"Push your legs out, so that you are fully stretched out, yes that's it. Now hold your arms out," I told her as I took multiple photos.

"You look beautiful like that, so natural in the rope, feel free to move about a little. Get used to how you can move your body while suspended in the rope." I took a few more photos, then I adjusted her chest rope and lowering her head.

Then tying her feet to the ring so she was now inverted. I set her spinning a little, but not too fast. I took several more photos and a short video, before gently lowering her to the ground.

I cradled her in my arms while untying her, keeping her connected to me as much as possible. I asked if she had enjoyed her first suspension and she replied simply with a massive grin. (Nuff said).

We rested in the sun, her head on my chest, relaxing and watching the dogs frolic in the water.

Eventually, asking her
"How had the deep throat training gone this week?"

"I am trying, Sir, but it is not easy. I even threw up one time… Sorry Sir!" she said looking downcast.

"Not to worry, it takes time. You will get there. Show me what you can manage." I said as I undid my fly, pulling out my cock.

She did not seem to need telling twice and set about my cock with gusto. This pleased me no end. (A proper cock whore this one.) She had changed her technique a little and there was a little less slobber and a lot more suction and even a little nibbling. She gagged a few times as she tried to take all of it in, but still, she could not quite get there. (A few more weeks and I would be able to pump that throat. (Well, at least that is what I hoped.)

I felt myself come again, quicker than I would like to have, but then again, I had had a stonker of a hard-on for several hours now… This pretty little eighteen-year-old was making me feel like I was thirty years younger.

She sat up and showed me her mouth, proudly showing me my cum on her tongue.

"Good, that was much better Rebecca. You may now swallow."
I smiled as I watched her swallow and then lick her lips to make sure she had got it all.

"Good girl. Let's head back now and get you cleaned up before your mother arrives…" Sending her off with the dogs, dressed in her sexy little outfit still, telling her I would catch up once I had put the rope away.

She walked off with not a care in the world, not worried at all about the possibility that someone else might come across her in the woods, dressed in only sexy little undies. She had not even bothered to change her footwear. What a sight that would be for someone…

I found her waiting at the edge of the wood, with the dogs now on their leashes, sitting patiently, tails wagging. Handing her the coverall so we could walk to the house without raising any eyebrows if spotted, unlikely but not worth the chance.

When we got home; I told her that her things were on the bed and to use the guest bathroom to clean up and remove the makeup.

Twenty minutes later she was down, dressed and waiting in the hall with the dogs, her mother due any minute now. When her mother arrived, we introduced her to the dogs, and I explained

that she had done very well today on her revision and that the tests at the month's end should be no issue for her.

"I will be going away next weekend for the night, but I will give her another revision test before I leave."

I also enquired,
"Are you certain you are OK with her staying overnight to babysit my babies?"

She assured me,
"Not at all; she is a grown girl and often stays with friends at the weekend now, anyway."

"That is great as I also have a long weekend planned in a few weeks' time and if you do not mind and things go well, I would love for Rebecca to look after the dogs for me, I will pay her of course!"

"I am sure that will be fine, but let's see how she is next weekend." Her mother replied, not at all looking concerned about her daughter staying over at a man's house.

I was pretty sure that her mum will be around next weekend, to have a nosey about. Rebecca had said the same, so we were going to play it straight next visit and do some proper revision, after all, I wanted her to do well in her exams as well.

I bid them goodbye and returned the dogs to the garden and decided to have a lie down in the hammock; it had been a tiring day. The end of the month was on my mind as I fell into a summer slumber.

Hard Lessons
The tuition of Rebecca

Chapter 7: Revision.

The weeks go by fast. Miss Lawson is learning, and her testing is going exceedingly well; going so well that I decide to reward her early.

"Rebecca, my girl, you have exceeded my expectations these last few weeks. Well done. I know the last few weeks have been hard. The lessons, the studying and also not being able to play has been rather frustrating!"

I smile and continue.
"For me as well, girl. Trust me, I wanted an excuse to spank that cute little behind! Strip you down and make you stand in the corner for hours, whilst I watch my game."

A small laugh and smile to show I was joking; I knew her thoughts on football.
"I also miss our oral lessons. I am sure you have advanced greatly in that aspect of your training, but exams are more important than the needs of our flesh, Rebecca, a few more weeks and we can celebrate."

"As you know, I am away next weekend, so you can use the house to study for the following week's tests. I will leave materials out for you and some guidance to point you in the right directions."

"But a good girl deserves a reward. So, if you go to the loft, you will see there is now a wardrobe next to the bed. This is yours." I say this, watching her face as it lights up.

"I am glad that brings a smile to that pretty face, Rebecca, but do wait until you see what's in it first!"

Watching her hesitate, I am certain she wants to go look but is waiting for my permission to leave; she has learned well.
"Go Rebecca, have a look. But look only. You can try them on next weekend, while I am away,"

I hear a distant,
"Thank you, Sir."
As she runs up the stairs, I smile, following at a more gentlemanly pace, wanting to see the glee in her expression when she sees the gifts, that I had purchased for her.

What I can only describe as a *squeee* emanates from the room as I reach the attic stairs; I took that to be a happy noise and continued in and found her holding one of the outfits against her as she stands in front of one of the large mirrors.

The dress; a Gothic Lolita style dress. Black and red with lots of lace and even came with a cape, so it had a little red riding hood about it. (A personal favourite of mine.)

She tosses it on the bed, just like the spoilt little girl she is, then pulls out another gift. I really have spoilt her but seeing her happy like this is a reward in itself.

This one is a rubber dress, red and black again, but this one is a rubber version of the LBD (little black dress) with buckles to make it more fetish appropriate. Again, I watch as she holds it against her. I can see she wants to try it on but when she catches my eye in the mirror, I shake my head and mouth next week.

She tosses that one aside and grabs the next outfit; I had purchased. I had bought four outfits along with lingerie, nightwear and matching shoes and boots.

The next outfit she pulls out is a black full-body rubber catsuit. This came with a heavily buckled corset and a hood with accessories.

"That, my dear, is the outfit for our first club night. You are quite beautiful, Rebecca, but until at least a year has passed, we have to keep our relationship a secret."
"You do understand that, don't you?"

I ask, waiting for her reply. It would be ruinous for my career. Should it be discovered I was dating a student, even an ex-student, even after she left the school?

Looking at me, she smiled and gave me a big hug.

"Yes sir, I know, it will stay our secret, and no one will recognize me in this outfit, Sir…"
All smiles, such a lovely smile, I think to myself for the millionth time.

She pulls out the last outfit, a mesh gown made of black opaque lace, off the shoulder and calf length.

"This will show off that body of yours perfectly. You can wear sexy underwear that you will find in the drawer at the bottom there or nothing at all!"
The look of lust I gave her then could have deflowered a nun at fifty paces.

"And on that shelf," I said, pointing to the uppermost shelf.
"You will find cat and bunny masks so we can keep your identity secret when attending events, plus I think you will look super cute in them…"

Going over to her and picking her up, I kiss her pretty little mouth. Kissing so passionately that we may as well have fucked. It felt so satisfying.

I dropped her off at home a little later, also a little less frustrated by all the deep kisses. Before she gets out of the car, I hand her one more gift.

"I know you have been practising your oral skills. There is one more thing you need to learn, and it is important that you learn this Rebecca as the time is coming where I will expect you to surrender to me fully."
Handing her a small box.

"You will know what to do with this. Get used to it, wear it at night, maybe practise with it while you practise your oral skills."
The thought of her spit-roasted came to mind.
(Later, you're a dirty old sod. Later.)

"Thank you, sir. I will practise. I want Sir to be happy with me." she says. Again, with that beautiful big smile.

I walk her to the door, greeted her mother and checked that all is ok for her to stay the weekend and look after my children (dogs) her mother assures me that it is ok, and she will drop her round. I know this to be a ploy on her part, as Rebecca has told me that her mother is quite nosey and has been asking questions about me.

I had known this would likely happen, so had a plan in place. The house would be sanitised, with all toys and kinky items put away. The loft cleared of all my rigging gear, shackles, and rings. The wardrobe locked. (Rebecca knew the location of the key.) The Dungeon was well hidden behind the pantry unit, so there was no chance of her finding that room. (That would have been impossible to clear.)

I thought that she might find it suspicious that a man of my age lived alone, so I put out a few pictures (Photo-shopped) of a

wedding, a wife and a faked memorial to make it seem like I was a widower.

The next weekend I checked in with Rebecca, late on Saturday evening, mainly to check on the dogs but also to make sure Rebecca was ok. She confirmed her mother had had a good nosey. She is such an embarrassment; she told me. I dismissed this, as I would have done the same in her boots. I was sure.

Placated her mother had left her to the dog sitting and told her to behave and not to have any boys over, she laughed when she said this.

"As if I want a boy!" she said and laughed again.

"Good luck with your exams next week," I told her, then I asked.
"So, what outfit are you wearing tonight?"

"The rubber catsuit, Sir, it feels amazing, so tight. The corset makes it hard to breathe but I love it, Sir, I really do."

"Can I send a video I made for you, Sir?"
A video, she says. I wonder what she has videoed; I hoped it was something naughty.

"Yes, please do, but use the computer, not your phone. As we discussed, we can't have anything that raised suspicions on your personal phone."

"I know Sir, I took it on your video camera. I will send it over now. I know it will make Sir happy," she said as she hung up.
Too excited to even realise she had not said goodbye.

The Video:

She is in the attic; the camera is pointing at an angle towards the tall mirror. I see her step into the frame in the reflection first. She is wearing the rubber catsuit, hood in place, and the blindfold pulled up so she can see out of the eyes. I watch as she licks the bottom of the dildo she has in her hand. It's not the training one I had given her, but one from the playroom! This one is ten inches at least and black like her suit. She looks over at the camera with a cat that got the cream smile on her face and places it head-height on the mirror, kissing the end. FML (Fuck my life).

I watch as she reaches behind her, unzipping the butt section of the suit, turning so I can see the pink of her arse in the mirror. I watch as she picks up another item, one I recognise. It was the gift I had given her the other weekend. She slips it into her mouth in a most suggestive manner and then again with a smile that would melt the coldest of hearts; she places the toy in the crease of her bottom…

I watch raptly as she slides it into place, to be buried deep in her arse, little pain on her face as she pushed it in, but it is fully in now, the base hidden between her cheeks.

She zips up the catsuit once again and picks up what I realise is a black silk scarf tied into a loop; she wraps it about one wrist, then after turning to face the mirror and the ten-inch black dildo, she pulls the blindfold into place. Then placing both arms behind her, she loops it onto the other wrist, twisting until her wrists are bound, bound as if I had tied them myself.

I watch fixated now, as she moves forward, tongue out, seeking the tip of the black rubber cock; she misses, and it hits the side of her face; I smile at this and smile broader when I hear her giggle. She turns her head, mouth open, and slides down the cock until she reaches the mirror, tongue wrapping around the rubber cock as much as possible. She must be aware of or have practised this, so she knows I can see her in the reflection clearly

as she slides up and down the shaft of the dildo before she takes the tip in her mouth…

She slowly bobs on the cock, taking a little more each time. I am watching, gripped by the sheer eroticism of what I'm seeing. She passes the 7-inch mark of her training dildo. It is now down her throat, and she does not stop there; she continued to bob up and down until she was almost to the mirror. I am amazed! Just six weeks since I gave her the dildo, to learn how to take my cock and now, she has surpassed expectations again.

How things have changed. The little exhibitionist that caught my attention by flashing her panties, now putting on a show that would be X rated on any site. Seems she really likes to put on a show. I shall have to remember that for future play.

Finally, her lips reached the base of the cock. I could see her throat swell as it went down a good 4 inches at least! I have to admit; I was masturbating! This show was more than a little arousing and certainly wank worthy.

She did not stop there, though, not satisfied with just getting to the end. She started to withdraw and then push forward a few inches at a time, so the rubber cock did not leave her throat! Face fucking her own throat. I watched as she pulled a little more and a little more back until she was at the tip and she would push forward again, each time showing me what she had learned.

I messaged her back on the PC. Sending along a picture of a cum splattered hand and cock, a tribute for such a good show... My girl, that was incredible, and you have been practising with the anal toy as well, good girl.

Graduation is coming and I think, Miss Lawson, that you will enjoy what is to come.

Meanwhile, it is time for you to find your kink name, choose well as it reflects on me
Rebecca.

Sir xx

Hard Lessons
The tuition of Rebecca

Chapter 8: Graduation.

The last of the exams had been completed, and the last days of school have come and gone. Rebecca had her birthday while she was away and was nineteen now. She had been away for a few weeks with her mother, as an unexpected reward for her hard work. Results won't be known for a few weeks yet, but I had assured her mother that she had studied hard and had done well in the mock tests I had set her in preparation for the real exams.

I had missed her while she was away and was saddened at missing her nineteenth birthday… I had sent her a message wishing her a happy birthday and hoping that she was having fun adding that the dogs and I look forward to seeing her in a week's time when she returned.

I grab the leashes from the hook and call Geri and Freki to take them for a run in the woods. While they run and enjoy their freedom, I set about mentally planning the final subjugation of Miss Lawson. I was more than a little taken with this young lady. Somehow, I had still managed to resist the temptation to rush things… To take her. To rush the process, so I could feel her submit her body to me.

She would have submitted to me that first day, I was sure. Almost certain that she wanted me to take her while she was strapped down in the dungeon! Especially after I had tongued her pussy and arse. But I had wanted to train this flower, guide her, ensure that she knew what I expected of her, how to please me and what she was getting herself into. She had trained with the dildo and butt plug, and I had experienced and seen for

myself that her oral skills were improving, culminating in the show she had videoed for me. (Watched several times now.)

I had a week to plan the perfect night for fun, tenderness, humiliation, pain, and submission, then finally her naming before I would take her as mine.

I ordered a new toy, one I had had in mind for some time, and I thought this would be perfect for next weekend and then spent the rest of the week preparing and cleaning my house and my equipment. The loft room was returned to normal now, rigging straps, mooring rings and cages all back in place. Ropes hung ready for use. I also brought up the St Andrews cross from the dungeon and set it, so it faced the window. A treat for sunset, I thought to myself.

Now I had but to wait until Friday afternoon for the graduation ceremony to commence. (Those five days felt like the longest five days ever.)

Friday: 17:00

I check my watch; checking the time again, a little late I thought. I had sent Rebecca the taxi fare, as I knew her mother was also away this weekend (a fortunate coincidence). I could have collected her, but that was not how I had this planned out and I was not going to deviate so soon from the plan.

I stood in the front room watching, I must admit, waiting; not all that patiently. A Little late, but there she was. The taxi pulled up, and she got out. She was in her summer dress and had her shoulder bag, a bag I knew to contain her uniform. I had asked her to save that so it could be added to the wardrobe up in the loft. I was very sure it would get some use.

I went to the front door, opening it as if to greet her.

74

No hello, no greetings or hugs today.
 "Strip!"
"Now…" I bark at her as if it was an order. Which it was…

I wait while she strips, playing shy, but I know that's an act… I liked it though. I take her clothes and her bag and tell her to stand facing the door and not to move.

"I shall return. Do not move."

I take her things up to her room (the spare room) I check that she is still standing naked facing the door; it has a glass front, but you would need to be right in front of it to see that she was there. Happy that she is obeying my instructions, I go to the guest bathroom and take a shower. I do this knowing full well she can hear it from where I left her standing.

Showered and fresh, I dressed in a three-piece suit; I felt it was appropriate to be properly attired on such a big day. I returned some fifty minutes later. She did not look back as she heard me approach, nor flinch as she felt my breath on her neck… Taking in her scent, her aroma, slightly perfumed, quite lovely. Just being this close makes my heart flutter (silly old bugger). I tie a blindfold about her eyes while I whisper into her ears gently.

"Do not speak, Rebecca, you will only speak if I ask you a question and I want direct, succinct answers only. Remember that you may call red at any point. As always, this will stop play."
"Nod your head, if you understand."

She nods, not saying a word, but I note that she bit her lip. I continue to whisper to her.

"Good girl. Rebecca, have you chosen your name?"
"You may reply with Yes Sir or no Sir only?"
Waiting patiently for her to answer.

"Yes, Sir," she says, in a low nervous voice.

This is a big step for her. This is going to be our name, the one we share and what I will call her in public when we are at any events or parties.

"Please tell me the name you have chosen."

"Cassandra."

I Repeated the name she had given "Cassandra." Calling her by her chosen name for the first time.

"A good choice. I like it. Well done."

knowing the name well, it was an apt name, as I was certain that she would shed a tear or three in the future.

I placed my hand on her shoulder and pulled as I stepped back, not to pull her over but to guide her, using gentle pressure transferred through my hand. I guided her into the living room, where I had set up a table for the first bit of play. This was to be sensual play, with maybe a little sprinkling of fear added in to spice it up.

Leading her to the table, I pick her up and place her down on the table, pressing her back so that she is lying flat on the surface. I placed headphones on her head covering her ears, so now she cannot hear nor see what I am doing, as I prepare the materials for the first session of the day.

While she lays there silently, like a corpse on the morgue table, not stirring, not making any noise. Her breathing was so shallow that I would be hard-pressed to notice the movement of her chest. I lit the candles and picked up a small bottle of sun-warmed baby oil. I begin gently massaging her, noting that her body is tense, but soon starts to relax as she feels my hands caressing and moving over her flesh.

My hands run up and down her body, moving her energy from her hands to her feet, also ensuring that I leave a thin film of oil on her skin to ensure the wax does not stick too hard to the flesh. I note also (as I took a very long look) that she has waxed this time; she is smooth, not even the slightest bristle. (I wanted to run my tongue down that tempting valley to feel the smoothness but kept to the plan.)

Picking up the first candle, I raise it a good few feet above her chest before letting it drip, a small drip hit her breast, and she shuddered, I knew from testing that at that height it would be only slightly warm, so her reaction was shock, at the unexpected sensation, not anything else. In fact, with these candles, I could drip it from an inch above her flesh and be sure that it would not burn; it would be hot, and she would feel it, but it would cause no damage.

I dripped more and then more on her breasts, alternating candles and breasts, so as not to overheat an area. Once a good covering was formed, I moved the candles down her body, running lines down her legs and arms. Then spreading her legs, I dripped it down that delightful channel that lay between her strong lean thighs, coating her soon to be plucked flower in a rainbow of colours and wax.

Taking up another candle, this one blood red, the wax dripping, moving it up from midriff to her neck. The candle held only a few inches away from her pale, trembling flesh as it dripped, intensifying the sensation as the wax fell dripping, running, so that looked like she had had her throat slashed. Then with a free hand, I closed her mouth and slowly ran the drips up her neck to her chin before coating those pretty lips in red wax, too.

I stood back admiring my work and the beauty of the colours decorating her, my flesh canvas. I picked up my camera and took several photos. I would show them to her later. I was

certain she would want to see how she looked lying there coated in wax.

Picking up my knife, a hunting one that was blunted slightly so it would not cut her, but she would feel the scrape of the blade still. I placed the icy blade on her belly so she would feel the weight and the coldness of the steel.

Picking up the blade and then running the back of the blade down the side of her face and pressing it up against her trembling throat, holding it there for a few seconds... A little fear is always a good thing in sensation play.

I placed the edge against the wax on her arm and began the process of removal, slowly shaving away the wax from her flesh. I did her arms and legs first, then I removed the wax from her mouth and throat. She sighed a little then; I was sure the sensation was turning her on; it was certainly having that effect on me. Leaving the fun parts to last, I took the blade to her breast, first cracking the wax with the back of the blade and flicking away the remains with the point, running little circles around the areola of each of her beautiful, firm little tits.

Finally, all that was left was the wax I had poured on her pussy...

I wanted this off whole, if I could, to save as a trophy piece. (I thought to myself absently that maybe I should order some plaster to take a mould sometime.) I spread her legs a little more, breaking the flesh seal, and gently teased the wax away from her perfect little cunt, getting most of it off in one piece. This made me incredibly happy. I would get a case to keep this in.

I took up some wipes and wiped her down. Raising her from the table slowly and wiping off any residue remaining from the wax and oil. Happy that she was clean, I checked my watch: 20:00. On schedule, I thought. Soon the sun would come down and I

wanted to get her on the cross. Placing my hand on her shoulder, I guided her up to the loft and fixed her in place facing the window, lifting the blindfold so she could see the sun setting in the distance.

Lifting the headphones, I whisper into her ear.
"No looking back at me, just watch the sunset, Cassandra…"
Calling her by her newly chosen kink name.

Stepping back, I picked up my floggers, a matched pair, and gave her a couple of gentle strokes across her back. I built up speed, florentining her back as the sun set in the distance. Keeping this up on her back for five minutes. (My arms ached like bastards, but I kept up the flogging.) I could hear her crying at the end, the pain and pummelling breaking her down as she watched the sunset over the woods.

"Cassandra's tears," I said warmly.
Forgetting that she could not hear me with the music playing in her ears.

I pressed up against her back and held her and joined her in watching the sun go down. Once the sun was hidden, I slipped the blindfold back in pace and led her away carefully down the stairs to the dungeon.

I led her over towards my latest acquisition, a vacuum bed. I had wanted to get one for a while, and Rebecca's graduation seemed like the perfect excuse to splash out.

Walking her over and standing her in place, I pressed down on her shoulder, and she knew that meant to sit. Once she sat, I pressed her back and laid her out on the base sheet of the bed. Deciding to leave the headphones on, though, I did change the music for some atmospheric audio I had found. (Dungeon sound effects, nice and creepy.)

She did not know what this was, as she had not seen it before, so this sensation would be something very new to her. I zipped the sheet over her pretty little naked body, placing a breathing tube into her mouth, covering it to show her that it controls her breathing.

I placed my fingers in her hand and she squeezed, a silent signal we had agreed on that told me she was ok. I switched on the vacuum. Such a noise in the enclosed space, but it was soon over, and the air had been sucked out of the space between the sheets. She was trapped like Solo in carbonite, and the black, shiny rubber showed her body contours rather well. Such pretty contours, too.

I ran a cloth with the rubber polish over her body, feeling her through the material. (And wondered if I could get one with a hole or fitting that allowed me to fuck her whilst in this device.) Her legs were parted, so I ran my fingers down her slit, slapping it now and then. Then, grabbing the Hitachi wand, I proceeded to force her to cum again and again. She would be laying in a pool of her own juices soon. Each time I felt her climaxing, I covered the breathing tube, counting to thirty before letting her breath again.

I kept up this assault on her pussy for half an hour before releasing her from the rubber trap; I had expected her to be a sweaty, pussy-soaked mess when I let her out, and I was not disappointed.

I towelled her down, removing the headphones (probably ruined as they were soaking as well). I could smell her scent now; she was bathed in her pussy juices. I did not really care; she smelled wonderful to me right now.

"Cassandra, you are a dirty little girl, you soaked that bed, you smell of your cunt, this room reeks of your sex…" As I spoke, I

was stripping down, I would be as naked as well for the next parts.

I stood in front of her now and removed her blindfold so she could see me. She blinked a few times, eyes focusing on me, on my nakedness and eyes lowering to my rampant hard-on.

I looked upon her kneeling before me, so pretty evening her sweaty cum soaked state. And with a serious tone, I said,
"Will you, Cassandra, do me the honour of being my submissive?" Offering the silver bangles, a matched pair that could link together to form a set of cuffs I had purchased to symbolise our relationship.

We had discussed the ins and outs; she knew what was expected of her and what her submission to me entailed, what the vow meant to me. That I would look after her, train her, help her grow, and guide her through life.
She knelt, and said, as I had earlier instructed a clear and concise answer.
"Yes, Sir."

That smile melted away any coldness I was feigning at the moment.

Two words only, but filled with so much meaning. We had discussed what I expected from her; her vows to be my faithful slut, my toy, and just simply mine, were imparted in those two simple words.

She lifted her wrists, still on her knees, and I fitted the silver cuffs on each wrist in turn and connected them, handcuffing her wrists together.

She lowered her arms, leant forward and kissed the end of my cock! Then she took it in her mouth and slowly swallowing until her lips met my balls, which she then flicked with her tongue…

A little bit of showing off which pleased no end. She did not bob but waited, cock down her throat. I placed my hands about her head, grippIng and then I started to fuck her face. I was so pleased to see her taking the whole length of my cock down her throat, I could have forgotten that I had another consummation idea in mind. But I did enjoy this for a good five minutes before stopping and slapping her face.

"You little cock sucking whore... That was amazing! The next time, I will shoot cum down your throat." I said breathily and with so much raw lust in my voice, I think I made her cum, or maybe she shivered in fear.

I handed her a towel again to wipe herself down. Drool covered boobs were pretty but messy too. Grabbing a handful of her hair as she finished, I dragged her over to the horse and bent her over it.

"Stay, slut," I order.

I went over to the rack and selected a 10mm thick cane, thick and thuddy. Then cock still waving about rampantly as I walked over to her again, I told her.

"This is the last step in your graduation before we consummate our bond. This will not be a hard caning as you are not ready for that yet, my sweet Cassandra."

"That said, I want a number from you. This will be a test of your commitment to me. Now tell me how many strokes of this cane you want?" I said this with as much seriousness I could, not easy for a naked man carrying a stick.

She was quiet; I guessed she was trying to work out what would make me happy. Too many and she would not be able to take it even if they were not so hard. They would really hurt, she knew. Too few and I would doubt her commitment.

"Thirty-six Sir."
Pausing a second before repeating,
"Yes, thirty-six Sir."

Good, she remembered I have a thing for 6 and multiples of such; I smiled at her and with the end of the cane I poked her bottom, aligning it for the first of the thirty-six strokes.

"You will count silently," I said.
As I delivered the first stroke gently on her beautiful pale backside. (Soon to be very red and a little sore).

After every second stroke, I increased the power behind the cane, moving it up and down her bottom so as not to hit the same place too often. After twenty-four, I was now hitting her as hard as I would normally start, so I levelled out the power and kept it steady for the next ten strokes.

She was crying now, sobbing; she was not prepared for how much the cane could hurt; I think. But even so, she was not moving, and that impressed me so much.

The last two were lined up, and I decided that she had earned full power, I had not planned this, but she had impressed me by not running away or wiggling, so I felt that she could taste the pain properly just two strokes, but they would mark her for days; I looked forward to seeing the bruises, bruises she would wear as a badge of honour.

We had reached the last few strokes; I was disappointed, but not in her. She had been amazing. No, I doubted now that she could ever disappoint me; I was disappointed only in that this had to end, so I reluctantly admitted.
"Last two…"

I delivered the stroke across her bum in line with that little rosebud of hers, and before she could dance out of the way, the second stoke followed the first in almost the exact same spot.

She jumped up, and I held her, comforting her, letting her recover from this her first proper caning. Her head on my chest, tears running down her cheeks and wetting my chest hair. I will be honest; her tears and the pain I inflicted, if it is even possible, made me harder.

It was time now, so feeling the warmth of her arse and slipping a finger down into the valley of her bottom, I found that little rosebud arse hole and slipped a finger in… Testing for resistance; I found it only a little tight but relaxed. Pressing all the way in, then slipped another finger in as I lifted her face to kiss her.

"Mine," I said.
As I fingered her arse, hard, not gentle, I had denied myself this treat, saving it up for her graduation and her submission and now I was going to take her as if she was mine, and mine she was now.

"Yes," a breathy pause. "Yours," she said.
She kissed me back as she leaned over the horse again.

I took her then; I was none too gentle going in and heard her cry out as I pressed into her, but I just pinned her down with a hand and started to thrust violently at first but calming down after a bit to get a rhythm going. Leaning on her to kiss her neck and at the same time pin her down, showing her that she was mine to do as I pleased with.

Grabbing my cock, I aimed it, as I started to thrust in and out of her arse; only allowing an inch or two to enter each time. Again and again, I thrusted into her arse until I started to feel that familiar feeling, and then I plunged again, listening to her as she

reacted, her own body falling into a rhythm with mine. She had cum a few times; the floor was wet. A squirter! I was certain she had the other week and from the wetness; I felt I was sure she had again.

I growled. She screamed; she cried out to her deities. I called out to mine; I cried out in pain, in relief, and release. She cried out in submission, release from constraint and acknowledgement of her own inner sluts' enjoyment of being treated like a piece of meat for her Sir's pleasure. without pulling out, I pulled her down to the floor and held her tightly to my body. Breathing slowly, recovering, my heart no longer racing, our bodies trembling in the aftershock of the coupling.

I kissed the back of her neck, that being the only place I could reach whilst in this position, cock softening but still embedded in her.

I held her close and whispered.

"Mine," I said.

I heard a quiet reply, almost below a whisper it was so softly spoken,
"Yes, Mine too."

A little later:

We lay there, sleeping for a while. I think time certainly seemed to have passed, and she was asleep when I moved her. I stood, then bent and collected her in my arms, carrying her up the stairs, careful not to bang her on the walls or framing. I carried her to my bathroom and set the shower running. She stirred, waking as I set her down on the floor of the shower and soaped up a sponge before joining her down there.

I proceeded to clean her, slowly, ritually, head to toes, cleaning each nook and cranny, then standing pulling her up, I used the shower to clean between her legs, feeling my blood warm and rush to my cock! Again, thinking about eating that pussy until she climaxed on my face.

Not wanting to wait, I dipped down behind her and bent her forward so she leaned against the wall, pushing out that tight little arse. Not needing a better invite, I buried my face in her cunt, tongue lapping her, drinking up pussy juices as she came again and again. Having my fill of her pussy, I decided to fill her pretty little cunt properly, the last hole for me to make mine.

Taking hold of her hair again, I lead her up to the four-poster bed in the loft and tied her down spread eagle on the bed and pounced upon her, driving my cock into her like my life depended on filling that tight little cunt. Placing my hand about her throat, thrusting in and out, choking her almost out several times but letting her cum when she could no longer hold back the climax, not denying her that pleasure.

Covering her mouth and nose as she orgasmed, I held until I saw her eyes flutter and her fight subsides, holding my thrusting until the moment, then I release before hammering into her soaking wet cunt again. No real resistance, though it was tight still and I could feel her clench and grip my cock as she came.

Feeling the tide turn, knowing that my control was slipping and that I would climax any second now, I choked her again, this time not letting up until she slipped under. Realising as I came, my cries were like those of a man finding his religion. As she came around, I kissed her as if my kiss had breathed life back into her.

Kissing her, I felt between her legs, fingers scraping up the cum I had left in her, and I lifted them to her mouth and watched as she sucked and licked them greedily clean.

Once she had cleaned my fingers, I slipped her ties off and added a new one, tying both her wrists together to the head of the bed. Covering her, I slipped off to lock up and check on the dogs before returning to find her fast asleep. For the first time, I slipped in the bed and spooned her, falling asleep soon after.

My dreams were filled with fresh adventures, adventures shared with my girl, my Cassandra, interesting times were ahead that was for sure.

Hard Lessons
(Book 1.5)
Debut

These short stories (interludes) fall some two years after the events of Hard Lessons, Rebecca now Twenty-one years of age, soon to be a collage graduate is ready for her and Mr Wyles relationship to become public.

Mr Wyles decides to treat her to an outing to a very exclusive club for her coming out debut. And a rather exciting limo ride around some of London's more famous landmarks.

Hard Lessons.
Debut.

Chapter 1: Debutante.

"Good morning, birthday girl," I say to her, as I unlatch the cage, the cage that she had slept in last night... She wakes, eyes squinting a little at the bright light, but still amazingly cheerful for someone who spent the night in a dog cage.

We have a little game of chance that decides where she gets to sleep.

1. A girl's choice.
2. In her own (previously the guest room).
3. The loft room tied to the four-poster bed, face up, or face down on the flip of a coin.
4. The cage in the basement dungeon.
5. The cage outside.
6. In the big bed with Sir.

Last Night she had rolled a Four. So, I had taken her down to the dungeon to put her to bed for the night. But yes, of course, we had had some fun before I left her there, to go rest in my comfortable bed, but nothing too hard, as I did not want her beauty marred by bruises and welts today.

Today marks her twenty-first birthday and almost two years since she had submitted to me fully and agreed to become my submissive. We had kept the relationship under wraps and for the first year. For that year, she had stayed in the local college dorm rooms (though more often than not, she had stayed with me).

Year two she had moved into my spare room, with her mother's permission. Her mother being no fool, but happy that her

daughter was happy and well cared for. Her mother had sold up and moved away soon after, gone almost a year now, living in Greece with a young waiter (we call her Shirley these days).

I led her to the kitchen where I had made her a special breakfast, comprising a stack of pancakes, crispy bacon, baked bananas, and ice cream smothered in maple syrup. She was a healthy eater and worked out daily, but today was her birthday and she could damn well enjoy a little cheat day.

She saw the food, already laid out, only needing the ice cream adding. She threw her arms around my neck and gave me a big kiss as a thank you. And without another word, set about demolishing the food I had laid out. I poured her a fruit juice and handed her a mug of barely stewed green tea, and left her to her birthday breakfast.

Heading upstairs, I set the bath running, adding scented oils, and getting her wash things ready for her bath. Another treat, one that I enjoyed giving her now and then. Not too often so that she would expect it, but two or three times every month, I would wash, shower or bath her, washing her hair and body almost ritually at times. Sometimes it would lead to sex, others I would dress her in her night things and put her to bed with her teddies and let her have her little time.

College was hard, and she liked to escape into different mindsets, and I played along with these, devising play based around her current mood. Of course, I could also set the mood and she would bow to my will, but never would I break her from her little space until she was ready.

The bath filled and steaming hot; I called down, letting her know she was clearly enjoying her feast as normally she would never keep me waiting, unless the brat was in the house, though I doubted that would be an issue today. Today was a big day, not

only twenty-one but her coming out party, well it was a party, and she would be coming out in a sense.

For the last two years, whenever we have been out to clubs, parties, and events, she has been in a mask, usually, a full rubber or leather catsuit or similar ensemble, always with her face at least partially covered. This was so no one would recognise her as an ex-student. I was not the only teacher on the scene, not even the only teacher at my school. We needed a reasonable space of time to pass before we could be seen together. I was sure a few eyebrows would be raised in the teachers' lounge, but at twenty-one, she was now a full-grown woman and there was nothing they could do about her and myself being in a relationship...

Today she would not hide away behind well-fitted rubber, no matter how hot she looked in that form-fitting outfit that showed off her body so well. I was going to introduce her properly and though she was known by her chosen name of Cassandra, no one knew what she looked like or had guessed at her being an ex-student. Most had thought that the masks were her kink.

She enters the bathroom, a big, satisfied grin on her face, and more excitement seeing that I had run her bath. Another treat for her today. Many more to come.

"Sie, you're spoiling me," she said, the smile wider and ever so beautiful.

A night in the cage had not dampened her at all. I think she secretly likes it. Though not so much the dog cage out the back, that could be cold and wet at times. (No, I did not make her sleep in it in the winter. What sort of man do you think I am!)

She was already totally naked; she spent a lot of time that way when home unless I laid out an outfit for her to wear. Of which there were many, as I did like to spoil my girl. She particularly

likes the Japanese anime outfits and wore them out at weekends and to college sometimes. the effect she must have on the males! I know full well the effect she has on this particular male; she is like walking Viagra to me.

Though when we go away, far away so we can have weekends out shopping and eating out like a normal couple. Though admittedly most think we are father and daughter until they see us kiss, that is. (Their faces.) I always insist she dress more appropriately, fifties attire at the least, or if it is warm enough, a summer dress is always a win for us.

She dipped straight into the hot bath, making a few oohs and ahhs noises as she settled into what she describes, as a monkey bath (so hot it makes you sound like a monkey when you get in). Once she had settled, I pressed her back and wet her hair so I could wash and condition her beautiful naturally coloured hair worn shorter now than when I had first met her. Her hair was now shoulder length, where before it hung down her back. I had carried out this routine many times over the last two years; It gave me more pleasure than I can or am willing to openly express.

So much of our play involves pain and suffering, but this simple caring almost parental act bonded us more than almost anything else. I never allowed her to call me daddy, though I know she has wanted to at times, especially in her little mindset. This act of bathing her, preparing her for the day, was as paternal as I got with her. I certainly loved her but not in a parental way, so I made the decision not to confuse things with DDLG play.

To complete the ritual of washing and conditioning her hair, I rinsed her off with the shower then plaiting her hair so she could style it later. I then took out the razor kit. Today I was preparing her for her coming out party and I wanted the honour of preparing her body. Using her body oils as a lubricant, I shaved her underarms, her legs and then her lady bits, this time

removing the little landing strip she likes to keep. (Fewer rashes that way.) Today though, she was to be as smooth as silk well at least until we bejazzled the area later.

Taking a warmed bath sheet from the heated towel rack, I wrapped her up, patted her bottom, and sent her on her way. She turned and came back towards me. As she stepped up to me, I could feel the warmth radiating from her body from the heat of the bath and the towel, and she gave me a loving peck on the cheek.

"Thank you, that was lovely." She said, then kissed me on the mouth, long and deeply.

I needed no Sir, as this was an act of love between us, one she enjoyed receiving as well as giving. (I did rather enjoy her bathing me.)

She left then, shaking her butt in an exaggerated manner. The little tease, I thought as I turned to clean up the bathroom.

Shortly after she left, I heard a squealing noise from her room; I guessed she found her birthday gift. I had purchased her a set of Kiss Me Deadly lingerie and a Vivian Holloway 1950 style pencil dress that I knew she liked, and a brand-new pair of shoes to match.

Leaving her to get herself ready, from experience I knew that it would be the best part of an hour before she would be fully dressed and made up. (I did not mind, the results were always worth the wait.) I picked up the leashes and took the dogs for a walk in the woods.

Getting back forty-five minutes later and headed to my room to get myself ready. I had chosen to dress up today as well, choosing my Glasgow brown tweed three-piece suit and hat.

My timing, as always, was perfect, and she was waiting for me as I came down the stairs, she was dressed in her new outfit. Hair styled appropriately for the style of dress she was wearing.
"Gods, you look stunning, my dear girl," I said, doffing my hat to her.

"Thank you, Sir, the gifts were beautiful and fit me so well…" she said, whilst giving me the old Anthea twirl. (Spinning around for those too young to remember.)

I picked up her bag, mine was already stowed away in the car. Hers was unusually light for a weekend trip, but then again; she did not need much tonight. We were off to London. There was a big party tonight, and she was debuting there, finally emerging from her cocoon.

I had booked a hotel on the Mall and booked a luncheon at the Ritz; she looked like a classic movie starlet, and I was going to show her off today.

She took my arm as we entered, announcing to all that she was with me and making it clear she was not my daughter, but my paramour. No more hiding from today. We deposited our things in our suite and took a horse and carriage to the Ritz, arriving in style. We enjoyed our afternoon of high society tea and cakes, before strolling through first Green then Hyde park's before heading back towards Covent Garden to have a light but needed dinner. (Needed for me anyway, I don't like missing meals.)

She ate little, nerves getting to her, but I made her eat a little more, insisting she finish her soup at least,
"It would not do you any harm Rebecca, and being hungry later might impact your fun," I told her, in my best fatherly voice.

As I ordered her a portion of chicken and sweetcorn soup. She was always this way on a night out, always worried about having a food belly and ruining the look of her skin-tight outfits.

She needn't have worried. She worked out almost daily and had the most amazing figure.

Grabbing a black cab back to the hotel, I told her to take a nap, if she wished, while I would unpack our things. Unpacked, I stripped out of the suit and took a shower before joining her on the bed for a little nap of my own.

I awoke to the sounds of a shower running, Rebecca singing away happily to herself... A habit I had gotten used to (eventually). Checking the time, I saw it was 19:25 as usual; I had woken a few minutes before my alarm was set. No idea how my body knew the time, but it has always been the case.

She exited the shower wrapped in a large white hotel towel and slippers, grabbed her vanity bag, then disappeared into the living area where there was a good-sized mirror to get herself made up. As always, she liked to get ready and let me see the end results. But tonight, I would not see until we arrived at our destination. I knew what to expect, of course, as I had given her instructions. But still, I would not see until after we arrived what she had created. I only knew that she would take my guidance and create something special for tonight's main event.

Grabbing my suit bag, I laid out my evening wear, a tux by DSquared and a pair of Ted Baker Oxfords. Happy that all was right, I went and grabbed a shave and shower myself, after all, I was part of her ensemble tonight and I had to look the part too.

Hard Lessons.
Debut.

Chapter 2: The Gentleman and the Debutante.

Showered, shaved, and dressed, I headed down to the bar area situated just off the lobby area and ordered myself a drink. Nothing too heavy but something cold and refreshing to start the evening off with. Rebecca is still getting ready and will meet me here as arranged.

It's her night, so of course, she keeps me waiting, but only for a little while. I will let that slide tonight. I'm sitting with my back to the bar, people watching but also with an eye to the stairs, waiting for her to make her entrance.

And what an entrance. Eschewing the elevator, she glides down the stairs, her feet coming into view first. She is wearing a pair of bejewelled stiletto-heeled pumps; her legs bare and still slender with the coltishness of youth.

She is wearing a red belted trench coat fastened about the waist by a belt and around her neck is the titanium dragon scaled collar I had put out for her to wear tonight. Her face, as ever, was perfect. Her makeup was applied with subtle touches of colour, except for her lips, which were done in ruby red rhinestones. Her shoulder-length hair fell down her face in ringlets (be still my beating heart).

She was beautiful looking every inch a movie star. Art in human form and every face was turned towards her as she slowly walked down the stairs, making an entrance. (Practising for later, I thought.) If onlookers only knew what she was wearing under that coat! I think there may have been a heart attack or two. Mine was certainly racing.

Enthralled by her beauty; I kept watching her, taking in every slow movement (she was really milking this walk). Eyes following her from all sides still, as she came up to me and not wanting to ruin her lips just yet, kissed me gently.

"Thank you for the new collar, Sir, it is beautiful…" she said, running a finger across the cold metal.

"Not as beautiful as you, ye god's girl, you fair near gave some of these chaps a heart attack with that entrance and my lord girl, those lips are amazing. Will they last the night?" I asked.

"Long enough Sir, I have my backup in my pocket for later." She replied with a literally dazzling smile.

I stood, signalling to the concierge, with whom I had arranged our evening transport to the venue at least.

A limousine pulled up, and she *sqeee'd* gripping my arm with excitement. The driver jumped out and opened the doors for us and we slid in; I was pretty sure he got an eye full, as she was very unladylike as slipped into the seat! The exhibitionist in her was strong.

I gave the driver a slip of paper with the address, a rather secret address at that. This party was rather exclusive and had cost me a pretty penny for the tickets, but as it happened to fall on her birthday, I could not resist. Plus, I had always wanted to attend one of these functions.

We sipped some Champagne; she used a straw so as not to disturb the bejewelling; they were pretty good at staying on as she had used them on her breast a few times for parties.

I had not seen the rest of her creation; I had only told her about the theme for the night. What she wore under the coat would only be revealed only when we arrived.

97

I took hold of her hand, noticing that her nails were done in a similar fashion to her lips, only with smaller jewels, and she had done a line of tiny jewels on her eyelids so when she blinked, you could see them. I really could not wait to see what else she had created for tonight...

Taking the scenic route about London towards the Strand. Taking in a few sights along the way, the palace being one and Big Ben; I knew she had wanted to see those.

"We can have a proper wander tomorrow, sweetie," I said, making sure she knew she would get to do the touristy stuff I knew she loved.

The party was being held in a place called the Vaults, hired by Killing Kittens tonight. They would fit this exclusive venue out in a manner reminiscent of the infamous Hell Fire Club. Pulling up outside, the driver again exited and opened the door for Rebecca. As I exited, I tipped him and asked if he would be free in three or four hours. He nodded as he slipped me his card.

"Call me half hour before you are ready to leave Sir and I will be waiting for you. Have a good evening."

We were greeted by the doorman, attired much like the doorman at our hotel, only in the red livery of a house guard. Given the exclusivity of some of the clients, he could well be one or an ex one at least. He scanned my phone and crossed us off a list.

As we entered and took the lift down to the vaults themselves, I noted the coat check at the reception and when asked; I said I would drop it off later if that was ok. This was, after all, not the place or time for her big reveal.

We were then greeted by one of the girls working the club (a greeter). The hostess was dressed demurely, in a long figure-

hugging sequined dress; she was quite stunning, but I expected nothing less from the organisers. She led us to our booth and pointed out all the areas we might be interested in.

There were dance cages, inverted crosses, and several St Andrews crosses against walls. In the cages were naked dancing men and women, all of them stunning. A young male was tied to the inverted cross (upside down) and was being flogged in a rather sensitive area by two tall and rubber-clad dominatrixes. I was not sure if they were guests or entertainment, but it was entertaining to watch. Though I admit to flinching a little, when they landed a rather cracking blow on his testicles… (ouch.)

The music was basey, and the lights were changing in time with the base, but it was not so loud that you could not talk at a normal level. These people knew their crowd and catered to their needs well.

On the table was a card with our names marked reserved, flowers (roses) and a champagne cooler with a bottle already chilling.

I asked the greeter where the display area was. This was a stage set up for those who wanted to show off their partners.

She gestured to the right, through an archway,
"The judges will be sitting in half an hour Sir she said." Smiling and giving an appraising look over at Rebecca.

I was not overly interested in the judging, but when she removed her coat, I wanted her to be seen by as many eyes as possible.

We sipped our drinks; she was still using a straw and even went off to the ladies' room to check on her jewels were all in place.

"Back soon, Sir…" she said, as she headed off to the powder room.

I got up and went to the stage area to wait for her; I was to escort her onto the stage. My Domliness would probably be assessed but mostly for my Suit and the confidence I exuded as I led her onto the stage. Hardly mattered to me, but I know she wanted this to be perfect. I was certainly not intending to trip up in front of all these esteemed guests. Heck, I even knew a few by name. The Headmaster was here as a judge and as a close friend, he would never let me forget it if I dropped the ball tonight.

She joined me a few minutes later, kissing my ear to announce her presence to me. I was preoccupied with checking out the stage and those being led up the walkway to be presented to the crowd. Whoop's whistles and handclaps were not uncommon. Some outfits worn were amazing, others were wearing little if anything, a bow tie on one young fellow's rather large cock, collars were of course worn by all signifying they were taken. The best was a furry dog girl, whose costume was amazing. The work involved in making that outfit was astounding.

Eventually, it was our turn; I went ahead, and she followed at my heel; I walked to the end and stopped; she stopped exactly one step behind me. Without looking, I put out my hand and she stepped forward, and I stepped back and one step to the side, so I was now behind her.

She looked up now, seeing her audience. No frightened rabbit this girl... No, she loved being seen. after all, being seen is how she got my attention and tonight she would have the audience's attention. Slipping my arms about her, I unfastened the belt on her coat, and then slowly undid the 3 buttons holding it closed. Then I stepped away as she shrugged off her coat, letting it drop to the floor.

Finally, she was revealed, exposed in the spotlight on stage for all to see, no longer hidden away behind a masque. I stepped

back several more paces after picking up the coat to allow her freedom to move about and show off her outfit.

Her outfit; or lack of outfit in this case: She was naked as I had instructed but had vagazzled herself, also at my request. She had created two serpents seemingly coming out of her vagina and wrapped about her waist, creating a heart shape with their bodies and heads. Each serpent's head curved in just below her breasts. Her nipples looked almost rouged; the illusion created by using the same stones she had for her lips.

There was a sigh of appreciation in the crowd for her, then the whooping, clapping, and whistling followed soon after.

I held out my hand, and she tottered back to me, with such a smile on her face, I was surprised the jewels did not ping off around the room.

I removed a length of silver chain from my pocket, clipped it to the collar and led her to the wall where the other submissive's were being displayed. I attached the other end of a chain and left her there without another word.

She would be on display for an hour and then I would release her, and she would be able to mingle and dance should she wish.

I mingled for a while, saying hello to a few old acquaintances and of course, greeted the headmaster, who patted my shoulder and laughed.

"I knew that girl of yours was one of ours! Kept her well-hidden, didn't you," he said.

Not that he could talk. His current partner was an ex-pupil herself, though many, many years had passed since she attended the school.

"Stunning girl, I can see why you kept her under wraps all this time... twenty-one now though eh, so no worry about disciplinary action, not that I would be saying anything, of course..." Laughing again.

"I will tell you all bout it sometime. She was quite brazen, a born exhibitionist!" Laughing as I said it, recalling the sight of her white panties from behind my desk.

In fact, that gave me an idea, and I decided to cut the evening short. We had done what we came to do, and although I had spent a bundle on this evening, I rather wanted the girl to have the best time. And I could not think of a better way for an exhibitionist to enjoy a trip to London, than putting on a show.

Taking out the card, I sent a text to the limo driver, hoping that he would be free for a few hours. Then returning to a very board looking Rebecca, many of the others having already been collected and taken away to play. I released her and led her back to our booth to ply her with a little more Champagne and await the limo driver's message.

I did not have to wait too long; the driver replying to my message, with a, certainly Sir, that would be my pleasure.

I led her to the coat check where I had dropped off her coat earlier. Introducing her to the Headmaster and his partner along the way. She, of course, knew them both, but they had never seen her face, and they both showered her with praise for her stunning outfit.

I lead her to the lifts, whereupon I put her coat back on her, whispering my idea for the evening into her ear as I kissed her lightly scented neck. She did a little bouncing jump and was clearly excited by the idea.

We stepped out; the limo arriving exactly on time, the driver, as always hopped, out and opened the doors for us both. We then set out on a sightseeing tour with a difference.

The first stop was Tower Bridge in front of the Tower of London. We hopped out, the coat unbuttoned, and I quickly took a series of snaps... I even brazenly asked a member of the onlooking public to take a picture of us both, as we posed next to one of the blue posts in front of the castle. Then some more with the towers of Tower Bridge in the background. Rebecca had at one point removed her coat and received cheers from some onlookers. Others were not so impressed, but it was Saturday night, and this was London. I doubted we really shocked anyone.

The driver then headed us back to Trafalgar Square, where we once again jumped out, while he would circle the square in the limo and pick us up in a couple of minutes. I got a few of her draped on the lions and then dancing in the fountain, naked again, this time joined by a few revellers who thought it was a hoot. I quickly got her back in her coat and headed back to the pickup point before any of the London bobbies could rain on our evening.

Dropping us off on the Mall, he said it would take him five minutes at least to circle back, so we took advantage of this and sought out a few good spots for more pictures. Not wanting to get arrested as security here was a bit strong, but we still managed to get a shot of her at the Victoria memorial; exposed but coat still on and another one of us both, thanks to a friendly passer-by. and then one in front of the gates to the palace before a guard ushered us politely on.

The limo arrived exactly five minutes after he left us. This man was earning his tip tonight and maybe a little show as well.

Enough photos, I thought, leaning over and speaking with the driver, then handing him some notes. I sat back and pulled her to me.

"Well Miss Lawson, did you ever think you would be flashing in front of the Queen?" I asked. Laughing at our antics, as I pulled her in closer to kiss her, no longer worried about ruining her lips.

"No Sir, I really am the luckiest of girls Sir… I'm so glad you noticed me that day." She said breathily, whilst kissing me back as hard as she could. Her hand grabbed and firmly squeezed my cock through my trousers.

I quickly removed her coat and leaned her back. The Driver had been told to circle London tourist areas for a while; he was welcome to watch but don't crash, that would be awkward.

I went down on her. This time, I was going to pleasure her first for a change. It was her birthday, after all; and anyway, I enjoyed eating this young filly out. I tongued, licked, sucked and I rimmed her smooth body, face buried deep between her thighs. Getting her thoroughly wet and then to cum, and even though the heat, the moister and the action was removing her jewels, I did not let up until I felt her shiver, spasm and climax…

Then she set about removing my jacket and trousers, my shoes were already kicked off. Pressing me back to the seat as she straddled my already hard cock. The driver, seeing this, slid back the sunroof so her head would pop out if she lifted enough. Ideal for a girl that likes to put on a show.

We drove about London, her head bobbing slightly through the sunroof, her cries audible to those walking by and when we were caught at lights she did not let up, even waved at a few gawpers.

104

I had an inkling that the driver was deliberately choosing a route that had heavy traffic control, so he could watch more of the show, and we seemed to circle Trafalgar Square more than a few times. She orgasmed at one point, and I heard a cheer; we were stopped, and it was obvious to all that could see that she was riding someone. Eventually, I shuddered, roared, and orgasmed as well, no cheer for me though. At this, she collapsed upon me and just lay there covering me with her body while my cock slowly shrunk, and my shivering body recovered.

After a few minutes, the limo pulled up; the driver alighted and waited at the door. We then realised we were back at our hotel and quickly dressed, downed another glass of bubbly, and exited ourselves.

I shook the driver's hand, tipping him another hundred, and thanked him for the evening.
 "No, Sir thank you and the lovely lady…" He said, parting with a bow and doffed hat.

Seeing the concierge, I tipped him again and asked for a bottle of wine to be sent up to our room, as well as two burgers (I was fairly famished).

What a night!

Hard Lessons.
Interlude,

Chapter 11: Succour.

Friday, the last day of hell week, is also known and as an Ofsted visit. After a stressful week of bureaucratic nosing into our classrooms and teaching plans. Honestly, if these people were any good, they would be teaching.

Parking the car out front, not bothering with the garage today, I had in mind an impromptu trip to a club tonight to destress and have some fun. Upon opening the door to the house, my girl greeted me. Not that unusual for her to do so but not always this way. She was kneeling on the floor of the hall, holding a glass of iced scotch. I might add that she was naked (Not uncommon for this young lady, she is quite the exhibitionist at heart and loved being naked about the house).

Holding out the glass, her back ramrod straight and eyes lowered, not looking at me, not expecting any acknowledgement, she waited as a good submissive should. Pushing the door closed behind me, then taking the proffered glass and taking a sip without acknowledging her at all. It was one of my favourites' single malts; Lagavulin, she had clearly known I was going to need a stiff drink after this week.

She stood up a moment after I had relieved her of the glass, then stepping behind me, she removed my suit jacket. Then her arms snaking about me, she set about undoing my tie... The school insisted on all teachers (males anyway) wearing these, to set a good example. A joke really, half the lads in the school think a tracksuit is the height of fashion and let's not start on what they do with their hands. (Why do they feel the need to hold their

106

nuts as they walk about? The mind boggles. Maybe they fear they will fall off.)

She whistles once and the dogs come out to greet me as well, and she then gestures for me to go into the living room. On entering, I notice she had rearranged some of the furniture, shifting it about the room. My big leather Chesterfield chair had been placed in the rear window nook, so the sun shone through the window onto it. I took the seat and placed the glass on the table that always sits to the right of my chair, especially for this purpose.

Scratching the dog's heads and ears (they rather like that sort of thing) gave them a good fuss, while I pondered on why she has brought up the play bench. This usually lives in the Dungeon, though I had an inkling of why she had brought it up. She really is such a good girl.

She returned, calling the dogs away as she entered getting their attention with two whistles, she pointed and the dogs went back to the garden (she had them well trained now, In fact, I think they responded better to her than me these days). I noticed that she was carrying my kit roll. She had ordered this for me for my birthday last year, based on the one that the protagonist in the Mummy carried.

Kneeling again, she laid the bag on the table, never looking up or saying a word. All I have heard out of her so far are the three whistles to call and then send away the dogs. Maybe she feels that I don't want to talk after the day I have had. (The opposite actually, but as she obviously has a plan in mind, it would behove me to spoil what she has clearly spent some time planning.) The straps undone, she unrolls the bag and I see my collection of straps, floggers, paddles, and the baby Bok had been added to the bag. There are a few other toys in little pockets, nipple clamps and such.

She must have realised I would need to destress after a week like this. A nice massage and a BJ would have worked quite well, but I liked this plan too.

She goes over to the bench and mounts it, reaching back to fasten the ankle cuffs and then the waist strap. She then slips both wrists into the cuffs left loose so she could slip her hands in or out. Leaving them for me to tighten if I wanted. Though I knew from experience, she would not remove them. She would consider herself bound and secured, so would not try to escape her bonds even if she could. By now, she was trained to accept the mentality of being restrained. If I told her she was bound to the wall by imaginary ropes and shackles, she would hold herself there as if she was physically bound there.

Sat in the rather comfortable leather chesterfield, looking very much the gentleman at home, as I sipped my gold watch (scotch) watching as the sun worked its way around the room, slowly coming to rest on her rear. This brought into focus the small, jewelled butt plug that she had inserted earlier before I arrived home, I guessed.

One of the agreements we had come to when we started on our journey was that anal was for special occasions. I had agreed to this stipulation. (At least she liked it! Some are not that keen.) Her cries the first time I had taken her anally, and the strength of her orgasm, had made it very apparent that she had enjoyed the experience. But we had agreed to keep it something special, a gift that she would give me when she wanted to treat me and she treated me bloody well, spoiled I am. The jewel catching my eye was clever; I had not noticed it until the sun alighted on her bottom.

I could just down this very fine scotch and take my pleasure of that little booty. She would not even care if I was to go in dry as they say. Though myself, I could never understand those that did not eat ass, as they say on the streets. I know myself the pleasure

108

of a tongue on one's arse is something to savour. She would unreservedly lick mine; I could do no less and anyway, I rather enjoyed her responses to my flicking, licking and probing tongue.

But no, she had laid out the toy bag and has been waiting there quiet for some time… While I sat sipping this scotch; the ice has melted now but luckily, I had drunk most of it before it got watered down too much.

No, a proper spanking was required. She clearly felt that I needed to release, and she was offering her flesh to grant me a surcease of sorrow. I could hardly just bypass all this to vent ardour on her little arse without the foreplay she thinks I need.

I slam the glass down dramatically for effect. Only my tension has already been released (the dogs always do that for me). I issue forth a frustrated sounding grunty-growl (for effect as well). Then, with purposeful strides, I walk over to her; I press her down to the bench, leaning forward and tighten the wrist straps and then, for effect, I fasten the neck strap about her too. Now she is fully bound in place. She could not escape unless I allowed it.

She knows now that she is mine to do with as I wish. This is her gift today. I could do as I please until sated or she called red. We had discussed this many times, though mostly bedroom talk, but if I so desired, I could make a call and have a stream of young bucks come to the house to use her while she was thusly bound.

She had fantasised about it herself, telling me that we could go to a club, and she would whisper in my ear that kitten wanted to be naughty! Fantasising then that I would then arrange for her to be taken, used, and abused by many men or women. Maybe even strapped into one of those Czech glory holes or thrown into a room full of men like a piece of meat for them to devour. She always asked if I would love her still after and of course, I

assured her that I would. That I would also be part of that pack myself, not only taking part in her debasement but encouraging others to use her as well.

The girl was an exhibitionist by nature and a bit of slut. But my slut, though. As yet, we had not gone that far, but we both knew the day would come when all the fantasy talk could; no would become a reality.

I stepped to her front, pulling her hair, lifting her view to my own, looking her in the eyes.

"You have been very quiet, my girl; you shall remain quiet! I want not a sound to issue from those pretty red lips, no cries, no sharp intakes of breath… Not a sound"

"You will take this in silence. Your gift to me will be your silence, as I do with you as I please. Blink twice for yes…" I say to her, my voice cold, as cold as the melted ice that ruined the end of my scotch.

I wait a moment and her eyes blink twice. The look of apprehension on her face is a picture. I rather wish this was being filmed. I think I would have enjoyed watching it later.

Normally I would warm her bottom with my hand but not today. She had laid out my tools and I would utilise some of them. I started by selecting the old belt, one I have had since my teens, made from a thick leather, and makes a lovely cracking sound when snapped out, very reminiscent of the sound my own father made when climbing the stairs to meet out punishments for my childhood misdemeanours.

I crack the belt a few times, letting her know what is coming and as is my usual, I decided to go with a pattern of six, though this time I would do six on each side, instead of moving about and keeping it even.

110

I hit her arse hard; I did not spare the leather, as they say back in the day. No warmup strokes this time, no gentle easing into the session, I had needed to let off some steam and relive some of my work-related frustrations and she had offered herself, her body as a gift to de-stress my soul and relive my burdens. I was pleased not to hear any cries, not even a gasp! (I had expected that at least, no matter what I had said.)

Not hearing anything issue from her mouth, I decided to see how long she could keep that control, to test her limits, so I leathered her bottom a further eleven times. I could see the welts already on her pale flesh, the outline of the belt etched on her bottom, yet not a single sound had escaped her.

She was a strong one; this girl; she submitted to me by choice, not because she was submissive in nature. No, if anything, she was a strong independent woman, who would do well in this world once she graduated college. She had chosen me, pursued me, demanded that I notice that she existed and made damn sure I could not ignore her attentions. Nothing phased this girl; I could walk her naked down the high street of any town and she would not blush or falter in her steps. In fact, I planned to do that very thing soon. A week in the south of France's nudist village was already booked to celebrate her upcoming graduation. (Village Naturiste Cap d'Agde.)

I picked up the butter paddles, something that has always tested her in the past. Silly really nothing but a small, ridged piece of flat wood but used right was bloody unpleasant! Or so she would tell me. Well, let us see if she can remain silent through a set of these. Again, I hit as hard as I could with this item, not as hard as the strap perhaps, but it was a very different sensation. With each hit, I left the stinging wood on her flesh for a second before raising it and hitting again and again. Yet still, no cries, not even deep breathing. She was holding herself under control.

I was not sure this was wise, as letting go would make this easier on her, as she could slip into subspace but keeping control like this would mean she felt every sensation clearly. Tough little cookie, this one.

Deciding to ease up a little, I picked out a medium weight flogger and eschewed the rule of six for a while, flogging her booty to warm her up. Only at the end, speeding up so that I knew that she would be edging her limits with this item.

Dropping it to the floor, in a display of fake pique; I picked up the prison strap and slapped it down on her ass cheek once, twice, then six times; the strap leaving four-inch-wide welts with every hit. I heard a tiny gasp issue forth but pretended not to hear it. I knew had I not warmed her with the flogger, she would never have been able to take this strap. The flogger had allowed her to slip into her subspace at least a little.

I moved around, walking past her face this time, and could see the dark trails of tears on her face now, tears that only lubricated my sadistic desires for her. I almost danced as I struck her six more times with the prison strap. her arse was on fire now, the heat was radiating, I could feel it without touching her.

She had kindly included the Baby Bok, like a Sjambok only smaller. This one fitted in the kit roll, a full-sized one would need its own case.

I had decided enough was enough. I would give her stripes now, well-earned stripes on top of those welts which I was sure would bruise even her now experienced flesh. Twelve (both sides) well-laid strokes later heard her cry out, not loud, but she had cried out. Her resolve had broken. I had broken her and now she had failed the challenge I had set her.

I stepped in front of her, bobbing down as I lifted her head.

"You failed me! I told you no noise… Not a whisper, but I heard you cry out just now," I kept my face straight, using my years as a teacher to give her my best-disappointed face.

"I think a further punishment is required, again do not make a noise, do not cry out. I want no sound to issue forth. I am going to take your arse now; you will not enjoy it. You do not have my permission to orgasm or to cum. Blink twice if you understand me, girl."

I waited, and she of course she blinked. This was after all just a game, her arse was already on offer, I was just playing my role as bad Sir, who is going to ravish his poor sub's tight little arsehole.

Unzipping my trouser fly, as I walked behind her, not even bothering to drop my trousers, I eased out my rock-hard cock. (Really what they say about pain and pleasure, well I get a lot of pleasure it seems from her pain and especially seeing her tears.) I popped out the butt plug, taking the time to place it in the whisky tumbler. Lining myself up, I pressed myself into her. She had prepped, and I regretted not tongue fucking that hole first, but I had a role to play, and I would play it through.

Once fully in, I started to hump her, occasionally interspersing spankings of each cheek to keep up the assault of sensations on her burning hot flesh. I would pull away and then push in, to the tip and beyond sometimes, fully out before I would just slam in. (This could be painful for me, especially if I misaligned a stroke, but it was worth the risk.) She was wet, I could see it dripping onto the hardwood floor, I ignored this, I could hardly blame her for cumming, though I still whispered into her ear,
"Don't you dare cum, girl…"

Grabbing the shaft of my cock, I started stabbing into her arse hard and harder, faster and faster until I felt myself getting ready to cum - then with might roar (I am really not a quiet man) I

came over her little rosebud, letting it drip down the crease of her arse and onto her wet cunt.

Stepping in front of her, I found her mouth open tongue out already; she knew her job and clean up was one of her favourites. Her tongue flicked and licked the end, licking away any cum that may remain, then she (with my help this time) took me into her mouth and sucked away, sucking out any that might have been still in my softening member.

Satisfied I was clean, I packed away my cock. My trousers were going to need dry cleaning. The stain might raise an eyebrow or two. (I found that thought rather amusing and laughed to myself.) Then I went and fetched myself another gold watch (in a clean glass) and sat and watched her; still held in place and laying there strapped and ready for round two. She knew that was coming; she had offered me this gift, and tonight I felt the need to indulge myself a few more times. Maybe I will bring out the camera and the fucking machine later, get her to squirt on film, that would be a pleasure to watch, again and again, I was certain but for now, while the sun slowly slunk away, I would enjoy my drink and the best view in the house.

The end for now.

Hard Lessons
Book 2
Exhibitionist Holiday.
By
M Alex Wyllie.

Continuing the story of Rebecca and Alex's relationship.

Rebecca graduation day is here and as a reward Alex treats her to a week away in the south of France a week away with a twist. A twist that will allow Rebecca to Indulge her natural inner exhibitionist tendencies and maybe find a woman to fulfil one or two of her other fantasy's.

Hard Lessons
Exhibitionist Holiday.

Prologue: Graduation Day Reward.

Graduation day at the college: My girl Rebecca is wearing her gown and mortarboard. Only she and I knew that underneath the robe she was naked! Well, almost naked, she wore nothing under the robe except for a butt plug that responded to a Bluetooth controller app on my phone. (I love technology.)

I was adjusting the device as she walked up to get her degree and flicked it to the maximum setting as she shook the hand of the prestigious looking lady handing the scrolls. The photo would take pride of place in my study and the look of delight on her face, definitely was not just for receiving this documental proof of her achievement.

A few years ago, she thought of only getting free of school and probably getting a child or two, so she could escape her mother's house. Now she had not only finished school with good grades much better than anyone thought she would get, but she had also managed to get a place in the local college and achieved something she never dreamed possible and then she actually earned a degree in English literature.

I was, of course, very proud of her; I had offered extra tutoring to her get her grades up at school and encouraged and supported her throughout college, but this was her achievement. She had done this herself, and no one could take that from her.

As a reward, I had booked a surprise for her. A resort she had mentioned a year ago; Village Naturiste Cap d'Agde a nudist village and the perfect location for an exhibitionist. It also had a good kink and swinging scene, it seemed, and I was sure we could have a lot of fun.

116

We mingled with her fellow graduates, chatting, and sipping the Champagne and all the while I was thumbing the control of the BT device, adjusting the intensity of the vibrations, as she chatted away. I must wonder at what some of her friends thought when they caught the odd twitches and micro reactions on her face as she talked to them. I know this was her day, but she had wanted to be naked, and she had chosen to wear the left Bluetooth device. Can hardly blame me for taking advantage of the situation.

She leaned into me, kissing my cheek. This raised a few eyebrows, seeing as many had probably thought I was her father! Far from it.

"Sir, you are so bad. I am so wet. I can feel it running down my leg," she whispered this into my ear, squeezing my arm and kissing my ear as she did so.

"Should I stop," I said, knowing full well I would not stop unless I board of the game, or she called red on it?

"No Sir, but you need to take me somewhere and fuck me!" She smiled playfully as she ran her hand across my crotch.

Well, I could hardly refuse such an offer, could I?

We said our goodbyes and headed to the carpark. This was a multi-storey carpark we were on level five, but I knew there were more levels above. The car park was not full on the level we were parked on, and I hoped that the ones above might be even less occupied.

I started the car up and slipped my hands between her legs to feel how wet she was, very wet indeed it turned out.

"Remove that robe…" I told her, an order not a request, one I knew she would obey this command.
She absolutely loved being naked.

Instead of heading out, I took the up ramp all the way to the top floor. As we drove up, there were fewer and fewer cars parked and none on the roof. It was wet up on the top floor, open to the elements and rain. This did not bother us at all though. It did pop into my head that this was probably going to ruin my suit, but what the heck, it was her day, and it would be worth it.

I got out of the car first, and went around and opened her door, as was my normal practice. I am a gentleman after all and a little old school about such niceties. Offering her my hand, she stepped out wearing only the mortarboard and her heels now… The butt plug, I noted, was on the car seat.

I slipped off my jacket, removed my phone and wallet and placed them in the car, then leading her over to the wall, I placed the jacket over the ridge and pressed her to the wall. (The jacket was, so she did not scratch her skin on the rough surface of the concrete.)

"Look out there, you can see the whole town, over there is the campus, and there is the venue we just left, with all your friends in it, some of them might be leaving now and if they looked up, maybe they could make out that there was someone up her looking down at them."

"Do you think anyone can see us?" She asked, turning to kiss me.

"Maybe, maybe the camera is working, and the attendant is watching us now, I know you like the idea of being watched, and being naked under that gown throughout the ceremony made you hot… I know it made me hot and uncomfortably hard." I said, smiling my most charming of smiles.

118

Rebecca *giggles* making me hard was her favourite thing in all the world.

"I'm going to fuck you now, right there. Lean over the wall, so you can see all those walking by," I said this slipping my engorged cock out from my trousers and pressing it into her.

She was so wet that I met little or no resistance; I slid in and began gently fucking her as she looked out over the wall, watching shoppers walk by. It was raining, so it was unlikely any would look up, but even if they did, she did not care.

Excited and turned on, I thrust, faster and harder and was pounding into her now, no longer gentle. She enjoyed gentle now and then, but this was not the time, this was fucking, and I was fucking her wet cunt with every drop of energy I could muster.

She slipped her hand behind and grabbed my cock and then guided it to her arse, her way of telling me I could have her arse today. (The cheeky mare; but I was more than happy to oblige.)

I had already surmised this by the fact she had removed the butt plug, but I guess she was making sure I knew what was on offer today... (We had come to an agreement that anal was for special occasions only and was her treat to give.)

I slid into her arse was already slightly loosened by hours of wearing the butt plug; I pushed my cock in all the way and I was none too gently either. My clothes were soaking now, but that did not matter. I could hear her moaning now as I fucked her arse. Nothing else mattered, not even the parking attendant I had seen exit the door, out of the corner of my eye. (Worst he could do is tell us to stop and get out).

Continuing to pound away while she watched the passers-by, I kept an eye on the attendant, wondering what he was going to say or do? As he approached, though, I saw him pulling out his cock and masturbating himself as he watched us. I turned her head so she could see the man. Not that old, maybe thirty, but a definite dad bod on him a result of too much fast food and beer, I suspected.

She smiled seeing him; she loved being watched and being caught like this, naked in public with her Sir's cock buried deep in her arse was a real turn on. Feeling her body shudder as she orgasmed, whether from being fucked or from the sheer naughtiness of the situation, really did not matter.

I nodded at him, and he came closer; I put up a hand to stop him before he got too close.

"Watch, don't touch," I told him.

Thoroughly drenched now but I could feel the time was close, beyond my ability to delay anymore. So, with a burst of effort, I quickened my thrusting, releasing my control as I shuddered and exploded within her. Coming with my customary roar of pleasure.

She pushed back into me, milking me with her arse, not ready to let me pull out just yet, so sliding my hand about her waist, I turned her to face the attendant as I pumped her for a little longer.

The attendant on getting a good look at her from the front, seeing the little heart-shaped dyed pubic hair and the perfectly formed breasts. A pretty and clearly young face. She was young, so young that I was often mistaken for her father. She liked that, enjoyed the shocked look on people's faces when they saw us kiss. I rather hated it, but it was something I had come to live

120

with and yes, the shocked looks were kind of amusing, even to me.

"Fuck me!" He said, the look of lust on his face was almost animalistic in its intensity.

"No, I don't think so, but how about you cum on her tits instead," I told him, smiling friendlily as I tossed my jacket down before her.

She knelt on the jacket and started fondling her breast in front of the attendant, pushing them up together and then tweaking her nipples, egging him on to cum. Unbelievably, this was as unlikely as it seems the first time we had done this, and I was pleased to see that she did not feel nervous at all. In fact, she seemed quite comfortable teasing this poor chap.

We had long discussions about these sorts of scenarios and had shared fantasies about all kinds of experiences and depravities she might be forced to endure and suffer. If suffering is the correct term, given that many of these were her own thoughts and fantasies.

She knew from my past and some videos I had that I have indulged other partners in this way. Submissive's who had been (willingly I might add) used by myself, the headmaster, his partner, our mutual friends and on a few occasions' multiple men at the same time (orgies or gang-bangs). But so far, we had not invited others into our play, although the headmaster had been mentioning it for a while, as had his partner, who flirted with Rebecca whenever she could. (Only fair, as I had had the pleasure of his partner several times in the past.)

I watched as she continued to fondle her tits and licked her lips suggestively; he was not getting anywhere near those, but she was teasing him with the suggestion. I watched as his face

reddened and he pulled a rather grotesque cum face and shot his load on her tits.

She smiled and rubbed his cum into her tits, then pushed her hands down to her bush, before turning away, walking back to the car. She pulled out the gown and dressed, blew him a kiss, and got back in the car... Leaving the poor chap with a now softening dick in his hands and a look of shock on his face.

I picked up my jacket, tossing it into the boot as it was soaking now. much as I was. Nodded to the man and got in the car myself, leaned over and kissed the girl.

"You are such a natural slut, my girl. Did you enjoy that?"

"Yes, Sir I felt very naughty, but I loved it when he unloaded on my tits. Am I going to be punished for letting him do that, Sir?"

"Oh, very much so I'm afraid," I replied with a playful smile.

"I may want to indulge your natural exhibitionism and feed your inner slut, my girl, but that does not mean there will not be an accounting my girl."

Pulling up to the house, I parked in the garage, stripping her bare as the doors closed automatically behind us. Grabbing a hand full of hair, I led her into the kitchen and then down to the secret dungeon. Tossing her to the ground. I shucked off my wet clothes and stood there naked as she was.

My cock was hard again, and I absolutely wanted to beat the girl for being such a dirty little slut, but I also could not mark her before we went on holiday, so I had another plan in mind. I led her over to the bench and spanked her, not so hard as to leave any marks, but long enough that she was sobbing by the end of the spanking.

Taking hold of her hair again, I led her to the centre of the room and told her to stand and wait. Going over to my box of toys and I pulled out the nipple clamps and some rope. I fixed the nipple clamps in place, ensuring they had a good grip on those pale little nubs. Then I tie the rope to her hands behind her back, then her ankles not so tight that she would be unbalanced just enough to hobble her. I then set the Acupressure mat on the ground and slid it under her feet. (This I knew was almost as bad as standing on Lego.) I then tied pieces of twine to each clamp and put them through a loop in the ceiling before adding two lead fishing weights (6oz).

The clamps alone were a punishment, but now her little titties were being pulled up while she was trying to stay balanced on the mat so as not to have more weight on one foot to the other. If she stood on tiptoes, she would take the weight of her nipples, but then the pain in her feet would be more intense.

Happy that she was now learning a lesson, I went off to shower and pack our bags for the surprise trip I had booked. She did not know about the trip. So, I was happy that I had found a way to keep her out of the way whilst I packed our bags.

As to where we were going, we would not need much. I packed away more toys than usual, having more space than is usually available in the cases. I set out a summer dress, shoes, and her shoulder bag to wear to the Airport (no panties, of course). Everything else was in the two cases.

Going down to the dungeon and seeing that she had chosen foot pain over nipple pain. (She was on her tiptoes.) Although she knew full well that there would be more pain as soon as I removed the clamps. Stepping onto the mat, I kissed her, tongue deep in her mouth as I release each clamp, feeling her shudder against me as the blood and feeling painfully rushed back into each nipple.

123

"Go, shower and put on the dress I have laid out for you. We are going on a trip. It's a surprise, so don't ask," I said, kissing her again, then patting her rear as she obediently tottered off to take a shower.

Whist she showered, I got the bags down, checked I had the ticket's passports and itineraries. Confirmed the taxi would arrive on time and then waited for her to get her shapely butt dressed and ready.

She came running in wearing the little yellow summer dress I had picked out for her. This one was not too short and would not expose her accidentally to anyone. Only she and I would know that she was naked under the dress. Unless he got searched at the airport, that is (had to smile at that thought).

Our lift arrived soon after and we loaded up to catch our flight to the south of France and our next adventure.

Hard Lessons
Exhibitionist Holiday.

Chapter 1: Exhibitionists Paradise Bound.

We arrived at the airport. She was guessing destinations, but I was not telling, a surprise I told her and wait' you don't want to ruin the surprise. Of course, she continued to guess, but I am an old hand at this, and I would not break, no matter where she placed her hand or stuck her tongue.

We arrived early and obviously at this point the cat was partially out of the bag; they revealed our destination at the check-in desk. We were booked on a flight to France's Montpellier airport. I think at this point she probably had a good idea of our final destination, but she still played the guessing game. Mainly, I suspect, to keep herself amused and probably to earn herself a spanking for annoying me too much. (A game I knew she liked to play, her being a bit of a brat.)

We arrived after a brief (two-hour flight) uneventful, seeing as I booked us on an EasyJet flight and packed in like sardines, hardly the place for any naughtiness at all. One day I will get to join the mile-high club. Maybe I should charter a plane for a few hours.

Moving through customs, my only worry was them looking in our luggage. Some of my toys might raise more than an eyebrow, even with the more liberal Gendarmerie, but luckily, they just ushered us through.

I had booked a private car for the journey; I liked to travel in comfort when I could. Yes, she was still making guesses. As we exited into the stifling heat of the Mediterranean, I was glad I had chosen a light linen suit now, a tad cold for the UK, but here it was perfect. Her yellow summer dress billowed in the warm

air but did not expose her inappropriately to the crowded airport public.

I guided us to the area where we were supposed to be met by our driver. Spotting the sign for Mr Wyles being held up by a rather well-dressed young man took our cases and put them in the trunk, then opening the door for us. Leaning close to her, I whispered in her ear.

"Why don't you sit up front and give this chap a little tip," kissing the nape of her neck as I did so.

She smiled a conspiratorial smile back at me as she went over to the driver,
"Can I sit up front please, and you can tell me all about this beautiful country?" she asked, smiling warmly at the driver.

Like how could he refuse? We had played this game before; I indulged her, as I knew she liked to tease and was always looking for opportunities to expose herself. I could hardly complain. It was how we met, after all.

I took a seat behind her so my view was obscured. Deliberately, the driver would think she was doing this behind her old man's back, but, of course, I knew exactly what she would be doing.

The young man opened the door for her, and she got in, hitching her skirt up a little as she did so, exposing a little more of her lovely legs. As the driver closed the door and went around the back to close the boot, I saw her lift herself briefly. This was to pull up the back of her dress, so she was now sitting bare-arsed on the leather car seat.

I sat back now; I did not need to see to know the scene that would play out before me.

The driver gets in and presses the ignition button, then checking on us both and hands a chilled water bottle to each of us. She by now would have raised the hem of her dress mid-thigh. Not too high, but he would have noted her legs now, and I caught a fleeting but obvious glance down as he passed her the water.

We pulled into traffic, and he started his local tour spiel. His English was rather good, I noted. He continued telling us interesting facts about the region as he drove. I knew she would be smiling along as he spoke and soon would ask a few questions, getting his attention. Then she would take a sip, probably let a little of the water run down her chin and down her neck. Then, If I know her and I do, she will place the chilled water bottle between her thighs.

I kept an eye on the driver and one on the road watching, waiting for him to notice the little game she was playing. Yes, again he noticed and looked. She caught this, smiled, and looked down, so his eye would look to see what she was looking at. She would slowly move the water bottle up her thighs, so it pressed up against her pussy.

At this point, I was sure he was watching her more than the road, but these young drivers all drove like they were Statham, anyway. I was monitoring the road and would pull his attention back if I felt it needed doing.

She took several more sips and slid slightly down on the seat, allowing her to show a little more of what she loved exposing. I was sure that by now her dress would be full up and she would be rubbing her lovely cunt with the ridges of the bottle. The Poor driver I was sure was glad he drove an automatic, as his own stiffening gear stick would be foremost in his mind by now.

Deciding enough was enough, I asked a few questions, getting his attention away from that delightful little pussy and colourful

bush. (Dyed pink at the moment, to match her Pixie coloured hair.)

With a squeal, she announced to me she knew where we were heading. Finally, she had guessed it.

"Yes, sweetie, you guessed it. I hope you like my little surprise."

"Oh yes daddy, I can't wait to run around naked. You know how I love being naked," she said excitedly, her smile was infectious. I had no choice but to return it.

The daddy bit, I think, was for the young man's benefit, a little more teasing. She never calls me that normally. I bet he had quite a shocked look on his face and probably a little guilty as well, seeing as he had been eying this little lovely's privates just now.

We drove into the complex, passing through the security gate. After showing my booking form, the driver seemed to know the area and took us to our booked apartment block and reception office. I dealt with the formalities and then tipped the driver. (Although after her little show; I felt that he had been adequately tipped well already.)

We made our way up to our apartment; I had booked on the top floor so as not to have anyone above us. Not the most luxurious of apartments, but I was certain we would not be spending much time in the room.

I placed the cases on the bed, opening them so she could see what had been packed, a few little dresses, shirts and shorts and slacks for me; sandals for us both and heels for her. Several spare towels, never enough towels at these places.

The rest of the space was taken up with toys, all sorts of fun toys. There was a thriving kink scene here, and I intended to indulge us both quite a bit.

I did not waste time either. The little show she put on had turned me on, even though I could not see her.

Moving quickly, I grabbed the front of her dress, pulling her to me, placing a deep kiss on her pretty lips. I then tore her dress away, ripping it almost in two. Then, as the dress remnants fell to the floor, I pressed down on her head as a clear signal that I knew she would understand.

She understood, but taking her cue from the way I removed her dress, she fought back. She was resisting just enough to make me force her down; I did this by grabbing her hair and tilting her head back, then pressing her down to the ground. I did this one-handed. The other was removing my belt and releasing my cock. Trouser dropping to the floor, I then looped the belt around her neck and twisted it in my grip, so she was now being choked.

I held this a little, not too long, but long enough to make my point. Making sure she received the I am not fucking about signal; she took my cock in her mouth and set about giving me a proper thank you for the surprise holiday.

I did not release the belt, however; I did twist it behind her so I could also grab her hair in the same hand and pull her head into my groin. I forced her head all the way down to my balls; she was an expert at this now, three years of training and she could swallow a 1twelve inch dildo if she wanted and sometimes even if she did not (I am evil at times, I know).

I face fucked her, feeling the tickle of her tongue on my balls a few times as she flicked it out to show her skills. I kept the face fucking up until I came with an incredible roar of satisfaction and relief.

129

I rather needed that, especially if I was going to be walking about nudist camp with this beauty. One does not want to get a stiffy whilst wandering around all that naked flesh.

As she was already naked, she really did not have to do much to get ready. She sorted her hair and makeup out; I had pretty much messed that up for her (I was sure she did not mind; I know I did not). Digging through the bags, I pulled out the case that held my favourite bit of jewellery for her to wear. It was a titanium dragon scale collar. Seeing me pull this out, she knelt before me and lifted her pixie-coloured hair away from her neck to allow me to fasten it.

I slipped out of my things and wrapped a small towel around my waist. That and a pair of sandals were going to be today's outfit. I had no issue being naked around people, but I needed to acclimatize myself to being naked, in a place where there are families likely to be around.

Rebecca, of course, did not give a jot. She disappeared into the bathroom and called me in a few minutes later.

I entered and found her sitting on the edge of the bath. She had covered her little bush in shaving cream, and she was holding out my razor, a clear signal that she wanted me to do the honours. Well, who was I to deny a lady's request? I knelt between her spread legs, seeing that her lips and bottom were as hairless as always. I carefully opened the old-style cutthroat razer. Knowing it was sharp, well, razor-sharp, obviously.

I slowly, with steady hands, scraped away the hair that she had carefully groomed into a heart shape over the last year. I had a steady hand, and she trusted me as much as I trusted her when she shaved me these days. It had taken a while for her to get the knack without nicking my face, but she had got there, and it was one of her greatest pleasures to shave me in the morning.

130

Though I admit, I am still hesitant to let her loose on my lower area.

Wiping away the remaining foam and feeling that she was now as smooth as she could be, I left her to have a quick shower and then join me for a stroll about this exhibitionist's paradise. I noted she did not bother wrapping the towel about herself and looked a little lost as to what to do with it. I relieved her of that burden and carried it in my free hand. The other was, of course, wrapped about hers.

Hard Lessons
Exhibitionist Holiday.

Chapter 2: Exhibitionist on Holiday.

We exited the room, then turned about and I re-entered and picked up the shoulder holster style bag I had brought to along keep our keys and cash in. (where did you think we were going to put our keys? The prison wallet!) Taking the stairs down, passing a few fellow naturists, all of them checked out my lovely partner. I doubt I even rated a second glance, and that is as it should be. She is the main attraction, a feast for the eyes to devour.

Exiting our hotel, the Le Jardin d'Eden and wandered aimlessly; although I had in mind as a final destination, the beach, for our first publicly nude swim. I admit the novelty of walking around shops naked and stopping for coffee, whilst being served while totally naked, was novel. It was not actually all that exciting to me. Rebecca, on the other hand, was loving it, loving the attention she was getting from passers-by.

The staff were friendly enough and, as usual; she got all the attention from both males and females. I did not mind, even being admittedly in good shape for a man of sixty years, I hardly expected to be considered eye candy by anyone, especially in the presence of Rebecca's beauty.

Though the shops and cafes were clean and modern the area was, unfortunately, as is common with French holiday destinations, a little run down and could do with some money being spent on prettying the area, but I guessed that was true with much of the world these days.

Finding ourselves eventually on the beach (as had been my plan all along) paying thirty euros for the hire of two sun loungers

and shades. (It was rather warm, and I certainly did not want to get sunburnt on my first day. Seasoned traveller that I am.) Wrapping my shoulder bag in the towels and sticking them under the loungers (not exactly safe but this was a secure resort, so I risked it) we ran into the sea holding hands and splashing about like small children on their first trip to the seaside. Then, as that brief childish excitement faded, we fell onto the sand just at the point of the breaking surf and kissed, making out like Burt Lancaster and Deborah Kerr (always loved that scene).

We kissed, the warm Mediterranean Sea gently breaking over us, as we rolled around in the sand and surf. The sun was high and the wind just enough to cool our wet, exposed skin. The sand, however, was getting in places I would rather not have had it, but we were loving every second of our Oscar-winning re-enactment.

When we broke, the usual issue was present. (It is not fair that women do not have an obvious display of their arousal. Maybe their tits should flash or something. (Come on evolution, how about a little equality!)

I stood, pulling her up with one hand, the other trying to hide my engorged manhood from the eyes of any youngsters that were on the beach. (There were few families present, and I did not want to add to their biology education.) Realising this was a lost cause, we re-entered the water to have a swim and a little more fun.

Swimming out maybe sixty meters, we were now chest-deep, and far enough away from the beach that I was not worried about being watched too much. She wrapped herself around me, legs gripping about my waist and wiggling herself into position. She knew exactly why I had led us out this deep. She had a mind that matched mine and wanted to fuck just as much as I did. (Probably more, my libido not being that of an eighteen-year-old

boy, but it was still a roaring hungry lion, even if it did sleep more these days.)

She wiggled down and, finding the right spot, lowered herself on me, while I concentrated on keeping my feet and not falling back into the water. I let her ride me; I was not able to do much other than try to keep afloat for most of it, even having to use my arms a few times to float over at the odd large swell.

We floated a lot; I was understandably distracted, and I had not realised we were being pulled out further from the beach. Remaining blissfully ignorant of the dangerous undercurrent, we continued frolicking. Until that is until a helpful lifeguard motored up on one of those terribly noisy water bikes things and insisted, he gave us a lift back to the shallows. He gallantly offered Rebecca a lift on the back, while I got to hold on to an orange flotation device and was pulled along behind, while she held on to the hunky, bare-chested beach guard! (No, I was not jealous, I genuinely did not want to hug the beach guard.)

Dropping us back in knee-high water, he warned us, in rather broken English, which was still better than my own French, I might add. That there was riptide, and we should avoid going out beyond the Buoys, which he helpfully pointed out (I had not noticed them, to be honest, mind elsewhere and all that). We thanked him profusely and she kissed him on the cheek as thanks as well.

Returning to our sun loungers and drying off on the slightly sandy towels; then lying down to soak up some rays, I made sure to keep the sunshade over my more sensitive areas while exposing as much of the rest of me to the warming sun. (Must bring the factor fifty out next time.) We laid there, hand in hand, resting, chatting, and chilling, as the sun worked its way about us, finally disappearing as it began its descent and settle behind the hotels.

Sunset here was about 22:30 and twilight was setting in when we finally roused ourselves from our repose. (I had dozed off at some point, happened a lot these days, old age sucks.) I was feeling rested but famished, realising we had not eaten properly today, and it had been a very long day since we had set off for her graduation ceremony at 08:00 this morning.

I led her to a restaurant that was set slightly off from the beach, the aptly named Le Glamour Beach Restaurant and cabaret, and ordered us both some food. As always, I ordered for us both; she let me have that little pleasure, not having experienced restaurant eating until she met me. Knowing I enjoyed treating her to new experiences, both physically and culinary, she would always let me order. I ordered her Ceviche (a South American seafood dish) and myself; I had Cabillaud (fish, probably cod) in cider source with fried muscles, along with two bottles of chilled wine. (I had asked for one to be left unopened so we could take it with us.)

The food was surprisingly good and sitting at the edge of the beach with the sound of the sea almost audible over the cabaret (not a highlight, but pleasant enough). For dessert, I ordered us Poires Belle Helene (pears with chocolate source and lemon sorbet for me).

Rebecca talked throughout the meal, excitedly expressing her pleasure at the food, the setting and the whole place and loving the freedom to be naked without judgement. All the people sat about us, all naked. Many were families, and no one was ashamed of their bodies, it seemed. That is how it should be.

She was right, there were all ages and sizes here and very few were what one would call models, but none of them seemed to care about that sort of thing. Though I did note that all would check out any newcomers to the restaurant, I had not noticed when we entered, but it was obvious after a while.

I was not sure they were judging, but rather they were maybe assessing the newcomers, as to whether or not they were swingers. I wonder what category we had probably been filed under, as a sugar daddy and his bimbo, away for a few days and having an illicit liaison in the south of France.

Rebecca, however, was anything but a bimbo, and yes, maybe I looked after her and made sure she had money to get through college. But she was determined to stand on her own two feet and had made that clear from the start when I had offered to support her through college. She intended to reimburse me for my help and pay her own way in the relationship.

Food finished and bottle wine down, we decided to take a moonlit stroll along the beach, while drinking from the bottle like teenagers (or winos). The cooling sand beneath our feet, the mid-summer Mediterranean wind enveloping our bodies in its warming cloak (or was that the booze). Venturing into the surf now and then as it rolled up the beach. It was a beautiful night to be out with my beautiful partner.

We spotted several other beach walkers, couples, then a few single males. All seemed to be heading the same way. Being nosey, we decided to tag along, following a small group to see what was so fascinating in this direction.

Eventually, we found ourselves in the dunes, and I recalled then that this area was quite popular with the swinger community. I had no intention of joining in such activities tonight, but watching, well, there was no harm in that.

What we spotted, and we kept back a little so as to show we were looky-loos, not participants in this scene. We found a group of males, a few females, possibly partners of said males were surrounding this couple. It took a bit of neck straining to see this, but a break in the crowd exposed the scene to us.

A lady, the owner of a fair-sized pair of knockers I noticed (I always notice such things) was sitting presumably on her partner's cock (may not have been her partner) riding him while she gave blowjobs to the surrounding males. They would switch out from time to time. Some might have cum, really could not see, but she was wanking of two and sucking a third, all the while grinding on the other fellow's cock. We watched as on a few occasions she would open her mouth and poke out her tongue to receive a masturbated offering from one of the attending males.

Some couples wandered off, resulting in the pulling away of a few of the hopeful males, who I am sure would make their own offerings soon enough.

We wandered back out of the dunes and to the beach, tossing down our towels to lie on and continue our earlier, From Here to Eternity homage.

She straddled me, taking over control. I did not mind during sex, this was lovemaking, not play and here we were equals. We both would take control of the lovemaking at times. She rode me now, raking her nails down my chest in a way she knew I loved.

She leaned forward at one point, never ceasing her grinding (I think I was going to need my little blue helpers this week if she kept this up).

"Do you think I could do that; would you want me to do that?" she asked?

Pausing to bite my ear.
"I'm not sure I could. That would be very intimidating, all those cocks being thrust at me!" she said as she rode me, never slacking off the rhythm.

I tried to talk though really, my only functioning brain matter was starved of blood right now, and even with that deficit of grey matter, I did manage to reassure her that I would never ask her to do such a thing. Only you can make that choice. In all honesty, she was not ready for such play, no matter the fantasy talk we had about sharing, gang bangs, and Bukkake.

I growled at her.
"Now shut up and make me cum, you sexy fucking little bitch."
(I can be such a smooth talker at times.)

I heard a giggle at that and saw we had our own looky-loos, who were enjoying our show. Well, that sent me over the edge, and I came again, 3rd time today! (My poor dick, I thought, though I had a big stupid grin on my face.) Although I had come, she did not cease the grinding, only slowed, and lowered herself to my chest, resting against me, feeling my body warmth and the shudders that post-orgasm always racked my body.

We laid there like that for ten minutes in blissful ignorance of those onlookers and passers-by, just cuddling, content to lay there in the late evening heat. When we rose, I picked up our towels, shook them off violently, trying but eventually giving up shedding the sand that had attached itself to them. We would probably be taking a few pounds of this stuff back in our luggage, I thought to myself.

Without feeling any worry now, I walked her back to our apartment uncovered, balls and cock swinging like a content pendulum with each step.

Back in the room, we shared a shower, washing each other as we did as often as not. Cleaned and refreshed, divested of sand that had invaded every crack and nook or our naked bodies.

138

We polished off the wine on the balcony and then deciding it was late enough for this day; I picked her up and carried her to the bed, where I had laid out two hanks of rope. I tied her wrists, then her ankles, loosely. She could walk, though, hobbled.

Then I wrapped a loop about both our waists so that she knew that I was bound to her as she was bound to me, symbolic of our love and commitment to each other. This was something she had suggested, abandonment issue still haunted her, I guessed, though I hoped she knew I was not going to be another absent male in her life (well at least until she killed me off with her appetites). we drifted off like that, covered in only a sheet, the warm wind billowing through the open door to the balcony, giving us all the warmth, we would need.

Hard Lessons
Exhibitionist Holiday.

Chapter 3: Never kissed a girl.

We rose early the next morning; I showered quickly, then dashed off to buy coffee and croissants, asking Rebecca to go find us two sun loungers by the pool before they were all gone. The good girl that she is. She did not even bother showering but grabbed the towels and dashed off. Luckily, we were on the top floor, so it was not far for her to go. She would hold them (if she found any free, that is).

I returned laden with coffee and pastries and found she had managed to bag us a couple of loungers and a sunshade, as I had asked her to. Good girl. I handed her a black Americano and a chocolate croissant, but instead of sitting with me, she returned to the room to freshen up. I ate and sat back, and for a change, I had no phone on me, no contact with the outside world, no daily news updates or messages from friends and work. Just early morning sun and coffee to keep me company (well, that and fellow early risers who were out to bag their own spots about the pool).

Looking about, I spotted some quite delectable sights. My girl was not the only stunning creature here, it seemed. My eyes were drawn to two ladies, one a mature lady of maybe 45 and another who maybe only a few years older than my Rebecca. The older lady, her partner, I guessed, given how close they were and where her hand was resting as they stood by the bar. A bar that annoyingly, I now noticed, served early morning Coffee's (well, I knew now). Her hand rested on the girl's bottom, and I could see quite clearly her index finger slipping between the cheeks.

Sex was supposedly forbidden in the public areas, though I had heard that it was not strictly enforced unless there were gentiles (non, swingers) about, so she was being a little naughty, but it was early, and no families were about yet. The Lady, as I said was mature, well mature compared to her partner (she was clearly younger than I am or had aged remarkably well) but very attractive, had a Scandinavian look to her, high, sharp cheekbones and her hair was that strawberry blond that looks so amazing in the sun, especially the early morning sun that was catching it now.

The girl was tall, statuesque, all curves and all of them very pleasant to view. I had spotted her earlier as she had approached the bar area and she was simply beautiful. Different to my Rebecca who still had the coltishness of youth about her, where she was lean this girl was rounded, strong thighs on long defined legs, her bottom was a well-rounded peach of a bottom, she had that hour-glass figure that Marilyn carried so well. Her hair was in dreads, dreads dyed many colours and interwoven with strips of linen, I think, very unusual but beautiful.

I watched as they walked my way; I was quite blatant in my admiration of both of them. No man could ignore such beauty. Their poise was genuinely self-confident. They were not in the slightest bit by the looks they were getting from the other early risers (TBH I felt myself rising a little too). They walked my way; I now wished I had a book so I could cover my now stirring manhood. Even better, they took the loungers only one set apart from us; I considered moving the towels on the pair of loungers between us, but not only would that be obvious, but it would also be a little rude to the owners of the aforementioned towels.

Rebecca returned shortly after, and I pulled her aside before she reached me so we could go get more coffee. This was an opportunity to give the ladies a good look at us. I hoped they were watching; I did not look back at myself, but Rebecca, being

a lot more brazen than I did and even waved. Of course, I filled her in as we walked, telling her of the two stunning ladies that were seated almost next to us. She was all for moving the towels, but I forbid that as would be crass and impolite.

Heading back to our spot, I noted happily that the older of the two were watching us; the girl was laying down sunning or maybe showing off that round peach of a bottom. With the sun shining on it, I also noted clear lines that implied the girl had had a cane across those cheeks in the last few days, fading now but obvious to one who has administered many such punishments himself.

Taking the seat closest to the couple, and seated myself back to them, allowing Rebecca the chance to get a magnificent view of them both. We spoke as we drank our coffee, quietly discussing them. She wanted to go over and say Hi. but I told her to be patient; they were here early to grab the loungers, so I suspected they would be here for the day, much like we planned.

"Wait, girl, the next time they go up for drinks or go in the pool, why don't you follow? Then say hi, see if they strike up a conversation. It would be rude to impose on them. They may not want to be sociable at this time of day," I said to her.

Keeping my voice low as we talked, but watching her closely, her eyes were on the girl and hardly left her to look at me. I could have been annoyed at this, but I was secretly happy. I had hoped to find a lady for her here, someone she could have her first girl on girl experience with and it seemed fate had given us a helping hand...

Soon two men, both shaven-headed and bearded, so alike they could have been brothers, but I guessed not as they were holding hands, came and took the separating loungers.

We returned to our sun-worshipping; I applied sunscreen to the delicate parts of myself and a lesser factor sunscreen onto Rebecca's flesh. She was a sun worshiper and had a nice tan already from lying about naked in the garden.

The lady rose after about an hour, about 10 am, the sun now well and truly beaming down on us. Felling the heat of the sun drove me to get up from the lounger and head to the cabana to grab a pitcher of iced water and some fruit.

As it happens, the lovely-looking lady with the strawberry hair also picked this moment to grab some refreshments. I used this convenient coincidence as an opportunity to catch her eye and say good morning in my plummiest English accent. I was, after all, a schoolteacher.

"Good morning," I said, smiling my most charming of smiles. I continued to say,
"Such lovely sunshine I do hope it lasts,"

Playing the part of the educated, mature Englishman I truly was. I held no illusions that I was this lady's type, but I fell that she was kindred in another way.

"Oh, hello, yes, it is quite wonderful, I will be nice and bronzed when I return home I think," she said, smiling warmly, friendly even, "You are seated with the charming young lady, no?" Her accent was cultured but definitely Scandinavian.

"Your daughter?" She laughed as she said that, clearly knowing she was not.

I laughed myself,
"No, definitely not my daughter," I winked.

"And your companion, I am certain, is not a relation; she has such interesting hair…"

143

Full-on charm offensive launched.

"No, you are right, but then again, I saw you watching us earlier at the bar. I thought you had seen me squeeze her bottom," she said with a conspiratorial smile.

"It is such a lovely squeezable bottom, is it not?" She laughed again. It was a rather charming and warm laugh that made me feel at ease.

It turned out she had spotted Rebecca earlier snagging the two loungers and had then seen me join her with the breakfast offerings. So, when she had seen me, people watching, she had deliberately squeezed the girls bottom, hoping that I might take note.

I introduced myself now, seeing as she had made it already clear that she welcomed my company, had even sought it in her own subtle way. I was now also sure our meeting here was no coincidence; she had probably been waiting for such an opportunity to arise.

"Alex, pleased to make your acquaintance, I said, holding out my hand. "British, as you can probably tell, and my companion over there is Rebecca."

As I said this, I turned to see that not only had Rebecca introduced herself to the girl, but she had also taken this lady's lounger and were in deep conversation already.

"Aha, my name is Lovisa," she replied, giving my hand a squeeze rather than a shake, "and my friend there, who I see has invited your Rebecca over already, is Gisela. We are being from Sweden." Her smile was warm and dazzled me a little.

I invited her to sit with me while the two girls chatted away, giggling, and playing with each other's hair; I think Rebecca

was quite jealous of Gisela's hair. We continued to chat about our homes, the village and eventually what brought us to this location.

As I had guessed, they were fellow kinksters and the scene here had attracted them as well, along with the chance to be naked all day and enjoy the sun. They were also quite looking forward to some more liberal fun that can be found in the evenings.

Looking over at the girls, I smiled and told her that I had been hoping to find a girl for Rebecca; she had as yet to even kiss a girl, though I knew she had fantasised about it. We had considered inviting the headmaster's partner to play, but they came as a package, and she was not yet ready for that.

That then led to a short explanation about the headmaster. I did not elaborate too much as I frowned upon outing someone. Then I just explained that he and his partner were close friends on the scene. I skipped over the part of him actually being a Headmaster IRL (in real life.)

"Ela has some experience," she smiled and raised an eyebrow as she said this. (I read that expression to mean Ela knew her way around a woman's body.) "Maybe if they get on, they can play. I would enjoy watching them, I think, especially a first time her virginity being taken in a way, yes?"

"Yes, I would think watching them would be very erotic," I agreed. I could also see that they were getting on very well right now.

We spent a good hour chatting away; I was enamoured of this wonderful woman already, that warm smile, that with her strawberry blond hair, the sun shining through it like a halo. She was making my heart skip, to be honest, but I had already read the tea leaves on this one and I would be barking up the wrong tree should I try anything.

145

The two men, seeing they were being gooseberries, spoke to the girls and between them reorganised the loungers. So now the girls could join us, and we then pushed all of them together to make a super-sized lounger and spent the rest of the day enjoying the sun and snuggling up with our respective partners.

Ela was very chatty and kept Rebecca talking all day and by dinnertime, they were firm friends and had shared many details about the grownups, as they called us collectively.

Ela was excited to hear I was good with rope. It seemed Lovisa was an accomplished mistress and dominatrix, but her rope skills were limited to restraints. She had no patience for all this knot tying and untying.

I overheard her ask her mistress if it would be ok for Rebecca's Sir to tie her sometime this week. Seems she wanted to fly.

"If Alex is agreeable, I don't see why not, there is a party tonight at Le TANTRA, maybe he would be so kind as to bring his rope and do some on you but do not pester the man dear, he has his own little girl to entertain, no?"

I told them it would be my pleasure and maybe they could join us when we go out to the hills around Lac du Salagou for a hike and some outdoor fun.

As we parted, hugs all around from both the girls, I also noted a quick kiss on the lips between Rebecca and Ela. Well, that worked out perfectly. Only our second day and I think we had found the right girl for her to experience her first girl on girl session.

We parted, promising to meet up later at the club. Rebecca was bouncing off the walls. She was so excited; it was cute if a little annoying.

"She is perfect, I am so glad we came here, thank you, Sir, I am the luckiest girl thank you thank you thank you," she said jumping up into my arms the moment we got back in the room.

"Do you want her to, Sir? She said you were quite attractive but she not sure her mistress would allow it," she asked, smiling that innocent little smile she used to avoid being told off for being impertinent sometimes. (Brats will brat.)

"Although I think you quite fancied her Mistress didn't you Sir?" she laughed, smiling, then kissed me, taking my cock in her hands, and continued,
"I saw this rise a little, a few times while you were talking to her."

"Yes, she is quite a stunning woman, but alas, I do not think I am her type, though I must admit that the idea of the four of us sharing an evening together does rather stiffen one's flagpole." I laughed at my own little joke.

"Let's see how this evening goes. Tonight is about you and Ela. It is well past time, that your fantasies became a reality, my dear, and I am sure we will share more experiences soon enough," I said.

I was rather looking forward to what was to come in the next few years as she grew into the sex kitten role; she was so perfect for. One day she will whisper those words, "Sir, kitten wants to be bad," and I would so enjoy unleashing this girl upon the world.

We went over to the beachfront restaurant and order burgers and fries, not being in the mood for anything exotic today and two Sundaes for dessert. (You can't go wrong with a burger and fries.)

147

We then spent a few hours on the beach sharing one lounger (you snooze, you lose) it was pleasant enough snuggled up, she even fell asleep in my embrace, and I have to admit I did the same shortly after only waking when the sun began its decline behind the hotel.

Waking bleary-eyed from our naps, we then retreated quickly to our rooms, both jumping into the shower and cleaning each other, soaping each other up and becoming rather aroused. Seeing my arousal, she took my cock in hand and soaping it, so it was slippery, began to wank me off.

Obviously, given the plans for the night, I was not going to fuck her. That pleasure would be Gisela's, though after I was going to be having my way with her. By then, my lust would be a roaring lion, chewing at its cage to be let out.

She slowly masturbated me, knowing the grip and rhythm needed to get me off successfully; after all these years, it was natural to her. Feeling when I was about to cum, she slipped her finger in my arse and took my cock in her throat. No playing about. She took the whole member down in one with a practised swallow. Finger my arse, milking me down her throat, not letting up until her need to breathe overcame her need to please.

I dried off and went out to pick up some wine for later. Easy for a man, no need to do one's hair, when running your fingers through was sufficient and no makeup required on this old face. Rebecca would be at least an hour doing her hair and makeup, so I had plenty of time.

I grabbed a few bottles, not knowing if we would have guests later or not. Better safe than a poor host was my motto.

I put out a little dress and her heels. She would not be wearing the dress long, but we would need to dress to get to the club, I had been informed. I slipped into casual linen slacks and a white

shirt. Then selected a silver collar for her to wear. (We had not actually done the collaring ceremony that was to come in the new year once she decided if she was staying on at college or going on to teacher training.) I matched this with a silver anklet.

Then, removing two lengths of my scratchiest rope, I had decided that tonight was going to involve Ichinawa; it was in my opinion, a good way to break the ice with a new bunny and something I could do anywhere. The club was more of a swinger venue, and I did not know if it had dungeon facility's and I figured Ela would enjoy the rope; I knew I would certainly enjoy wrapping it about that curvalicious form.

Deciding I did not want to carry the rope, I called Rebecca and had her stand still while I fixed it about her waist in a corset tie. Patting her bare behind and admonishing her to hurry up her pretty self, before warming up that bottom.

"Yes, Sir," she replied, heading back to the bathroom to continue with her makeup.

But I knew full well she would take as long as it took. No way was she going out tonight looking anything less than stunning. Funnily enough, if she turned up looking like one of the dogs after having rolled in a mud pool, I would still think she was stunning… (Ahh love blind, you silly old fool.)

Ready finally, dress covering the rope as I knew it would, we made our way downstairs and grabbed the stretch golf cart that ferried guests to the club. Entering the club, down some warmly lit stairs, we entered a neon discotheque bar area that was heaving and rather loud.

There seemed to be public booths and some private booths around the room. I asked how one could get access. Long story short, money changed hands, and we got one of the more remote booths to ourselves. The booth came with table service, so I

ordered champagne, which arrived in a bucket of ice, along with four glasses?

I raised an eyebrow at this but then saw the waitress was followed by Lovisa and Gisela, both of whom I might add, were already completely naked, though Lovisa was painted from head to toes.

We rose and greeted them, then I stood back to admire the body paint; it glowed in the neon lights of the room; she was purple with gold and lots of neon lines work. That showed off her curves spectacularly.

"Do you like it? Ela is quite an artist. Maybe you will let her paint your Rebecca sometime?"

"Absolutely," I said, turning to see that the girls were saying hello their own way.

I mean, they were kissing, not a peck either. This was a full-on snog of a hello. Well, I guess my girl had finally kissed a girl and she liked it. (Oh dear, that song will be in my head now.)

Waiting for them to part, I took the opportunity to greet Ela myself, and with her Mistresses nod of approval, she kissed this old man in a manner likely to cause cardiac arrest. This Marylinesque beauty came in for a proper kiss and pressed her body firmly against mine. (Oh, another shrinking violet, I thought. #Not.)

I invited them to join us, but being the good host that I was, I did not want them to feel uncomfortable. So, I removed first Rebecca's dress, this was accomplished by the simple process of untying the wrap-around belt and letting it fall away, revealing the rope corset wound about her.

I, being of a more dignified nature, picked up the dress and went to the changing rooms to divest myself of my clothes and put everything in a locker.

Turning about, I found Lovisa standing there in all her painted glory, waiting for me, I surmised.

"Ahh Alex, a quick word, if I might?"

I had expected this, so just nodded.
"The girls tonight yes, they can play, Ela is quite taken with your girl, and I believe rather likes you as well... I think your rope will send her over from liking to wanting and that is ok, but not tonight, tonight we let them play, yes?"

"Agreed; tonight, is all about them. I have wanted this for Rebecca for some time. We just had not found the right girl."

"So, it is agreed, you can tie her, you have in mind Ichinawa I hear, that is good, she will like that I think." Again, with that disarming smile, this woman certainly knew how to charm a man.

"It is a shame I do not have the skill for this, but it is good that you do." She paused and looked down a moment. I had not noticed, but my old chap had perked up and was taking note of the fair Lovisa.

"You may touch her, but not sexually, and of course keep that to yourself tonight, maybe later in the week," she said and winked and flashed me a winsome smile.

"No, not me," she said, smiling. Then continued to say, with a little laugh. "But I think maybe I will let you borrow Ela sometime this week. To be honest, I don't think I could keep her away anyhow, but maybe you will let me borrow your Rebecca as well?"

151

She said this standing there magnificent in her blue and gold body paint; her face warmly lit by her dazzling smile and fiery blue eyes.

"I don't see how I could refuse such an offer. I think it would be an interesting experience for her, though I will have to ask her first, you understand?"

"Yes, of course, with her consent and your agreement. She is quite an attractive young lady; you are a lucky man. You must tell me how you met."

And with that, I walked her back, by way of exploring the club, giving the girls time to relax without their respective dominates there to supervise. Recounting the tale of how my young student got my attention during an English lesson.

We were laughing like old friends when we returned, Lovisa leaned into Rebecca, close to her ear as if to whisper but given the ambient volume of the club she still had to shout a little and I overheard her say, "White panties indeed, you must wear them for me some time," and kissed her ear.

Hard Lessons
Exhibitionist Holiday.

Chapter 4: Ela Unbound.

We drank a few bottles, talked, laughed, and generally relaxed, enjoying the ambience of the fluorescent decor, Lovisa insisting she purchased her share of the wine. The girls danced while we talked, then insisted we join them, much to my embracement (my dancing being of the dad variety these days, and I rather did not want to look the fool in front of Lovisa). Still, we had fun and our two girls were getting on famously.

Ela, at some point, unwound the corset from Rebecca and as a hint, handed me the rope with a bit of a curtsy, just in case I did not get that subtle hint. Rebecca nibbled on my ear and whispered.

"Tie her for me, Sir. Please…" she said, using her little girl voice, this and kissed me again before dancing off.

I looked over to Lovisa, who had guessed the subject of our conversation even if she had not overheard. She just gave a simple nod. I think she wanted to see this, too. We both knew where this was leading.

I picked up the rope; the rope being my palm tree coir, about 4mm, I used this as it was light, thin and very scratchy; perfect for Ichinawa. I got up and led the ladies into the play area in search of a free space that was large enough for me to tie in.

We found a spot quick enough; I had spotted a few earlier and though it was currently in use; we did not have to wait too long for it to be freed up, although we did, however, have to clean it ourselves. (Some people are just uncivilised.)

Unfurling the rope and laying it on the bed, I realised I had forgotten a key part of this scene, a blindfold. This would be a much better experience if she could not see. Sometimes, I even blindfolded myself to perform this tie, wrapping the rope about the subject by feel and response only.

I looked about and caught Lovisa's eye and made an eye covering gesture. She seemed to know what I meant and disappeared into the crowd, returning shortly with a red scarf. No idea where she had got this, though I guessed someone had donated it or had had it liberated.

I knelt on the round bed, rope to my side, where I could reach it with ease. I beckoned Gisela over, gesturing for her to sit in front of me. She did, kneeling much as I was (the position called kiza in aikido).

Leaning forward, I bound her eyes with the donated scarf, tying it firmly in place so it would not slip off during the movement of the rope dance.

I then spoke to her, softly explaining that I wanted her to move with me, feel the tug of the rope and not resist each movement but flow like water disturbed by a branch, move with me let the river flow around me.

Ichinawa is a form of rope that can be used in many ways, often it is tied in a sensual and relaxing manner (this is how I was taught to tie it) but others use it as a takedown tie. Ichinawa is a Japanese term, stemming from the words Ichi mean one means one, and Nowa means rope. The purist will only use one rope, but I always felt that when ropes are joined, they become one, so I do not prescribe to this purist doctrine and use two. My version has evolved over the years, and I now describe it as the Ichinawa tango.

As this was her first experience, I was going to go for the more sensual tie this time, rather than the more fighty tango style I often used. Gisela was a statuesque woman, tall and strong, but this girl also had curves, curves that I could not wait to feel bend and flex under my touch. I wanted her to be in a state of arousal or, given the way they had been behaving earlier, more aroused.

Still, she was also not my submissive. Lovisa had not given me permission to be sadistic and this tie could be sadistic as well as sensual, so I would not be punching in the rope tonight.

Taking up her hand, placed it on my knee, then tied a quick column tie to that wrist, before pulling on the cord with my opposite hand, this pulled her towards me and I used the movement to turn her, so her back was now to me. Sliding my other hand down her free arm and taking hold of that wrist, twisting and pulling it behind her, then leaning her back into me to hold it in place.

This freed my hand up, swapping hands now, taking up the cord in the freed hand, pulling her tied limb across her body, placing her open hand on her left rather ample breast.

Keeping tension, I wrapped the cord about her, crossing the arm that was behind her, the tension never being released on the rope. Her body moved to my touch and with my own movements. I was also feeling her bottom wriggle slightly, the better to feel the hard cock that was pressed to her back. Both arms now held in place, I moved her body about, using the tension to control her like a marionette.
(Hey, you tie a naked beautiful woman and try not getting aroused.)

I still had a metre or two remaining on this piece, so taking it in both hands I sawed it across the exposed nipple of her right breast, then moved it so it pressed against her neck, adding only the slightest bit of pressure to this stranglehold but even that was

enough to send her off. I felt her melt becoming limp in my arms, as I saw the coarse cord back and forth, pressing lightly against her pale throat. Continuing upwards, rubbing the scratchy palm tree rope against her flushed cheeks, caressing her tenderly like a lover with the roughness of the rope, then I kissed her with the cord.

Moving the cord against her lips in such a way as to mimic the press of my lips, slipping the cord between the full moist open lips, her tongue coming out to lick the rope with a gentle kiss. I slipped out from behind her now, pressing her back as a lover would; the rope still held between her lips, pressing her down to the bed. The tension on the rope was still there, though less tight whilst caressing, brushing her lips as if the rope was kissing her.

Pinning her down briefly, kissing her myself, the cord still pressed upon her bottom lip, my tongue finding hers briefly but satisfying, my cock hard as iron now, was pressing against her. She felt this and wiggled but this was not to be, not this time and lifting myself off her, I slipped the remaining cord behind and pulled her up to a sitting position, legs out before her.

Joining the second piece of the cord, I wound it about her waist, pulling tight so it squeezed her tightly; like an over-enthusiastic hug. Then tying one of her legs into the rope, pulling her into another position, as I moved back behind her. This is why I describe the tie as a tango, I lead the dance and guide her as I move; she moves, but the tension always remains.

I pulled her into me now, holding her tight with the rope, keeping the tension and connection between us, I bound and unbound her body, pulling her this way and that always we were connected by touch and by feel, I wound a loose end about her throat again, looking over to her mistress for permission. She had read the scene, watched as her lover, her partner and her submissive, had melted and been seduced by an old man's rope. She had seen her wiggle, trying to feel my hardness, watched her

shudder with pleasure as the rope sawed on her flesh and now had given me permission to subdue her totally.

I wrapped the remaining cord about an ankle, lifting the leg as I pulled most there about her neck. She would choke herself if she allowed her leg to drop, but she held it there. My free hand (the one not holding the end of the rope) flowed over her breasts, down her mid-drift, and touched her wetness, fingers running back and forth, feeling her get wetter and wetter. I did not enter her, but coated my fingers in her juices. Brining my cunt-soaked fingers up to her lips, circling them, wetting them with her wetness.

Slowly again, I ran my hand down her body, this time not stopping at her cunt but sliding up the raised leg. I pressed down gently, increasing the tension about her neck bit by bit. I pressed harder until I felt her subside. Feeling her breathing through our physical closeness, shallower and shallower, as she choked herself slowly out. Finally, sensing that it was time, I released the pressure and took the weight off her leg, releasing the cord with my other hand before lowering her unbound leg. Lowering her body to the bed, and rolled away from her now resting form.

I told Rebecca to go to her now, hold her for a while, let her recover in your embrace, Lovisa agreed, and ushered her over herself with a pat on her bottom.

"You are a skilled man, Alex. That almost makes me regret not being a switch," she said. The smile on her face made me regret not being a switch too. She was an incredibly stunning woman.

Hard Lessons
Exhibitionist Holiday.

Chapter 5: Tell it to the Bees.

I watch as Rebecca gently, hesitantly even, crawled onto the round bed and snuggled into Gisela's prone body. With one hand she untied her, removing the last of the rope bindings (the one from her wrist) dropping it aside, then her front to Ela's back she spooned Ela. Ela's hand in response came up, slipped behind her, grabbing at Rebecca, pulling her closer and content. They just lay there for a while.

Lovisa took up guard duty, glaring at anyone who approached, telling them in no uncertain terms to let the girls be. I leaned back against a wall to continue watching, a voyeur for now and in what was to come.

Rebecca was technically a virgin; at least when it came to girl-on-girl sex. She had, until today, to my knowledge, never even kissed another girl and now; she lay on a bed with her naked body wrapped about another nubile young, beautiful woman's body.

She had expressed more than a little interest in finding a girl to experience girl on girl play, and there had certainly been no end of ladies at parties that had shown more than a passing infatuation in her. We had discussed it many times, pillow talk, fantasy talk, about me bringing home a girl and inviting her to join us in bed, but this was perfect. This was someone she chose for herself, and it seemed fallen for.

I am not a jealous man; I am a lucky man. Lucky in her unexpected interest in me and finding that in her, I had found what I had been missing for many years. No, I did not fear

losing her to this girl; I am excited to witness the next stage in her evolution.

Rebecca was not as tall, nor did she have the curves of Ela's body. They were opposites in a way, one athletic and coltish of limb, the other tall, curvy, and statuesque. Both were beauties though, with a style of their own and even though both were submissive to their respective partners, they were strong young women. Independent of thought and action and they submitted to no one, but those they chose. Lucky for Lovisa and myself, they had chosen us.

Resting my back against the wall in this dimly lit room, lit mostly by LED strip lighting around the edge of the bed, admiring Lovisa as she guarded the two girls, much like a lioness guarding her pride.

My eyes, now drawn back to the bed by movement, Ela stirring now, turning on the bed to face Rebecca; fingers caressing her face, following the contours of her eyes, circling her lips, pressing her bottom lip, exposing the moist flesh inside. A hand slipped behind Rebecca's neck, pulling her in for a kiss.

Ela was not new to this. Her partner, her lover, her mistress was a woman. Knowing that this girl before her was inexperienced, Ela would take the lead. Ela would Lead Rebecca, not in a top and bottom way; no, I suspected Lovisa, and Ela made love much as Rebecca and I did. It would not be a scene, not be play but lovemaking and they would flow naturally, learning each other's needs as they went. Ela's experience would allow her to guide Rebecca so they would not be like two virgins on their first awkward fumble. Rebecca's imagination would fill in the gaps.

They kissed, gently at first. I found that amusing as earlier they had their tongues buried deep in each other's mouths. Their kisses were slow, probing and nibbling, biting at each other lips,

tongue darting into parted mouths, only to pull back to stare at each other. Both had a hand full of hair, holding as if they feared to let go, least the other would vanish away.

They would pull each other toward the other, kissing harder and harder, longer, and longer, deeper and deeper, their passion, their heat building, until Ela pushed Rebecca to her back. Gripped both wrists and pressed her down with ease, using her much taller and stronger frame, overpowering Rebecca, her breasts caressing each side of Rebecca's face as she pressed her down.

Now I am watching this, as were many others, including now Lovisa, who has stopped her pacing of the room as well, finding a clear spot to lean back and watch. The room was filling, but no one was approaching the bed. No one would disturb these girls, all could see this was between them. We could be voyeurs only.

Ela moved down, hands sliding from Rebecca's wrists, down her arms, until she was face to face again, kissing her now, taking charge. She kissed deeply and long, then nuzzled Rebecca's neck, clearly biting at one point before sliding down further, kissing her shoulder, her chest and slowly running a wet tongue down to a nipple, circling. Then suck, a hard suck pulling her small but only in comparison to her own, breast up with the force of her suckling mouth. Her other hand was fondling, needing the other breast, pinching the nipple between finger and thumb, and pulling as she twisted.

This cause Rebecca's back to arch up. I knew from experience that this was a pleasure and pain response, and she loved both equally. Ela swapped mouth for hand and continued the hard play with Rebecca's breasts, as she slid her tongue down to the navel, circling and tonguing that small erogenous mid-point, one that thrust up to meet her mouth as she twisted each nipple in turn.

Ela undoubtedly knew what she was doing. She was getting Rebecca to the point of cumming without even touching her (I had no doubt) moist and willing cunt. I could see her arching, offering, her legs spreading. She was with her body, begging Ela to take her. Then slowly, so incredibly frustratingly slowly (even to us onlookers) she started moving down, still licking and nipping at Rebecca's flesh. Not in a straight line. No, that would have been too quick: she meandered about Rebecca's abdomen, teasing, making Rebecca beg even more with her body's movements.

Her hands stopped the hard fondling of Rebecca's breasts, and I saw her claw down the side of Rebecca's chest, down to her thighs, over the top and between her spread legs. Apparently not spread enough though, as she pressed them apart, pushing, seeing how flexible her lover was.

Rebecca is fit. She exercises daily and does yoga and some other callisthenics dance classes, so in other words, she was very flexible. I should know. I have tied her into some rather trying positions over the years.

So, when Ela spread her legs, Rebecca obliged and almost did the splits. Ela lifted up to look about, seeing that there was quite an audience now. There was quiet humming from the background music, but the watchers were almost silent as they took in the show, rapt in their attention on the scene unfolding before them.

Rebecca's eyes were closed, a shame as I know she would have enjoyed being watched by so many eyes, a true exhibitionist at heart. She always wanted an audience. Her eyes were closed, her bottom lip held between her teeth as she waited for Ela's first true kiss.

Ela paused, holding the legs apart, her eyes darting about the room, seeking her Mistress, seeing her, then seeing me next to

her. She smiled and leaned down to place the very first kiss on Rebecca's sweet flower. She blew first, a cooling breath across moist flesh. This made her lover's back arch, and her hips rise to meet her, demanding that she fulfil the promise of that teasing breath.

Ela did not tease again. She kissed her lover's lips, a lover's kiss much like their earlier kisses, gentle kisses, lips and tongues exploring the other's lips.

She released Rebecca's legs. Now, Rebecca responding, wrapped her legs about the waist of Ela, pulling her into her, telling her not to stop. I could no longer see what she was doing, but I could see my girl, her lover, and see her reactions.

Her hands were clawing at the mattress, then at her own body, raking her nails down her own moist flesh, reaching for the matted dreads to Ela's multi-coloured hair. Her finger slipping between the dreadlocks and gripping, pulling and at times pushing as Ela's kisses drove her into a frenzy. Body arching, her hip grinding into Ela as she held her head and writhed on the bed in reaction to her first true kisses from a girl.

Rebecca's body was soaking now, her pink hair plastered to her face, as Ela drove her beyond frenzy into one orgasm and then another. Ela herself was soaked now as well, not just from the heat of passion, also probably from Rebecca's wetness. Rebecca could squirt, and I think Ela had found that out. It did not seem to phase her in the slightest, in fact, I was certain even though I could not see that several of Ela's fingers were now deep in the moist, tender flesh of her lover's sex, building her up to another climax and possibly another gush.

Lovisa leaned into me, and then against me, seemingly unconcerned that my hardness was pressing against her painted flesh. Sensing it was OK, I wrapped my arms around her, not trying anything, just holding her; I think she needed comforting

or contact with another body as she watches this unfold. I realised then that I had not asked if they had shared before. Maybe this was her first time as an outsider too.

We stood there wrapped about each other, watching as our girls made love on a round, orgy bed surrounded by couples and men, some now making out as well, the scene before them driving them into their own sexual frenzies.

Ela seemingly loved eating pussy and was not letting up, even when Rebecca tried pushing her away. She kept her face buried deep between her legs, not satisfied until she had licked her lover into multiple orgasmic spasms. When she finally did let up, her face was flushed and her makeup in ruins. Still, she had a grin, like the proverbial Cheshire cat.

As she lifted away, Rebecca shot up to embrace her, and kiss her, tasting her wetness on Ela's lips, kissing her with a passion that would cause jealousy in lesser men, I was sure. (Not me, I was happy to see her fulfil any of her fantasies and this one, in particular, pleased me.) They embraced, then I heard Rebecca say clearly, though a little huskily.

"Your Turn."

Rebecca was new to this; this was her first girl on girl experience. I had just witnessed her taken in a way that drove her to a frenzy. She had climaxed multiple times, was a hot, sweaty mess, but she was not done. Her lover deserved no less attention than she had received. I knew her to be a generous lover, having been on the receiving end of her attentions for nearly four years now.

She would never let me go unsatisfied; my burden unrelieved so to speak. I have known her to suck my cock for almost an hour, never ceasing her attention until I gave her my gift (her words). I

was indeed a lucky man. And now it seems Gisela was about to receive some of that same enthusiasm.

She was now taking the lead, kissing deeply, her nails racking down Ela's back, digging into her shoulders before raking them down her side, leaving red trails on Ela's flesh. Kissing deeper and harder, as she would grab a handful of that curvy bottom, lifting her, pulling her closer to her own body. I watched her finger slide between Ela's cheeks, touching, circling, then probing.

I recognised these moves. These were how we made love as equals. My body was hers to explore as much as hers was mine. After sex, I could at times look as if I had been wrestling with a bag of cats. I would have so many scratches, some would even have drawn blood! A real wildcat.

Yes, her finger was in Ela's arse, and I saw now that her hand had worked its way between her legs as well, inexperienced she may be, but she knew her own body and knew what felt good to her would probably feel good to Ela. And was now fingering Ela, kissing her, their body writhing together like two mating snakes. Ela's arms wrapped about Rebecca, holding them both together, keeping Rebecca pressed up against her heaving bosoms (they really were magnificent).

Lovisa was stirring, I think, touching herself as she watched the scene before her, her body still up against mine, my arms about her waist, my hardness pressed against her bottom. Her hand reached behind her and touched my face, caressing.

"Just hold me please, I feel you, I know your need, but I cannot," her voice soft, apologetic.

She knew that her body against mine was doing, knew that the sight of our two girls was arousing me to the point of distraction. Yet I knew that she was not on offer. She needed my embrace, my warmth, not my cock.

My growing frustration of being just a voyeur to the unfolding scene, my beast's hunger would just have to wait, to be sated later.

Ignoring with difficulty Lovisa's movements as she dealt with her own hunger's need. I am certain this would have tested me had I been younger, but I have been tying pretty young things for years and have learned a modicum of self-control.

Turning my attention back to the girls, I saw Ela reach the point of her own release, her back arching, her head snapping back to setting free her primal scream. Rebecca did not let that movement go to waste. She pressed Ela back on the bed and, for the first time in her life, drank another girl's orgasm. Much like her kisses, she did not explore gently as Ela had her, but pressed her mouth up against Ela's lips to taste her as deeply as possible.

It was hard to see what she was doing but Ela's reaction was easy to read, inexperienced Rebecca might be, but she had a vagina and knew what felt good to her and was now showing Ela what pleases her, the sensations, and touches that she enjoyed. I was pretty sure that her tongue would not just explore Ela's cunt but delve deep into her rosebud (that is what she called it) while her fingers would explore, seeking those spots that would elicit a reaction from her lover.

She rose after the next spasm; her face soaking with sweat and Ela's fluids, both their make up in ruins, their hair wet and matted to their face. They embraced and kissed and rolled about the bed, coming down now slowly relaxing and eventually just lying there, wrapped about each other, legs, arms inter-woven, tying them together as if they never wanted to be parted.

Hard Lessons
Exhibitionist Holiday.

Chapter 6: Serre-moi fort.

We left them there, letting them come down from the sexual high they had taken themselves to. Lovisa moved away from me. I felt a slight loss at that, a dissolving of our connection as our bodies separated.

The crowd also started to wander away, though one couple was still fucking in the corner, possibly waiting to use the bed themselves. We sidled up to the bed, each taking a side, the side with our partners on. Both almost at the same time reach out to touch, then gently, then slowly pull them apart and to us.

Rebecca flung herself about me, head nuzzled into my neck like a little girl in her fathers. Seeking comfort, kissing her cheek, tasting Ela on her clammy flesh, the scent of sex hung about her like cheap perfume, not unpleasant, just heady in the air about her.

I looked over to Lovisa, who was similarly comforting Gisela. Brushing the matted hair from her face to kiss her, I guessed that was hard for her to watch as well. I also wondered if she was tasting my girl on Ela as well. The girls were slowly coming down and recovering, so we guided them away from the bed.

The couple in the corner, I noted, did not wait for us to clean the bed but grabbed the spray and cloth to do so themselves. I nodded my thanks to the lady as she came over with my rope. I guessed they realised we had our hands full at the moment. We did.

Finding out the booth was still empty, I placed Rebecca down and handed her and Ela a bottle of water each, hydration being important.

We sat and talked some more, though loudly as the ambient noise level had increased (annoyingly). I had to ask Lovisa about how she was feeling, as I had picked up on her earlier discomfort at seeing the two girls like that. As I thought she had never shared Ela with another, though she knew that she had had girlfriends before her. I admitted the same, telling her the closest we had come to that was allowing some random man to jerk off on her tits when he caught us in flagrante delicto, as it were.

It seemed we both had the idea of allowing our girls to find others to play with, Ela as she wanted dick (Lovisa word) and Rebecca as she had wanted to experience what it was like to be with a girl. Though I think we both thought of finding a third for a threesome, this had worked out better. Although she said she still had to find Ela a man, she was looking at me rather intently as she explained this.

"She likes you. What you did with the rope, you could have taken her there, I am certain." She looked over to Gisela, as she said this, who, it seemed, had been following the conversation…

"Goddess yes, but only if Rebecca is ok with it; or better still, if Rebecca joins us." Worried eyes flashed over to Rebecca to see her reaction.

Rebecca looked at me all serious,
"I would like that Sir; I would like that very much, but Sir I would also like to spend a night with Lovisa and Ela…" She said this with that big-eyed look some girls perfect, to get their way. (I assure you she had it down to an art.)

I had not considered this; her spending an evening with someone else other than myself; I had to think about this. And her toes on

my cock were not helping me think straight at all. The sneaky girl.

I sat and thought deeply for a few minutes, then spoke quietly with Lovisa for a few minutes, then I made my decision.

"Yes, I think that will be ok. We have discussed this and a night with each of us, a night where we both entrust our most precious with the other." I had a quite serious look on my face as I said this, as this was quite a serious decision. But the looks on their faces cracked my stern visage a little, and I let a small smile cross my face.

The girls kissed, then kissed us both in return. I must say, being kissed by both Ela and Rebecca was quite invigorating and reminded me that I had to relieve a little pressure of my own.

I figured it would have to wait, though; I was not of a mind to pull Rebecca away from Ela and although she remembered I was there; her mind, though, was clearly focused on Ela this evening. Focusing on Lovisa (hardly a chore, as she was quite lovely) getting more information about her, her past where she lived and how long she had been on the scene.

She was, of course, Swedish from Jönköping on Lake Vättern. Living now in Copenhagen with Gisela, who was German and had moved to Copenhagen from Hamburg to study. Finding the BDSM scene at an early as a submissive but grew to realise she preferred to be the one in charge. She had met Ela at a party two years ago, and they had been inseparable ever since.

I had already imparted the tale of how Rebecca and I had met, so I filled her in a little about my history on the scene, being introduced by my school's Headmaster, some twenty-five years ago after running into him and his then-wife, at a swinger's club! Wholly embarrassing at first, I must admit, though seeing as we were both there and at the time on opposite ends of his

wife, we found it funny. They took me under their wings and introduced me to the kink world. Somewhere I had been interested in for some time, just unable to find a connection.

Much like Lovisa, when I first entered the kink scene, I was unsure of my place and experimented a lot, had a lot of fun. Eventually finding that I had a love of bondage, particularly rope Shibari, in which I have become quite skilled. From there, and after much experimenting, I found my place in the community and never really looked back.

We must have chatted for some time. The wine was all gone (four bottles of it, whoops) the girls were snuggled up asleep in the corner. I had not noticed when they drifted off; I guess the night was too much for them, bless.

We woke them gently, suggesting that we return to our apartments, reassuring them both that we would meet up in the morning for a country picnic in the countryside a trip to the lake was in order, I handed them their clothing, having retrieved ours and theirs from the lockers, Lovisa had stayed to keep an eye on the sleepy lovers.

Taking the stretch golf cart back to the apartment block and we bid each other a good night with several embraces and kisses for all, we parted and headed to our rooms. I almost had to carry Rebecca. She was so tired and probably tipsy; it had been a big night for her. Putting her to bed, tying the waist rope about her, her eyes already closed, asleep before her head hit the pillow, I think. I placed the bottle of water on the side and headed for the shower. A very cold one.

Showered, and dry, I slipped into the bed, tying the rope about my waist, trying not to wake her. She stirred slightly, and I heard her say quietly.

"Serre-moi fort." (Hold me tight.)

169

Hard Lessons
Exhibitionist Holiday.

Chapter 7: Converfucking.

Awaking in the morning, still holding her tightly to me, cradled in my arms. Being the big spoon, she called it. We had kicked off the sheets and untied ourselves at some point during the night. I stayed there, not moving, listening to her shallow breaths.

Aroused still; not that surprising given the events of the previous night, aching with lust, a need that I knew would not wait much longer. But wait it would, kissing the exposed nape of her neck and just lay there, just holding her, waiting for her to stir. Usually, she rose before me to bring me a cup of tea, always nice to wake up to. I suppose after such a big night she was tired or maybe did not want to wake from whatever dream she was having.

Still, the ache, the throbbing hardness of my cock pressed against her naked bottom was distracting. I knew from past times that I could wake her with sex, sleep sex, she called it. She loved being fucked awake and a few times I had woken to find her on my cock, taking advantage of morning wood either slowly grinding herself off or even more pleasant, waking to find her mouth wrapped about my cock. (Can't think of a better way to wake up.)

But that was not what I needed now. I needed to see her eyes, watch her as she takes my cock in her, see her and feel her reactions to our lovemaking. I had seen the way she looked at Ela and though secure and not of a jealous bent; I had felt some envy. It was our first share. The first time I had seen her with anyone other than me. I had always hoped to be part of that experience. Being a bystander was harder than I would have

thought! Lovisa, I believe, had felt the same, though she had had me to comfort her, and I had felt her arousal as much as she could feel my own more obvious arousal.

I had been lying in the same spot, watching as the sun crested and lighted our room through the big double doors that led to the balcony. The sun in our faces would wake her soon, and I stayed patient, just nuzzling her neck, waiting for her. I would know she was stirring as she would press back against me, trying to gain a little more connection, a little more warmth from my embrace. There she is. I felt her move, felt her press, felt her bottom press against my hardness, heard the murmur of satisfaction knowing I was hard for her.

"Mmmmm, morning Sir," she said. I felt her wiggle and manoeuvre herself, sliding my cock between her thighs.

"Morning Princess," I said in return, adjusting myself so I could press my cock into her. No foreplay, not waiting for her to be ready. I had waited long enough, I felt. Pressing into her, feeling her tightness, feeling as her resistance receded, as she was instantly wet. I rolled upon her, raising myself on my elbows, and thrust myself several times deeply into her sweet little honeypot.

"I enjoyed last night, seeing you with another girl, but I wanted to be in there with you so bad, wanted to taste her wetness on your lips, wanted to see you taste my cock on her lips. See you lick her pussy clean after I had fucked her. You know this we spoke of this, and this is how it was supposed to be." I talked as I thrust. Letting her know how frustrated I had been just being a voyeur last night.

"Sorry, Sir, I know it was supposed to be like that, but it just happened."

I knew this, of course, and in reality, I was pleased with last night's outcome. She knew this as well, but went along with the narrative; it was a game we played often.

"I will bring her to your bed, Sir, I promise. She wants to join us. I want to taste you on her, drink from her after you have filled her. Teach her how to please you as you taught me to." She looked at me, eyes wide, smiling innocently at me. What chance did I have against that arsenal of cuteness?

I rolled her about, facing her now, looking into her eyes as she mounted me, leaning forward to kiss me.

"Will that please, Sir? Will seeing me lick Sir's cum from Ela's sweet little cunt make Sir happy?" She smiles. She is almost irresistibly cute as she says this.

"I think I will enjoy the taste. She has a sweet pussy. Do all girls taste so sweet, Sir? I think I would like to taste more." Again, with the big eyes and the smiles, her words working their magic on my soul, the thought of her licking Ela after I had cum almost made me cum right there and then.

Well fuck me, I thought as I watched her grind on my cock, moving a little each time to matcher her movements, she grabbed my face to hiss at me hissing she wanted to take Ela on my lips and then rising and racking her nails into my flesh harder than I think she ever had.

My mind drifted a little, recalling Lovisa, her beautiful painted body wrapped about Ela, and wondered if they were having a similar converfuckingsation right now.

Rebecca rode me, harder and harder, she knew what it took to get me to cum, knew that even as aroused as I was last night, I never came easy or quick (well almost, little bugger has a mind

of its own sometimes). I was panting now, edging closer and closer to the point of release.

She knew this as my growls started to build in my chest, a rumbling growl as felt the pressure building to the point that it could not be contained. She rode me, staring deep into my eyes, watching me as looked at her. My love, my adoration, my lust for her written there clearly, unable to hide behind my English reserve at the point I exploded in her, with a cry like a man going into battle.

I had cum; she rode me a little more, before sliding down to take my cum covered cock into her mouth, slowly little by little, licking and sucking away the residue of our fucking from my softening cock. This often became too much for me, the sensitivity of the old chap racking up in intensity by the second, but she knew this and would just swallow my cock wholly and release slowly, allowing it to fall from her lips with a kiss.

We embraced in post-coital bliss for a few minutes before I picked her up and carried her to the shower.

"You smell of sex," I said, placing her in and turning on the water, cold at first, cold enough to elicit a wail of protest, but it soon warmed up and I joined her in the shower.

I cleaned her, using the scrubby puffy shower thing that she always seemed to pack, covered it in shower gel and scrubbed her down, cleaning her from head to toe. Then she returned the gesture and cleaned me up as well, before grabbing my razor, a disposable safety razor as we had used my cutthroat to shave herself the other day.

I dried myself off, grabbed shorts, a shirt, and waling sandals, and headed out to grab supplies for our excursion with the girls. A day in the hills by the lake would be bliss, and I might even

find a tree we could tie from. Rather, a happy thought of both girls hanging from a branch overlooking the lake came to mind.

Rebecca would be awhile getting ready, so I had time to go pick up the car from the hire place and do a little shopping before she and the ladies would be ready at ten.

Hard Lessons
Exhibitionist Holiday.

Chapter 8: Exhibitionists Excursion.

Meeting up with the two girls as planned at 10 am out the front of the apartment block, they were dressed for once. I hardly recognised them (only kidding). The two girls raced to each other, hugging, and then kissing. I could see how this day was going to go already. Lovisa gave me a friendly hug and kissed each cheek. Lovisa received a full-on French kiss from Rebecca! Not wanting to leave me out, Gisela pressed up to be giving me the benefit of a very booby hug and not settling for anything less than what I would call a snog from me.

They both had dressed in long hippy style skirts and halter neck style bra things worn as tops, while I had picked out a little summer dress for Rebecca. Loading their bags into the boot, everyone jumped in, and we set off for the lake, a drive of about an hour.

The two girls took the back seat and were both chattering away excitedly. I did not bother trying to follow their girly, giggling back and forth, but chatted to Lovisa, both of us describing our homes, lives, loves, and ambitions. She chatted about her home village, telling me she still had a place there and spent a few months there in the summer.

The drive was scenic, with lots of well cared for farmland in every direction, until we reached the hills, and drove into a more rural wooded area. Winding up the hills into the Mont Redon area. Reaching the parking area, I had picked out on the sat-nav; I was happy to see thick woodlands leading down to the lakeside.

I had chosen an area away from the campsites and main trails, hoping for a little privacy. It was a weekday and not a public holiday, so we had a chance that we would have the area to ourselves, mostly.

My backpack contained my rope, so we split up the picnic food and drink between the three other bags and set off towards the lake, taking a small trail. The trail headed up, then down the hillside and wound through some good-sized trees that I noted as we passed. Trying to find one that gave me a view of the lake from where the branch hung. The trail was dry and rocky; the ground was some sort of red clay and covered us in red dust as we walked.

Finding a small clearing by walking along the beach and a little away from the path, increasing our chances of being left undisturbed further still. Selecting a less rocky looking spot and unfurling the blanket and towels, laying them on the rough grassed area rather than the dusty clay beach. I had a feeling we were going to be a little mucky when we got back, but hey another shower with my lovely girl, so bonus.

The water here was nice and clear and a lot warmer than the sea. The sun being high overhead now, the heat of the midday sun was beating down on us, the girls all three of them stripped down to their bathing suits and went for a dip. I joined them after wrapping the cheese and wine in a damp towel to keep cool. They quickly removed their tops and swam half-naked; we were far from the tourist area, and this was France after all; I suspected no one would bat an eye at the pleasant sight, even if they stumbled upon us.

Splashing and swimming about, playing tag, I was quite happy to lose that as it involved a kiss; even Lovisa joined in there, a pleasant surprise. I have to admit to being quite taken with her.

Lovisa and I both tired of the game, went and lay in the sun and had a little talk about each of our girls, their limits, and things they liked. A conversation that we both would repeat with the girls later, before any play.

Eventually, the girls came out, stripped off their swimwear and layout in the sun to dry off and tan their bodies… Rebecca had no tan lines and Ela only had the faintest one that showed she wore a thong usually. Lovisa's skin was pale, and I had rubbed factor thirty on for her, noticing several clusters of freckles she had that fair skin one associates with redheads. (I rather like a freckle or two on pale flesh.)

Myself? well, I was pale, mainly because of working indoors in a suit and not being a sun worshiper. Though she commented on my salt and pepper chest hair, she seemed to find it attractive on a man. (Be still my beating heart.)

Leaving them for a bit, I walked back to the trees, assessing them and testing branches for strength and location. I had in mind a double tie, something simple that I could tie quickly and not too stressful on the new volunteer bunny I had with me today.

Grabbing my bag while they continued to sun worship, I set up my ropes and tested the branch by tying myself and bouncing up and down; it seemed strong enough, and it took my weight without flexing or moving; I considered it safe enough to hold their combined weight.

After fixing two rings to the branch, I lay out my ropes, safety knives and carabiners on a mat that I kept in the bag, to keep them away from the dirt (also less likely to lose stuff in the grass this way).

Returning to the naked sun worshipers, joining them sitting, relaxing in the sun, and admiring the breath-taking scenery, the

lake was quite beautiful too. But it was the three beautiful women that I had for company today, that I was truly admiring.

Making myself a quick sandwich (I am always hungry). We had packed a simple fare of French bread, cheese, fruits, and chocolate spread. I poured Lovisa (who was not whispering away as the two girls were) a beaker of wine and one for myself (a small one) sat back, ate and chatted some more. I rather enjoyed her company and could tell we were kindred souls, both educated, educators, and had a love of literature and beautiful girls.

At one point, I heard Ela laugh and then turn to Lovisa and explain what was so funny.

"They have two dogs called Freki and Geri," she said.

This also made Lovisa laugh, such a lovely sound (yes, I know I had a crush). I raised a quizzical eyebrow. (A skill I had learned during my many years as a teacher.)

"This is such a coincidence. The gods have interceded, we have been predestined to meet, I think; As I have two cats named after Odin's Ravens, Huginn and Muninn. Because they are both black with yellow eyes."

This started us talking about Norse mythology, a subject it turns out we both loved, it seemed. Time passed fast, and it was well into the late afternoon before I roused the girls for some rope fun. We had been lucky so far and no one had wandered in this direction, so I hoped we would remain undisturbed.

I told them to put their bikini briefs back on nevertheless, as there really was no need to tie nude today. I started with Rebecca and explaining as I tied, I would use the same tie for Ela. The tie I was doing was a chest loading one. One that would

179

leave your arms free, although I will tie them at a later point, but they will take none of the strain.

I tied the harness on Rebecca, tying an up line to keep her in place on her toes (she liked that and would lift her legs and spin). Tying Ela in the same harness, though it looked somewhat different, as the rope tie accentuated Ela's breast, quite a lot (very distracting to all there it seemed, as all eyes were on them.)

Tying her to the other ring and lifting her onto the balls of her feet (I was playing nice). I then tied simple butt harnesses on both and attached a rope to one ankle and one wrist in preparation for the next stage.

Attaching another up line to each butt harness, I started the process of suspending. Lifting Rebecca by her butt harness so she was about four feet off of the ground, then raising her another foot by her chest harnesses up lines. Tying her legs up next by throwing the spare line over the branch.

I then repeated the process with Ela. checking that she was ok at each stage, I did not need to raise her though, as her centre was higher than Rebecca's, to start with (her being taller), I had tied them, so they were almost facing to face now. Taking the wrist tie on Ela's, I attached it to Rebecca's, pulling them into each other so they were now facing each other. They kissed as soon as they were able to, which was my plan. Finally, tied off Rebecca's free hand behind and into Ela's dreads so she was cupping Ela's head.

Lovisa was snapping away, so I did not have to worry about picturing myself and for a change, I would be in them. I moved them about, lifting legs, dropping bottoms, and pulling them apart so they could not kiss. They complained bitterly about that (I just laughed).

180

Releasing Ela first as she was the newbie, I did not want to cause her any distress, suspensions being hard even on experienced bunnies. I told her she had done well as I lowered her, getting a free booby hug as I did so. Handing over her aftercare to Mistress Lovisa, while I set about freeing up Rebecca, but only after inverting her so I could lower her down headfirst into my lap. (How I wished I was naked at that point, oh well, another time.)

I held her there for a bit before she snuck away (I let her) to snuggle up with Ela. She did not need comforting; the tie was not that tasking, but I let her have her fun and Lovisa I think enjoyed having both girls snuggled up about her.

Seeing them like that touch me, touched me in my darkened soul; I made a hard decision; I had had fun with her girl twice now (tying her both times) and Rebecca had made love to her. It was only fair that she gets her chance to enjoy their company.

All hungry now, we ate some more French bread and chocolate. While I drank water, they polished off the wine. I caught Lovisa's eye, pulling her aside, and whispered to her my plan for the evening. She kissed me on the cheek and cupped my face. (I quit telling my beating heart to be still and enjoyed the warm feeling that spread through my body at her touch.)

"Thank you. I will look after them well and tomorrow, I will bring Ela to you. I think you all will have fun as well." She smiled at me, her eyes radiant and affectionate.

Then another kiss on the lips, and not one that a friend would give another, either. She may not be into men, but she sure knew how to make their hearts skip a beat.
We decided not to tell the girls, let it be a surprise.

We spent another hour or so soaking up the sun and letting the food and wine settle before making our way back to the car and eventually back to the complex.

Hard Lessons
Exhibitionist Holiday.

Chapter 9: Polyadventurous.

Returning to the village, a little worn out from the fun and heat of the day, we dropped into bed and slept for an hour; I am sure this was for my benefit, but Rebecca always liked to snuggle up when I took a nap. (Yes, I like to nap, I'm old, get over it.) I awoke to the smell of food… Rebecca had evidently woken early, and she had been out and picked up a takeaway pizza. My belly told me I loved her; I let her in on the conversation; she laughed.

The pizza pulling off, that trick it does by vanishing long before it should; I took her hand and led her to the bathroom, telling her I had a surprise for her later. I was sure she could guess, but she liked to please her Sir and would play along.

Turning on the shower, getting it good and steamy before I led her in and washed off the day's dirt. A lot of red clay washed away that night. Washing and conditioning her hair, tying the still-wet hair into a plait. I took up a safety razor and set about shaving her underarms and then other more sensitive but fun areas, ensuring she was good and smooth.

I could not stop myself from checking how smooth, with my tongue, and after several minutes of intrusive and very thorough checks. I was happy to report that she was indeed velvety smooth and tasted of strawberries (although that may have been the body wash).

I left her then to finish drying and setting her hair and applying her makeup (I have tried to do this for her, but the results are often frightening to small children). While I picked out the outfit for the night. An easy job, given that we were in a nudist resort.

Selecting a collar and matching colour ribbon (pink if you are wondering to match her hair). I also decided on a bunny tail, which also matched in colour and last of all, I pulled out a blindfold, alas, not a colour match as I only had a red and black one with me. Not an issue, though; as the red one would match her lipstick, I made sure of this by telling her to wear the red tonight.

When she was done making herself presentable for the night, her hair hung in ringlets, her eyes were smoky and her lips ruby, she stood there naked, turning slowly so I could get the full effect of her almost Aphrodite beauty. She came and stood before me, ready for me to put the finishing touches on her outfit. I did so love dressing her in pretty things; I placed the collar about her neck, careful not to snag her hair in the clasp. Then tied the ribbon about her waist, adding a bow to her front.

Turning and presented that bottom, the tease, and wetting first the tip of the bunny tailed butt plug, then deciding it would be better to moisten her beautiful pale butt hole. (I was sure she bleached. If she did, she kept that a secret and I would never ask.) Wanting to be sure she was well lubricated; I pressed my tongue in deeply several times before remembering this was not about me and pressed in the tail. She wiggled her cute little bunny tail behind, checking herself in the mirror. Finally, seeing it was almost time, I added the blindfold.

She was bouncing off the walls; she knew in her heart why I had done this; the ribbon was a clue; she was to be a gift tonight and there was only one person that could possibly be for. I told her to stand still and not move while I dressed myself, choosing to don my linen slacks and shirt. Then, placing a hand on her shoulder, I guided her to the door.

We had done this many times in the past, so she could follow my touches and would know from my finger movements when

to stop to start, to turn left to turn right and if there were stairs. Leading her down to the lobby, passing several other guests. It was past 11 now and the night-time people were out. We would fit in perfectly with the swingers and kinksters that were heading to the clubs.

I guided her across over to Lovisa's apartment, whispering in Rebecca's ear as I reached the door.

"I will leave now. Tonight, you are a gift from me to Lovisa and Gisela. Enjoy your night. I love you," I Kissed her neck, letting go of her shoulder and knocked on the door, stepping back as I did so; waiting only to ensure that the knock was answered.

They both answered the door, Ela. Taking Rebecca's hand and leading her into the room, Lovisa stepped out to embrace me, reassuring me that she would take care of Rebecca and return her in the morning. I smiled, embracing her back and stepped away, leaving my partner in her care much as she had left hers in mine while I tied her the other evening.

I knew in my heart that they would look after her, that she would have a night of experiences the likes of which she had never had before. This was the whole point of the trip to expand her horizons and experience; what she was about to experience, though I had never imagined that I would not be there to share that experience with her. It was harder than I had thought it would be, but I knew tomorrow Lovisa would be in the same boat as she left Ela with me, and I now pitied her a little.

I took myself off to a bar to drink away my blues and watch the entertainment. A belly dancer performing with fire was just the thing to distract me for a few hours.

I dropped into my bed, not even bothering at first to undress. A bottle and half of the wine will do that to a person. In the night I must have kicked off my clothes as when I was roused from my

slumber by the touch of another sliding up next to me, holding me from behind (the little spoon spooning the big spoon for a change). I turned, about to look her in the eyes. Her smoky eyes were now those of a panda. She kissed me on the head, the nose, then the mouth and thanked me for the night and promptly fell asleep.

We slept in, something we seldom did, but I did not want to wake her and was content just to lie there holding her against me. I could feel my arousal at her presence, but I was not going to satisfy that desire now. No tonight would be our turn to entertain, and I wanted as much sexual energy and hunger as possible. (I will also probably pop a little blue helper; one does not want to flag on an evening, like the one I had ahead of me.)

Sleeping in until noon, before rousting her from the bed and making her go and shower. She rather smelled of sex, lots of sex, and as pleasant as that was, it was not a scent for dining out. Once freshened up, we set out to grab a late breakfast and some sun on the beach.

She filled me in on some of the night's fun; I let her tell me what she wanted and did not question her, as she would tell me everything in her own time. The highlights were enough to cause me to roll over on the sun lounger. (Yes, for that reason.) I had rather expected Lovisa to play the dominatrix, but it seemed she went for lovers' last night, Rebecca becoming the meat in an all-girl sandwich…
(Damn I wish I had seen that.)

There had been plenty of double-ended dildo fun and a lot of strap-on play as well, sounded like a lot of fun. Kissed, clawed, eaten, fingered and fist fucked, and the highlight was a double penetration for Ela and her. Surprised, still, that there was no impact play; I had given my consent, stipulating as long as Rebecca gave hers on the night, I would be ok with that.

I certainly intended to indulge my inner sadist a little, though only a little: Ela was not my submissive, and I did not know her limits, nor was tonight about finding them.

Rebecca fell asleep again. It really had been a long night, and I was ok with her resting as it would be another long night for her. Leaving her to her slumber, I went and sought drink and sustenance, for I was certain of one thing, I was going to need the energy tonight.

Finding Lovisa at the bar as well, getting coffee, black coffee (I guessed she was a little worn out too). I greeted her with a traditional continental hello, but she insisted on giving me a lovely warm hug and a big kiss on the mouth (I think, maybe; she was warming up to me).

"Thank you so much for your lovely gift last night and wrapped so prettily. We had the most wonderful evening, and Rebecca told the tale of how she got your attention after realising she had a crush on sir. Such a naughty girl. No wonder you had to chastise that lovely bottom." She said, before kissing my cheek again.

"I would love to see you punish her one night and maybe Ela, I only punish, I do not play this game you do, funishments! this is new to me but sounds like a fun way to enjoy your dynamic." Her tone was friendly, playful even, and her smile bright as the afternoon sun. (Ok, I was enamoured of her.)

"Of course, you are welcome to watch us play anytime. In fact, I will give you my address. Why don't you join us for a few days this summer? I have the room and you can use my dungeon." I said, hoping she would take me up on this offer.

"Yes, that seems a good idea, and you both must visit me in my summer home, come and enjoy the woods, the sea, and the mountains."

187

"I would love to, and a certain young lady would also love to tag along," I replied. (Knowing full well Rebecca would kill me if I thought about leaving her behind.)

I then filled her in a little on my plans for tonight's play, making sure she had no issues with what I had in mind.

Hard Lessons
Exhibitionist Holiday.

Chapter 10: Funishments.

The evening was approaching fast, and Rebecca was in full flow now; she insisted on showering and shaving me, including my more delicate areas. It seemed she and Ela had decided that tonight was about me. A thank you for the rope, but also for allowing them their night with Lovisa.

While she set about cleaning and shaving me, I thought through my plans for tonight. Lovisa had green-lit my funishments idea and as long as Ela still consented, I thought that would be a fun way to start the night.

As we were at a nudist resort, one with families and we absolutely did not want to have to wear clothes, I had to make sure not to mark the girls too much, so I designed a funishments wheel with that in mind.

Toys in my bag:
· Short cane
· Flogger x 2 (set)
· Paddles Various
· Prison strap
· Ruler
· Rubber strap
· Old leather belt
· Clamps Various
· Ball Gags
· Cock and Ball Gag (Purchased for the trip)
· Pin Wheel
· Bear Claw
· Vibrators and dildos, various
· Violet Wand

· Rubber bands
· Cuffs various
· Scarfs Multiple

Enough for a fun evening, I thought. Though some will have to remain in the bag, the prison strap always left a mark, therefore could not be used on any part of the body safely. (I would put out a few of the more intense toys that we were not going to use just to play with her head a little.)

I use an App for the funishments game, a spinning wheel of fortune game that I could fill in with my own options.

Leaving out the prison strap, my old leather belt and one brutal looking paddle, these would not be used but she did not know that, nor would Rebecca.

Flogging:
Bottom
Back
Breasts
Pussy

Cane:
Feet
Palms
Nipples

Paddles:
Bum
Calf's
Inner Thighs
Ruler:
Palms
Bottom

Clamps:
Nipples
Tongue (spit)
Pussy

Rubber Strap:
Bum
Tits
legs

Butt Plugs:
Vibrating
Small
Medium
Anal Beads

Chocolate Spread Lick:
Sir
Sub

Hands:
Bottom
Tits
Face
Thighs
Cunt
Choke

A few spins of this to start the night, break the ice and then the real fun can begin.

Rebecca was excited, reciting what had passed between them the other night, the conversations about what she and Ela had about me. Ela telling Rebecca that she had a thing for older men, seems they both had than in common (lucky me). We had a few ideas of what we wanted to experience tonight; it was not my first threesome, but it would be Rebecca's first! No, that's

wrong, now it would be her first MFF, her having experienced an FFF just last night.

I planned to let things flow naturally, although I did intend to explore that magnificent statuesque body of Ela's and Rebecca wanted me to cum only in Ela tonight, as she had planned to taste both Sir's and her lovers cum cocktail. We will have to see how that goes; I had popped a little blue helper to make sure I would rise to the occasion (I had little doubt, but a little insurance of performance never hurt).

Rebecca was a ball of energy, so excited she was tiring me out just watching her, So I grabbed my rope and tied her to a chair for a while as a way of admonishing her to calm the heck down. Meanwhile, I laid out all the toys on the side, chilled the wine in a sink full of ice (the fridge was small and pretty useless) food and snacks laid on. Also, there was a selection of spray cream and cheeses and a tub of peanut butter for recreational use only.

Once Rebecca had calmed down, I released her from the chair and blindfolded her and told her to stand and wait in the corner. Knowing that Ela would only be another quarter of an hour, the quiet time for her would allow me to enjoy a glass of scotch, undisturbed. Though admittingly I was almost as excited as her, luckily my English reserve allowed me to keep it under wraps...

There was a quick rap on the door, and a *squee* from Rebecca (really, when do they grow out of that noise). I opened the door to be greeted by Ela, who was I noticed wearing little white panties. She bounced up and hugged me, her bountiful breasts pressing up against my white shirt as she kissed me hello. (Yes, I was fully dressed; we require some decorum even for funishments).

Lovisa I was happy to see was naked except for spirals painted about her breast to her naval (they really liked the body painting). She kissed me again the continental way, both kisses

192

feeling like bursts of sunlight on my cheeks and finally an open-mouthed kiss that shook me to my shoes.

"We share lovers no, so we are lovers now and should greet each other as such. You don't mind, I hope." She said smiling tenderly.

"Tonight, you have Ela. She is yours, as Rebecca was mine last night..." She kissed me again and left. I watched her depart, admiring the curve of her back, the self-assuredness of her stride, knowing that she was probably heading off for a drink herself much as I had needed last night.

I closed the door, mind racing a little at that last statement. Sharing lovers made us lovers! well, when in Rome, I guess (I definitely had a crush, that's for sure).

I led Ela into the room and told her to stand; I left her standing in front of all the toys I had laid out for the evening's entertainment. Let her see and wonder and maybe a little worry when she sees the prison strap, which I think is formidable and quite intimidating.

Calling over to Rebecca, telling her to turn and remove the blindfold. I then counted to 60, before telling her she could come over and say hello (I am a git sometimes). She ran over and straight into Ela's arms. Ela, being bigger, caught her and lifted her into a passionate embrace. They really were hooked on each other, these two.

I handed them both a glass of chilled wine, then explained the rules of the game we were going to play tonight, the rule of six (six being my favourite number) six strokes or six minutes, depending on the funishment selected.

Of course, we could have just skipped past this play and gone straight to naked writhing, wiggling, perspiring flesh on the bed.

But I thought a little game would be fun, and I knew Ela was unaccustomed to impact play for fun only, something I and Rebecca preferred to punishment. Punishments meant a failure, and neither of us like that. Luckily, she was a good girl and seldom broke a punishable rule.

I said, to make things easier, one spin will be for both (with exceptions) Rebecca will receive first, so Ela will know what is to come and could choose to opt-out, should she not want to experience this. She, of course, insisted she was up for anything.

"I love the white panties. May I remove them?" I asked. Rebecca leaned in and whispered in her ear; I expect explaining what I really meant.

What I meant was to tear them from her, rip them, shred them, destroy them in one swift tug. Which I promptly did the moment she nodded that pretty head of hers. Moving her about two feet in the direction I pulled. They came away in three pieces and elicited a small cry of surprise from Ela. (One of my admittedly many kinks, was the shredding of white panties worn by naughty girls.)

Opening the wheel of misfortune on my phone, showing the girls as it spun, it came up spanking on the bottom. Not a surprise, as I had added this three times. An obvious favourite and the perfect entrée to what was to come.

I pulled up a chair and explained again the rule of six. With my hands, it would be six per cheek, as I could only hit one at a time. Seating my knees together, I beckoned Rebecca over, who leaned over my legs and wiggled her bottom at Ela; for that bit of bravado, I shall not start gentle, I told them.

Rebecca placed her hand over her mouth in a mock whoops gesture, showing off for her girlfriend! (Well, I will show her.) "Count," I said and hit her bottom full power with my hand.

194

"One," she said.
"No, count properly GIRL," I barked at her. We had played this game before, so she knew what she was doing.
"Two, Sir," she said.
"NO, no, no, start again."
"One, Sir," she said, finally getting it right.

She counted off the next two lots of 11, correctly, and had a nice red glow on her bottom for her cheek.

Ela whispered in Rebecca's ear, and Rebecca whispered back in mine. Seems Ela did not want to call me Sir, she wanted to call me daddy! Now I generally shied away from this with Rebecca, as she was so young when we found each other, and I was not looking for a little. But I saw no harm in indulging Ela's request this one time but would need to have a very deep discussion with her and Lovisa should we all decide to continue after this holiday.

"You may address me as Daddy tonight," I conceded. This made her smile and jump up a little in excitement, which did wonderful things to her breasts.

I gestured down to my lap, and she placed herself hesitantly over my knee; I felt her arse, such a great arse, firm rounded a booty that made my anaconda get sprung to misquote the vernacular.
"Count for me, Ela," I said, my tone friendly and calming.

"One, Daddy, two Daddy," and on.
Ending on a "Twelve Daddy, thank you, Daddy," kneeling before me, looking up at me with big eyes and a winsome smile on her pretty face.

Do they teach this in some secret class I wondered to myself? Her look was so sweet. I gave her a comforting hug.

Spinning again, we got cane and feet, which caused some squealing as each stroke was applied to each, in turn. As I had said, this was punishments so most strokes were less powerful than I would apply if this was a scene. (I am not always so nice, but I can be at times.)

We then spun again and got clamps. These were applied to nipples. I left them on, stating that they would remain for six minutes. We then got my favourite toy, the ruler and of course, the rule of six applied.

Again, Rebecca went first, bending over the back of the chair so that her bottom was high in the air. There was no cheeky wiggle this time. Her nipples were clamped, and she knew the ruler stung when applied this way.

This time I counted as I danced from side to side, hitting each cheek in turn, enjoying myself as I struck her tight little booty. Though keeping the level low, so as not to leave a bruise if I could help it. (I had stealers wheel playing in my head as I danced about, yes, like Mr Blonde.)

Then I was Ela's turn; she leaned over the chair, less of a stretch for her taller frame. This pose displayed magnificently her full booty. I danced about her much as I had Rebecca enjoying the simple pleasure using my old school ruler brought me.

Next Spin, we got floggers and tits. So, I had them stand shoulder to shoulder while I florentined them both in turn, removing the clamps in the process, to some rather loud squealing. Keeping to the rule of six, I continued for six minutes (or thereabouts, I may have gotten carried away, distractions and all that).

Next up, was floggers again but pussy this time. (At last, and good timing, I thought, I was getting aroused to the point I

wanted to shred my suit away and dive onto the bed between these two beauties.)

"Floggers again but this time pussy's," I said, pulling up a chair sitting, then holding one out to each girl.

"I think I have worked hard enough tonight. Why don't you take care of this one yourselves," I said, raising my eyebrow in a quizzical manner (I'm a teacher, they train you for this).

"Yes, Sir," said Rebecca.
"Yes, Daddy said," Ela.

"Good girls, you will flog yourself for six minutes, you will keep the stoke even and hard, no letting up or slowing down. Now start," I said. As I settled in to enjoy the show.

I sat back and watch them, as they both stood side by side in front of me, legs spread to allow access and a damned good view I might add. They started flogging almost together, and I watched their faces as each stroke landed. Rebecca had done this before and knew what it would do to her, eventually. Ela, on the other hand, had not, and her face was a distinct pleasure to watch as she slowly built-up speed and impact level.

I watched as Rebecca climaxed for the first time and the look on Ela's face as the flogging got her off made me wish I had a camera recording this. She picked up the pace as she built her climax, and she was going to orgasm before I called time.

Rebecca was already down on her knees, forced there by her orgasm, and was kneeling in a puddle as she had gushed at the end. I checked my watch and six minutes had passed, but I could see that Ela was close and would not ruin this new experience for her. She orgasmed and fell into the open arms of Rebecca, who had been watching, waiting for this.

197

"Oh, my goddess," was all Ela could say. This made both me and Rebecca smile.

I decided to forgo the next spin and call a refreshment break so they both could compose themselves and Rebecca could mop up. While they recovered and we sipped our wines, I loaded a new wheel of fortune, one that was loaded for one particular activity.

When I spun the wheel again, it came up with chocolate spread; I showed the girls, and they both laughed and even louder when they saw that all the segments had the words Chocolate spread and Sub on them. I pulled off the bedding, exposing a plastic sheet that I had put on the bed earlier.

Then I had them stand still as I applied spread to their nipples, the pussies, and the bottoms, getting them to bed over while I applied the messy stuff. I removed my shirt and trousers at this point, not wanting to get my only good clothing covered in hazelnut chocolate.

I then told them to lick each other's nipples clean and watched as they set about each other tits, in turn, licking like cats cleaning their fur. sucking nipples and getting it all over their faces. This did not matter, as they were about to get their faces even more covered. But first I wanted a little taste.

Telling Ela to bend over, I ran my tongue up from her chocolate-covered clit to her chocolate-coated arse hole, digging my tongue in, in a manner that would have looked rather disturbing had you accidentally witnessed this act, not knowing it was chocolate spread. I then watched as the girls fell on the bed and consumed each other's chocolate-covered cunt. I rather wish I had had some cake to throw in the mix (next time maybe).

They kept at it until they were both licked clean, amazingly they then set about cleaning each other faces and fuck me if that is not one of the most erotic sights I have ever witnessed.

Ordering them both to the shower to clean off any residue while I fixed myself a scotch. My, that was a scene and a half. I wondered to myself if I could get Lovisa to join in on that one night. Maybe a paddling pool, cake, tins of cream and custard! Oh, my word.

When the girl came back, I held out two blindfolds to them, tying each, in turn, getting close to each of them pressing against their backs as I fastened them, my cock trying to escape the confines of my briefs as it pressed into them.

"Ok, girls on the bed are two ball gags, one is a cock gag whoever gets that one will be will have her face and the cock attached to the gad rode by the other," I told them this moving the two items about on the bed, so they could not just go for where they saw them last.

As luck would have it, Ela got the cock gag and Rebecca, the ball gag (no, I did not move them, so this would happen, honest). I tied the gag about her head, inserting the two-and-a-half-inch end into her mouth, leaving the six-inch end, protruding from her mouth. I then tied the other in place on Rebecca, ensuring it could not pop free.

Laying Ela on the bed and spreading her legs with the aid of a scarf tied to the post, her wrist tied to her waist, ensuring she could not roll over either. I then guided the still blindfolded Rebecca into position, guiding the tip to her cunt but telling her to hold that position until told otherwise.

At last, it was my turn to taste the sweetness of Ela's cunt directly; I had tasted a little when I kissed Rebecca the other night. Now I was going to taste directly from the lips of that

honey wine scented cunt. I slipped my briefs off, no longer needing the constraint, and leaned in to blow on her lips. I could smell her now, such a lovely scent, a mix of the scented soaps in the shower and her very own natural scent.

I blew up and down her glistening moist mount, my lips brushing ever so lightly that I am sure on a less sensitive body part she would not have known I had kissed her. I flicked my tongue out, sliding down between her lips a little more with each pass, running my tongue until it reaches her arse, making tiny circles about the hole before poking it in as deep as I could.

Then sliding it back until I could press the full length of my tongue into the velvety smooth channel that nestled between her legs. Reaching up as I did so to press Rebecca's leg, a signal to start her own movements on the gag dildo. I ate pussy like a man who had been in prison for twenty years; she tasted like a heady spiced red wine, her hips moving now, grinding back against my probing tongue, wanting me to keep licking, nibbling, and teasing her cunt.

All the time Rebecca was riding her face, I looked up to see Ela was at times pushing her head into Rebecca's cunt, coming up to meet her thrusts. It occurred to me that she had probably worn one of these before or been on the receiving side. I felt as she shuddered and cum but did not let up until I saw Rebecca do the same; I hoped she would gush, was pleased when she did, seeing Ela's face covered in her juices, and knowing a lot of it would have gone into her mouth.

I reached up and released the catch on the gag dildo, allowing Ela to spit it out and get to Rebecca's cunt with her tongue. Which she did, with as much gusto as I had hers. I also released the tie binding her in places, freeing her to move. When I did, she stopped eating pussy and came up to kiss me. I could taste Rebecca, a taste, an aroma, a fragrance, and I knew well, one I now savoured for the first time on the lips of another.

200

As she kissed me, she mounted me, not waiting anymore. She had wanted me for days and now she had me; I heard her whisper fuck me, Daddy, in my ear so low I don't think Rebecca heard her, as she started to grind on my cock. Rebecca came behind her, nuzzling her, kissing her neck, whispering her own words into Ela's ear.

Ela, who is a tall, curvy statuesque girl, pressed me back on the bed, I could have resisted being no lightweight myself, but I went with what she had in mind, I was sure it would be pleasurable whatever it was she had planned.

What she had planned was the reverse cowboy it turned out and Rebecca finally got her wish, as Ela rode my cock (I was doing my part, I assure you) I could feel, Rebecca's tongue sliding down my cock, licking my arse and knew without a doubt that she was also sucking Ela's clit on each pass.

Now there are days when I take a long time and a lot of stimulation to come. Today was not one of those days. I had been with Rebecca for four years and in that time; I had not been with another; I had experienced threesomes and moresomes in the past, but now with someone, I loved as I did Rebecca, someone that knew my body as well as I knew it.

She poked a finger into my arse and bit down on my shaft as Ela ground and rode this bronco; I bucked as I felt myself starting to cum; I roared as the pressure released and screamed a shout of joy as I felt Rebecca's mouth swallow my cock.

I felt her suck all she could from me, licking and testing both her lovers cum, not satisfied, I watched as Ela lay back on my chest and spread her legs letting Rebecca go down on her and lick her pussy to get every bit of cum, she could. Before coming up to Ela, holding her chin and leaning in for a kiss, I saw their lips not quite touching as she passed a mouth full of a cum cocktail

between them, then kissing her for so long I wondered if they had learned how to do without breath. Licking her lips, Rebecca kissed me, sliding away from Ela so she could turn and kiss me too.

I ended up resting with one on each side, heads nestled into my shoulders, recovering slowly but knowing this was but round one.

Round two started not long after. Both girls, knowing I would need a little time to recover, decided to start making out while lying beside me. I watched as they kissed, occasionally remembering I was there and turning to kiss me, sometimes both of them almost fighting for my lips. I tasted each again and again as they would turn and kiss me, sharing the wetness of each other's flowers as they made each other climax again and again.

Eventually, they decided I had had long enough (I had, but I had also been enjoying the show) and I felt them spreading chocolate and peanut butter over my now stiffening cock. Fully erect by the time one of them (I did not see who) stuck the jar over my erect member.

They then both proceeded to give me the licking and BJ of my life. The girls licked the spreads off first, slowly sucking away the sticky, gooey mess until they had cleaned me completely. They then smeared some on my arse (Rebecca's idea I was sure) and took turns to give me a tongue bath, spreading more on when they were done, so both had a good long lick... (FML)

Happy that I was about to explode, both girls settled into a rhythm of licking and sucking on my cock, taking turns, and at other times running their tongues and lips up and down my shaft meeting at the tip, both sets of eyes coming to rest on mine as they kissed with my cock in between both of their lips. (Best blow job ever...)

I came. I could hardly stop myself. Rebecca, knowing the signs, held her hand up to Ela' to stop her from taking my cum in her mouth, not wanting her to spoil this treat too quickly. She massaged (wanked) me until I had blown my load and it was all down my cock and on my belly. Quite a bit on her fingers, which then had the pleasure of watching as she fed each in turn into Ela's mouth.

Ela obligingly sucked each clean in a manner that was likely to get me hard again very soon. Hand now clean, they both set about licking the remaining cum from my belly and worked their way up my cock until they took turns sucking on the now very sensitive end.

They then kissed and came up and kissed me. I did not care where their mouths had been. I kissed them back as passionately as they kissed me.

I think I then died and when to heaven as when I awoke; I found myself between two angels.

Hard Lessons
Exhibitionist Holiday.

Chapter 11: Exhibitionists New Family.

6:30 am walking an exhausted and satisfied Ela back to her apartment; she was wearing my shirt to stave off the early morning chill. She was leaning in on me for support; her legs a bit jelloish; it seems after the night's adventures. I have to admit my legs were a little shaky too; so worth it, though. What a night.

I dropped Ela at her apartment, watching as she let herself in before returning to my apartment and the warm spot next to my girl.

Once again, we slept in late, this time doubly tired, not surfacing until well into the afternoon. (Slugabeds the pair of us.) a quick shower and visual inspection for bruises and marks that would be a little embarrassing, there were a few marks, mostly scratches from Ela, my back and chest had clear claw marks, so we decided on a shirt and bathing suit for me and a sarong for Rebecca (she had a few marks that were clearly not from falling if you get my meaning) at least until we got to the loungers.

I grabbed us both strong black coffee, ham and cheese paninis, cold orange juice and iced water, settled down on the lounger after demolishing the late breakfast and promptly dozed off again. We spent the day recovering and recuperating, well I did. I'm sure Rebecca was fine, but she kept me company and I treated her to a lovely meal at the local restaurant before we retired for the night with a bottle of chilled wine.

It was nice after several days of activities to relax with my girl snuggled up in my arms. We drifted off like that and for a

change; I did not need to tie her; she seemed content just to be the little spoon to my big spoon.

When I awoke, it was still bright and early, so I carefully separated myself from Rebecca, not wanting to wake her from her; she was so cute when she slept. I dressed and set off in search of coffee and fresh bread (one thing the French do well). Returning, I found they had slipped a note under the door.

I trust you both have recovered. Ela slept most of the day, a tired girl (smiley face). We are up now and will grab some sun loungers by the pool and an extra two for you both. See you soon.

Love L and G xx

This was our last night and seeing them again very much called for. Hopefully, we can make plans to meet up in the future. I had already told Lovisa that they both had an open invitation to stay any time. Rebecca, I know for sure will want to go visit Ela and vice versa.

I placed the coffee by the bed, broke the bread and spread jam and chocolate on it, knowing the scent of coffee and fresh bread would drag Rebecca from dreamland soon enough.

Sleepyhead woke slowly, needing the coffee before she was able to deal with the morning, bless her. She demolished the breakfast baguette and, on hearing the plan, was showered in minutes and ready to go. She had it bad for Ela and I have to admit a sense of loss at the thought of not seeing the lovely Lovisa for a time.

We found the girls roasting in the sun, a big jug of sangria by their side, and as promised, two sun loungers for us in between theirs, looked like we were the meat in a very attractive sandwich. They greeted us in the now familiar and very

welcome fashion: big hugs, big deep kisses from Ela and slightly more restrained ones from Lovisa.

While the girls all started chattering away, I went and purchased some more drinks and fruits to snack on. I admit it was heavenly to be laying out in the sun, enjoying an iced beer and having the company of 3 beautiful women. Was that a look of jealousy I spotted from a young man walking past…

We lay there chatting away, discussing the events of the other night, Ela having filled Lovisa in with all the details of the funishments games. I promised to send her a link to the app and the rules of the game. Seems Ela really enjoyed the experience and wanted to play again. (What can I say, I am a bad influence aha)

We also exchanged numbers and emails with addresses, so we could keep in touch and make plans to visit soon. Ok, very soon, as the girls both insisted that it would be weeks, not months.

We agreed to meet up later for a meal and one last night in the local club for some dancing, drinks and more rope play, Ela insisted on more rope. I could hardly say no to such a beautiful bunny.

"Yes, Ela, I will bring my rope," I assured her, a broad smile crossing my face at the thought of tying those breasts.

Rebecca and Ela went off early. Apparently, Ela wanted to paint Rebecca for the night, leaving myself and Lovisa to have a chat about them without them overhearing.

As the girls were pretty much smitten with each other, we decided to make plans for us to meet up in two weeks, a surprise trip to be organised as soon as we returned home.

We went over Ela's daddy request as well; she explained that Ela had had a DDLG relationship previously, but it had not been a healthy one and hoped that maybe I would show her what a proper DDLG relationship should be like.

We discussed this at length; I had done this before and knew the amount of work involved in maintaining such a relationship, especially one that was distant. Lovisa understood that it was a big ask. But all that aside, I liked Ela and if she (Lovisa) was happy for me to step into this role with her partner, even if most of the time it would be online, I was willing to donate my time to being a daddy to Ela.

Meeting up later for dinner, Rebecca surprised me in full body paint with lots of colourful swirls wrapping about her body and what's more, Ela was painted similarly, though maybe not as well. I guessed Rebecca's handiwork.

"You both look amazing," I told them. I meant it too. If they had turned up wearing sacking, they would have looked as stunning. These two were just that hot.

Then Lovisa arrived, dressed head to toe in rubber. I guess subtle was not on the menu tonight. I stood, greeting her, and telling her how amazing her outfit looked (it did, it really did).

We definitely got some looks while we ate but it was our last night, so what the heck might as well enjoy it, Though I felt underdressed in my white linen shirt and slacks. It was far too hot for a suit! I have no idea how Lovisa could wear such an outfit in this heat.

I spoke with Ela for a while, telling her that if she wanted, I would be a daddy for her from now on, telling her I would message each night and give her little tasks, I would also be in contact with Lovisa making sure there was no bratty behaviour and that the tasks I set were carried out. We would work out the

details over the next few days and talk more when we meet up next.

She bounced up and gave me the biggest and, unfortunately, for my shirt, body hug and kiss, a kiss that promised so much. This was going to be interesting, and Rebecca joined her in kissing me, thanking me for making Ela so happy.

Grabbing the limo golf cart to the club. I had sprung for a booth, and Lovisa purchased two bottles of bubbly to celebrate Ela's new DDLG relationship. We spent the night dancing and chatting and drinking, so much so that it was no longer advisable for me to tie. The girls were disappointed, but they understood that their safety came first; I suggested the jacuzzi which meant that the girls had to shower first.

Such a hardship, but myself and Lovisa took the opportunity to have a little fun and swapped partners to shower them, I got to play my new role with Gisela, washing away the paint with lots of suds and rubbing of the pink shower thingy (all showers seemed to have these).

Lovisa was quite enjoying showering Rebecca and was also quite a sight for onlookers as she had forgone removing her rubber outfit (it's rubber, so the water was not an issue). I watched as Lovisa caressed and fondled Rebecca as she showered, her hands and fingers exploring every nook and cranny, and eventually her tongue, making sure those nooks and crannies were deeply clean.

Not to be outdone, and one for enjoying the simple pleasure of cleaning his girl, I followed suit, my hands and body rubbing, caressing, and fondling every full-bodied inch of Ela's beautiful body. I also decided that deep clean required a deep inspection and took the opportunity to taste the sweetness of my new girl. She, in turn, made sure that I was clean and used her mouth to great effect.

208

All three of us, Rebecca Ela and I decided that Lovisa needed a proper shower and insisted that she strip that rubber suit off now. It was not like she could wear it in the jacuzzi. Unfastened and released from the confines of the rubber suit, exposing the lean and trim body of Lovisa. The two girls set about showering her. I figured this was a girl thing and was about to pick up the suit to put it away in the locker when a hand grabbed mine and pulled me into the middle of the three girls.

"No, stay. We are family now, all lovers together. You have held me, comforted me, and not once did you think to take advantage of my emotional state. We share lovers, maybe I will love you too…" she said, this pulling me into the middle, pouring soap over me and all three of them made like loofahs and rubbed me with their bodies.

This was a new experience, and I thoroughly enjoyed it. Titties and arses rubbed me down and hands seeking all sorts of places and received kisses from all three, which made the shower seem twice as hot.

Then the girls pulled Lovisa into the middle and set about giving her the deep, clean treatment. I slipped out during this and took the rubber suit to the lockers. Returning to find them all still soapy and laughing, I was certain they had not noticed me go, nor did they take any more notice of the dozen men and women watching them.

All three of us are now very, very clean. We made our way over to one of the Jacuzzi's and squeezed in, a little crowded, but we enjoyed it. Rebecca sat on my lap while Ela sat on Lovisa's lap. Sipping our drinks, chatting, and enjoying the play of bubbles on our bodies as one does.

It was rather a pleasant way to spend an evening, but we could not end the night this way. Both I and Lovisa seemed to have the

same idea and the girls swapped places and whispered into our ears pretty much the same thought.

"Let's go find a room."

We wandered until we found a vacant room (our lucky night). Locking the door behind us, both Lovisa and I transitioned straight into Dom mode. Now we both had been drinking a little and experience as we were, knew better than to go too hard, but we both as one grabbed our girls about the throats. (We had discussed this between us both, deciding on the format for tonight.) My grip, at least I knew, was not a chokehold held lightly, not pressing, but it was still enough for Rebecca to get the point.

I walked her over to Lovisa.

"Lovisa here has offered to share her girl with me. I feel I can do no less."
"I would like you to properly thank Mistress Lovisa on my behalf." My words were not harsh, even though I still had my hand about her throat. I was asking her, not telling her.

"Yes, Sir, I understand my duty…" she replied, her face serious, even a little feigned fear about her eyes. She really was such a special girl and always knew how to play the role I gave her.

She dropped down as I released my hold on her.
"Mistress, Sir wishes me tonight to convey his gratitude for your generous gift. How may I serve you this night?" She said this looking up from her knees, knelt in front of Lovisa. Those eyes are kryptonite to the strongest of wills. I wondered how she would fare.

Lovisa looked down upon the kneeling form of Rebecca. She did not speak for a few seconds, as if pondering her response.

"Well girl, I cannot refuse such an offering, can I now."

"Bow down before me, while I give Sir Alex his gift." Her voice was devoid of any warmth, her eye seemed hard the lines of her lips showed not an ounce of what I knew her to be feeling inside, she was cold as stone, even sent a shiver down my back, or maybe it was just a draught.

(How do women do that?)

Rebecca bowed down head to the ground and waited, while Lovisa, taking a hand full of Ela's hair, pulled her over to me, forcing her down to the ground, head to the floor.

"Girl, this man who stands before you, has offered to take you on as his little. You will be his special princess and do as he command's you. Do not disappoint him as it will disappoint me, and you don't want to do that do you girl?" Lovisa's voice was cold, emotionless, scary even.

This was Lovisa in full Dominatrix mode, our styles were very different I already knew, she clearly used words and her voice to chastise and punish, it was rather effective too (made me shiver a little) though I knew she would break out the cane if Ela ever pushed her luck.

"Mistress, no, I won't disappoint you or Daddy!" (That word again, that is going to take some getting used to).

"I am so happy that Sir Alex has granted me this wish. I will be the best little girl for him, I promise," Ela said this her voice cracking with emotion, fair touch this old man's heart. (I have one, you know! The cold-hearted bastard thing is just an act.)

I pulled myself together remembering I am supposed to be the mature adult and a Dom, damn it, looking down at her.

"Look at me child, you are now my little princess, my little one."

211

"I will care for you and support you, give you chores and give you praise when you are good, but also punish you, should displease myself or the fair Lady Lovisa. In short, my little one, I will be your daddy for as long as you wish me to," I told her this. As she looked up at me, big eyes watering, I held out my hand to her and she took it.

She stood now; she was so tall, only a few inches shorter than me, and looked me in the eye unblinking, but her lip tremble gave away the emotions that were boiling away inside her.

"Thank you, Daddy," she said, her face beaming with joy, but her body betrayed her, and she fell into my arms. I picked her up and carried her to the bed.

I held her there while she cried. Her tears were happy ones, but there were tears all the same. So, I just held her, making her the little spoon. After a time, her tears stopped and her breathing shallower. She turned to me, looking me in the eye, and said a phrase that echoed one that Rebecca and I had discussed as a release to be naughty.

"Daddy, Kitten wants to be naughty…" she said, voice cracking with emotion. With those words, she kissed me and slid down my body and took my cock in her mouth and my feigned cold Domly shell cracked.

Leaving her to suck on my cock for a while, before placing a hand on her head to get her attention, gesturing for her to come up to me, I kissed her, rolling her to her back as I did, and slid between her leg sand entered her. I was gentle; I was loving; caressing her, holding her, telling her how lovely she looked, how good she felt, how I enjoyed feeling her surrender.

We kissed and kissed, as I slowly, lovingly, I took her for the first time as my little I did not call her names or belittle her; I did

not slap her or spank her. This was loving Daddy compassionate Daddy; bad Daddy's time would come, but that was not today.

We continued like this, making love as it was love that I was showing her this night, sealing a promise with this act of love and when finally I came, I tried my very best not to roar with passion but sigh with contentment.

I looked up and saw that Rebecca and Lovisa were watching us. Both had tears in their eyes. There was no jealousy in their eyes, there was only joy. Rebecca's lover was joining her family becoming like a sister and Lovisa knew that she had not lost a lover but gained two who were also her family now.

Holding Ela, I beckoned to them to join us; the bed was big and could accommodate more than the four of us, so plenty of room. Lovisa whispered into Rebecca's ear, and I saw her nod in response.

Her face changed, softness vanished, a hand slid into Rebecca's hair grabbing a handful of pink fairy coloured hair and pulling her head back. Lovisa's free hand slapped Rebecca, then grabbed her about the throat and pushed her to the foot of the bed.

Now I had seen them converse and the nod from Rebecca. We had played rough many times and she knew to call red should she be unhappy, so I was not concerned about what was going on. I just watched, holding Ela close to me, her face still nuzzled up into my neck.

"You, little girl, you will please me as I have seen you, please my Ela," She was glaring at Rebecca now, still holding her hair and throat, her posture full of potential violence.

"Do you understand my GIRL? Your Master gave you, gifted you to me. I expect you to pay that debt. Do you understand?" The last words were said loudly, almost barked out.

Rebecca looked up, no defiance in her face, her eye big, a look of fear seeming to cross her face (little actress, she knew how to play her part).
Rebecca replied, an impish smile on her face as she spoke.

"Yes, Mistress, I am here to serve you at my Master's bidding."
"What do you desire of me?" How Lovisa kept a straight face, I do not know. I am sure I would have cracked a smile at that last bit.

Lovisa threw her down onto the bed, pushing her onto her back, and pressing down, a clear signal not to bloody move.

"We are going to play a game, child. If you lose, you will be punished."
"I am going to sit on your face, Girl."
"You will pleasure me while I slap your lovely little pussy."
"If you cum, orgasm, or squirt before I do, I will punish you severely."
"Is that clear GIRL?" she settled herself above Rebecca's face, waiting for her answer.

"Yes, Mistress, I understand." The cheeky smile was gone now. She was playing her role for her new Mistress and would play it well.

And with that, Lovisa settled down on Rebecca's face, leaned forward, and spread her legs, and started slowly, rhythmically slapping Rebecca's little, slightly pouty cunt with her open hand.

There was no way Rebecca was going to win this game. Lovisa was an experienced Dominatrix and I bet dollars to doughnuts she had full control of her orgasm. Also, Rebecca loved having

her cunt slapped. (And I loved slapping it.) She would try to control herself as commanded and please Mistress Lovisa, but alas I fear she was also destined to be punished tonight.

I watched Lovisa face as she had her pussy eaten by my girl, a girl that had never touched a woman like this until the other day and now she was tongue fucking, pleasuring a Dominatrix who had threatened her with punishment if she failed to please her.

The slapping went on for a while, but then I heard distinctly wet sounding slaps, followed just after by a moan of pleasure escaping Lovisa's lovely lips. A failure but a close-run thing, Lovisa did not let up on the slapping and Rebecca, knowing she had failed once, did not stop her attack on Lovisa's now wet cunt.

I could see her grinding into Rebecca's face, getting her deep into her parted lips. Rebecca for her part had a hand between Lovisa's legs rubbing at her clit, something I was sure she knew how to do well. But still, she lost the next round, as she orgasmed and then squirted a fountain of pussy juice, soaking the bed.

Lovisa stopped slapping her cunt but kept up the facial grinding. I was not sure that she was even giving Rebecca a chance to get a lungful of air. She demanded satisfaction and was not letting up until Rebecca delivered.

Both of Rebecca's hands now gripped Lovisa's thighs as Lovisa rode and ground her wet cunt into Rebecca's face. I watched Lovisa and Rebecca with some envy. Part of me longed to make her mine, make her ride me like she rode Rebecca, but I knew it was not to be, so I would just have to enjoy the view.

Lovisa was crying out now, moaning as she was pleasured. Her face was changing, a look I had seen on many faces over the

years. Her resolve was breaking, as the assault on her lady bits became too much to deny or control.

She orgasmed and then squirted, only lifting away at the last second, so she showered Rebecca's face with her juices. Rebecca caught as much as she could in her open mouth, sliding from under Lovisa and offering Ela a kiss, which she accepted, sharing a trickle of pussy nectar between them. She then kissed me, giving me a taste of Lovisa, one that I savoured, savouring the taste of this beautiful woman even though it was second hand. It tasted sweet to me.

Exhausted by exertion we all lay in the bed, Lovisa spooned Rebecca, while I spooned Ela, and we all lay like that for a while, until some rude person started knocking and jiggling on the door handle. A pet hate of mine.

The girls laughed and rose from the bed; I guess we had hogged the room for quite some time, only fair to let others enjoy the evening.

The bed, though, was soaked, So I picked up the towels, using them to wipe down the bed as best I can, before spraying it down and wiping it clean. (It would be rude not to.)

Lovisa, though, had not forgotten that Rebecca still owned a punishment for failing her game. She made her crawl from the room, leading her to the dungeon playroom. Where she strapped her down to the spanking bench and asked various men to spank her bottom.

She had obviously heard about my rule of six and told each man to spank her six times as hard as they could. Six men she chose, and all six struck each bottom cheek six times. Seventy-two slaps of her bottom left it nice and red and pleasingly they were not gentle as Lovisa would have tongue-lashed them had they

not put some effort into each spank. (She could be a scary woman.)

After her punishment, we returned to our booth; the girls going for a dance. Where do they get the energy? I ordered more champagne (not a fan of the stuff really, but the girls like it) and we did have something to celebrate tonight: the joining of our two kink families.

The girls danced, I watched, we talked and when we parted there were tears and promises to meet up soon. (Already in hand, but we kept that secret.)

I had to comfort Rebecca for some time when we got back, nearly spilling the beans about the planned reunion in a few weeks' time. I had to bind us together again this night. She needed the comfort that being bound to me brought her.

Hard Lessons
Exhibitionist Holiday.

Epilogue: Exhibitionist and the Chauffeur.

Before she fell asleep, she told me that she loved me and was so happy I had agreed to take Gisela under my wing, though just mentioning her name made her cry again. So, I just lay there cradling her in my arms until she fell asleep.

In the morning, we found another note pushed under the door, a parting message from the girls.
Dear Alex and Rebecca,

So glad we met you, thank you for such a lovely week, we had the best time ever!
See you both soon.

Love Ela and Lovisa xxx
I sent Ela, the first of many messages I would send, wishing her good morning, Princess and telling her how happy I was with her and that we both enjoyed our time last night.

She replied, quickly. I guess she had her phone with her now that they had departed the site.

Thank you, Daddy xxx,
Thank you for adopting me. I will be the bestest little girl for you. I promise xxx

I replied, letting her know I would call her tonight xx

It really was going to be a lot of work all this Daddy thing, but I liked Ela, Rebecca I think loved her already, So I would play my role. It would have its benefits, I was sure. (Ela is a stunning, sexy young woman.)

A quick black coffee for us both and then we were packed and ready, waiting for the driver to take us to the airport. I had chosen a little yellow summer dress for Rebecca to wear today, the one with the belt fastening, easy to undo and open. I figured she might as well give the driver a show.

The driver this time, however, was a woman, dressed in a chauffeur's outfit, rather handsome I thought. I sent Rebecca to the front of the car again, wondering if the lady driver would show an interest. We would of course not foist out kinks on the young woman, but if she looked interested, Rebecca would put on a show.

Her dress hiked up already, showing far more thigh than was decent. The driver saw and took note. As usual, handing out bottles of water to each of us. I watched as she leaned over and checked Rebecca's seat belt and quickly pulled on her dress's belt as she did so, releasing the bow that held it closed.

Well, this looked like an interesting drive, after all, I thought. As we pulled away, Rebecca pulled open her dress showing the driver, and any that got a look in the window, that she was naked. The drive back was slower than normal, mainly as the driver took us along back roads and had to drive one-handed most of the way.

My little exhibitionist girl was definitely becoming an exhibitionist slut.

End.

Rebecca's Story.
Crush.

Part of the Hard Lessons trilogy.

This is Rebecca's story as told by her.

All characters are fictional any similarities are purely coincidental.

Rebecca forms an inappropriate student teacher crush in the final months of her education. Her attempts to get her crushes attention lead her further and further down a very slippery slope. Eventually, she goes too far, an action a cry for attention that leads to detention and possible suspension but then the fun really begins for Rebecca.

Rebecca's Story.
Crush.

Chapter 1: Crush.

Hi, my name is Rebecca, and this is the story of how I became Sir's girl.

I'm eighteen, but I will be nineteen soon. This is my final year at school, and we are now in the last few months of school before exams start.

I live with my mum (single) in a split-level flat. I have not seen dad in six years. Mum did not want him to come around any longer. I suspect she has told him not to bother me and I think he was glad to be free of the responsibility.

My mother had me when she was my age! She never even finished school! Yet she has the nerve to tell me I must do well! Or I will end up just like her, stuck in a crummy flat with a crummy job (and spoiled, ungrateful child... She doe does not say that last bit, but I can read the subtext).
Way to make me feel unwanted, MUM!

I sometimes wonder if I should just do what she did and get pregnant! Maybe have a baby or two. To be honest, I don't see much else in my future, best I can hope for is a crap job if I am lucky, probably cleaning like mum does. But if I have a baby, I will at least be able to get my own place to live. Anyway, I will be a better mum than my mum, could not be worse.

My friend Paige had a baby last year, and she even has her own flat now. She gets money to live on and does not have to go to school anymore. She lives with her boyfriend, and they seem to be ok, though he does not work and spends all day playing

games. Still, he is nice to her, and they are planning on another baby soon.

God, I hate school! Always have. Well, maybe only since I moved up to this school. The school was ok but then I moved up to senior school and it was not the same. I really struggle now, and I am not doing very well in my classes, they are so boring. The teachers are dull and too serious, most don't seem to like me. Most would not even know my name without the register...

Even this class, the one I am waiting outside of now, is boring! I mean used to be boring. English lit, lots of dusty old books, and worst of all are the written essays on the tedious books...
Yawn.

That was until the other day when sir told me off for not reading in class. (I had been on my phone.) I got a funny feeling after he told me off. He did not actually tell me off, just stood there and tapped my book with a scowl on his face.

At times I feel invisible, like I am not there, School, home mum, dad it is like I am invisible or something. Would anyone notice if I was just to vanish? Maybe that's why I get in trouble, so I am noticed, so people know I exist! Sir noticed me when he saw I was not reading the book assignment and I felt weird when he told me off. A good kind of weird, but different this time.

I felt guilty and sad that I had disappointed him! I did not understand why I felt so bad and why could I not stop thinking about him during class. I even deliberately got caught with my phone out again so he would tell me off again. It's weird, it is like I enjoyed him telling me off! I liked it when he noticed me!
Is that weird?

I found myself watching him as he spoke to other students, feeling a little jealous that he was not talking to me. At one point, I caught myself checking his butt out! He really is kinda

fit for an old guy. Looking at him made my belly feel weird, and I could feel a little tingling between my legs! I was getting a little turned on at the thought of him standing over me and telling me off again.

That is so weird, right!

After the lesson ended, I stayed back, waiting to get my phone. I had to wait until he noticed me. He was marking papers. I think he likes to make students wait. I did not like that he was ignoring me...

When he eventually noticed I was there, he stopped writing, but he still did not look at me. Just *sighed* and handed my phone back telling me that the exams are coming up and that I should apply myself more. His voice sounded a little disappointed like he was tired of repeating himself all the time.

It had felt nice when he spoke to me, but it also felt kind of bad; almost like I had failed him. I really did not like that feeling at all.

As I was leaving the classroom, I deliberately wiggled my bottom, hoping that maybe he was watching me leave and would notice that I have a nice bum. I even stomped my feet a little, hoping he might turn and look at me as I walked from the room, hips swaying exaggeratedly.

I do have a nice bum. I have been told by my friends and several dirty old men in the park. Mum's boyfriend thinks it's cute too...

After school, I went home, catching the bus and this time avoiding the pervs that like to eye me up! Sometimes it's fun to tease them a little, but not today. I was not in the mood, so I stayed downstairs near the driver.

Arriving home, I found a note from mum letting me know she would be working late and would be going out with friends

after. Nothing usual then. Yep, and as usual, there was no food left out for me... I suppose I could cook something but really mum! You could have made something for me!
I hate cooking.

Settling for a bowl of Shreddies for dinner, at least they are not fattening. I took the bowl up to my room. I wanted to think. I could have sat in the front room, but for some reason I wanted Teddy...

I could not stop thinking of Mr Wyles. It was like I had a crush on him or something... But he was old, old like dad maybe older. Even later when in the bath, I was thinking of him... Put that phone away young lady; you need to apply yourself, Miss Lawson, see me after class, Miss Lawson... Please try harder Miss Lawson, exams are important, Miss Lawson. Miss Lawson, Miss Lawson, Miss Lawson!

The bathroom is my private space, the only room mum does not walk in unannounced. It is the only place I can play with myself without her catching me! And I was touching myself while I soaked in the hot scented water. I was remembering Mr Wyles, telling me off, standing over me, remembering the look of disappointment he gave me.
He had kind eyes.

I did not like that; I wanted Mr Wyles to be happy with me. I wondered if Mr Wyles even knew my name; I don't think he called me by my first name in the three years I have been in his class. It is always Miss Lawson, Miss Lawson, put your phone away, Miss Lawson. Please stop talking in class, Miss Lawson, your report is due.
Blah blah blah.

Drifting off into a half-asleep state, daydreaming and fantasizing while I was relaxing in the bath... I kept thinking about Mr Wyles, Mr Wyles standing over me, telling me I was a good girl,

that I had pleased him, and then he as he kisses me! He tells me I'm his best student and calls me Rebecca! |Calling me my name as he pulls me into his arms.

I bet he could lift me easily.

Then suddenly I am sitting on his lap, straddling him. I can feel his hard cock pressing against my panties. He is hard because I made him hard. My kisses, my touch, the feel of my body against his made him hard.

See, sir, Rebecca is a good girl.

He slides my panties aside and fills my tight little pussy with his cock as he calls me a good girl again and again. He is so big it hurts a little, a little pain, but a nice pain. I liked how it feels and the way his cock fills me up. I was so happy but then suddenly I hear the bell and I realise we were in school! In class and everyone is watching me as I was fucked by Mr Wyles.

Oh My god!

Mr Wyles, though, just keeps fucking my little pussy. He brushes the table clear, papers were thrown to the floor. Mr Wyles pushes me onto his desk, taking me from behind now, so I could see the class watching me! Watching me while he proceeds to teach the lesson. I was naked in class and Mr Wyles was fucking me over his desk and everyone was watching me…

Wake up, Rebecca…

I woke then, choking on bathwater as I slipped under. I must have dozed off. It was a dream… I had dreamt about Mr Wyles making love to me! I must really like Mr Wyles if I was dreaming about him fucking me! I was also quite turned on by the thought of being seen while having sex.

I am such a perv.

That night, I Google Mr Wyles; finding out his first name, Alexander. I hoped he went by Alex. I like that name. Then I

checked him out on Facebook and IG and although there is not much info on his profile. He does seem to have a lot of female friends, many of them a lot younger.

He does not seem to be married, or at least there is not any family listed on his FB (Facebook) profile. He has two dogs though and gosh, they are so cute. I love dogs and miss my dog Wooffus who passed away last year. Mum won't let me get another. She says they are too much of a bind.
Bitch.

I looked through his photos and there are a few pictures of Mr Wyles on holiday, and he looks very fit for his age. He must work out. Finding nothing else interesting, I start checking out his female friends' profiles. Now, these are more interesting, some of the girls are very pretty, others are not so much, I guess they are ok for their age. Some of the women and girls have pictures of them at parties and in a few, they are wearing rubber dresses, corsets and catsuits!
That rubber dress, though, is dope!

She looks so hot; I wonder what I would look like in some of her outfits? I think I would look badass in that rubber dress. Then I find a picture of a girl tied up in rope! Really pretty rope. I read through the comments on the pictures and see in another image's comment list, someone that looks like Mr Wyles had commented. He must have another profile.
Bingo.

I clicked on the profile and the same girl was in rope again in one of the images, and Mr Wyles is holding the rope! In the comments, another message from Mr Wyles. He thanks her for a great time and promises to show her his dungeon next time she is up…
Dungeon, DUNGEON!

He has a dungeon! OMG, he is a perv, kinky like in that film, fifty shades of something that Lucy and I watched before her mum told us off for spanking each other. (That was fun.) I had enjoyed being spanked by Lucy, shame her mum had to spoil it. I bet her dad would have just watched us... He is always watching me when I stay over. I like it a little and occasionally let him see me in my nighty.
Dirty Perv lol.

I decided then that I wanted Mr Wyles! I wanted him to notice me. If he like girls who wear kinky rubber and likes to tie them up and even has a dungeon, I'd bet, he enjoys spanking their bare bottoms too... Maybe if I get in trouble, he will spank me, I would like that I think. I go to bed and dream about Mr Wyles's big hands on my little bottom, the sting of his hand as it slaps my tight little round arse.

Over the next few days, I try to get Mr Wyles to notice me in class. I wear a dark bra, leave a button or two undone so that he might notice my breasts. I ask questions, even deliberately get caught using my phone. But he does not notice me and ignores me when he hands me the phone back...
Humph!

He has even stopped walking up my aisle and I was sure he could see my breasts the other day. His eyes must have seen down my top while he answered a question about the book I was reading. Why is he ignoring me?
Notice me!

Boys like me, though they are so dull, talking about football and x station and call of Fortnite or whatever. I bet Mr Wyles does not spend all day playing games and watching sport. I think he would talk about places he's been, exotic counties and people, even art. I would like that, even if some of it sounds a bit dull. I bet from him it would sound exotic and interesting.
Please notice me!

227

And this is where you find me today, waiting outside the class, waiting for Mr Wyles to let me into the class. I am at the front of the line, ignoring my friends. I want the seat in the middle of the front row. So, Mr Wyles can't ignore me and will be able to see me from his desk.

I am so nervous, but I am going to do this. I want Mr Wyles to notice me; he must notice me. This will work…
It just has to.

Rebecca's Story.
Crush.

Chapter 2: Notice me!

Sir opens the door and we all file in. Quickly, I grab the seat in front of Mr Wyles. The girl who usually sits here glares at me, but I just ignore her. Once everyone is sitting, I slide up my skirt a little. Just enough so that now that I have opened my legs a little, Mr Wyles should be able to see my inner thighs.
God, Mum's right! I am a cock tease.

He looks up as he takes the register; I think he noticed I was sitting in front of the class, right in front of his desk. Did he see my legs were wide and my skirt was hitched up? Am I being too subtle, I wonder? I lift my skirt a little more.
Come on, look, sir.

Now he should be able to see the white of my panties. He does not seem to be looking at me at all. I am watching him. My eyes were on sir, not reading my book, just willing him to look.
Please look at me…

He is not looking though, just working on his papers. So, I decide to get his attention by asking a question, yes; he looked at me. Did he see? Does he see what I am showing him? After answering my question, he returns to his papers. Did he see? Did he notice will he look again if he did? I watch him hoping he will look up, but he does not seem to be looking, just writing in those stupid papers.
Grrr, the least he could do is look!

Something is odd though; he is not walking around the class today. I wonder why? Usually, he wanders about answering questions and talking over some of the material, but not today. He just seems to be marking papers.

Notice me!

I decided to spread my legs wide, hitching my skirt so he cannot miss what I was showing him. I could get expelled, I realise, for what I am doing. It would be hard to convince anyone that my skirt just rode up like this by accident. But I decide to risk it.
Look at me, sir...

My legs are wide, which stretches the thin material tight across my pussy, so tight I fear they might slip and slide between my lips and expose my little pussy. I think I would like sir to see that. Maybe I should not have worn any panties. Then I bet Mr Wyles would look up from those stupid papers... Should I go to the toilets and remove them? No, that is going too far.
I am not a slut.

Notice me, please. I feel like crying. Why does he not look?
I decide that for the next lesson (tomorrow) I will not wear my panties and shave all my hair off! Maybe sir likes the smooth hairless look. The Hollywood they call it, it is all the rage now with my friends. I bet that would get his attention.
Ok, maybe I am a slut.

The lunch bell goes. I close my legs and slip my skirt down in case any of my classmate's notice. As I stand, Mr Wyles calls my name.
His voice is quiet, but I hear him clearly.
"Miss Lawson, please wait..."

I sit down, worried now, I am in trouble; he did notice, and now he is going to call the Headmaster maybe even my mother. She will send me away if I get expelled. Maybe I will have to live with dad! wherever he is now.
Gulp.

He is making me wait, still marking his papers. My friends have gone to lunch. They won't want to be late and miss the good stuff.
Maybe now he will notice me!

He is still ignoring me though! Even after what I risked today. He is ignoring me...
He tells me to wait behind and ignores me.
I think I'm going to cry.

He looks up, looking at me coldly, and calls me over.
Gulp again!

I walk over to his desk; I can't look at him. The disappointment in his voice hurts. I feel sick inside. I can't bear to see that in his eyes.
Please, not the disappointed look.

He is talking; he mentioned my skirt. Oh, hell, I am in trouble. He is threatening to call the Headmaster and my parents; I don't want that. I look up at him. Can he see the tears forming, the fear I feel right now?
I am going to be grounded for life.

He tells me to take my seat again; I go back wondering what he is going to do. I sit with my knees together while he looks at me, staring at me with cold, disappointed eyes.
But he is looking.

Then he tells me to show him my white panties... Mr Wyles knew I was wearing a white thong! He wants to know if I wore them, especially for him...
Well yes, yes, I did.

He did see. He noticed, sir, noticed me... I am happy inside, though I am scared. Mr Wyles is looking as I open my legs and

hitch up my skirt. This time I spread my legs as wide as I can, hoping the material slides into my pussy.
He has noticed me at least.

He does not look happy, but he is looking. He is noticing me. Noticing that I am a girl, a woman that I am offering myself to him.
I want to be yours, sir.

I stay sitting like that, looking at Mr Wyles while he looks at me, he is looking directly at my panties. How I wish I had not worn them now. I bet he would like my pussy. I have little hair, a strip only, but I am fair-haired, and the hair is barely visible. I wonder if he likes girls with hair or shaved? Shaved is normal now. Many of my friend's shave every day to stay smooth. I like having a little strip of hair, fewer rashes but have shaved in the past. Mum says it makes me look like a little girl still. But she shaves hers off when she has a date. The bath is always full of hair. So, I don't really understand what she means by that.

Sir takes out his phone. I panic for a second but then realise he is taking the picture, so I try to spread my legs a little wider.
Slut! I am such a slut!

He tells me he now has proof of my behaviour, that he really should go to the headmaster, warning me that this could mean suspension. My eyes start welling up again. I realise that I have done something monumentally stupid and now I am likely to get expelled.

I plead with him; tell him I am really sorry, sir. Promising that I won't do it again. He is looking at me with that disappointed look again, butterflies are pogoing in my stomach.
I was really am going to be sick...

He feels sorry for me, I think, and the look of anger and disappointment slips from his face. He tells me that maybe

233

detention would be enough this time. But warn me never to do that again.

He asks me why I did it, why I exposed myself to him.
I look at him, smile because I am happy. I got away with it…
Mr Wyles has noticed me. He will think of me later. I am sure maybe he will dream about me and take more notice of me when in class. And he has that photo of me now. I hope he looks at it often and thinks about me.
Maybe it will make you hard, sir.

So, I smile and tell him,
"Sir, I wanted you to notice me!"
And it worked…

He tells me to come to his office after school, calling me Miss Lawson. I want to hear him call my name, so I tell him.
"Rebecca sir," I say, smiling.
Call me Rebecca, please.

He snaps at me angrily and dismisses me until after school. I stomp out of the class but hope he is watching as a wiggle my skirt into place again.
He noticed me. What do I do now?

Rebecca's Story.
Crush.

Chapter 3: Detention

The last bell rings and I make my way up to Mr Wyles office. My stomach is churning, butterflies are dancing, making me feel nauseous, but I know it's just my nerves. I'm scared about what is going to happen, although I have been daydreaming about this all afternoon. Hoping that he closes the door and pushes me over his desk, pulls down my panties and fucks me right there in his office.
I'm so horny right now.

He opens the door but tells me to wait. So, I sit and sulk a little relieved as I need to get my shaking under control. I sit and calm down, waiting for him to call my name. Hoping he calls me Rebecca, that would be a good sign if he calls me that.

Half an hour he makes me sit there. If he wanted me, he would not make me wait! I am scared now. What if he has changed his mind and is waiting for the headmaster or my mother to arrive? But then he opens the door and tells me to come in.
I am definitely going to puke!

He orders me to stand in front of his desk. There is no chair there. Usually, there is a chair to sit on in the teachers' office. I have been in a few times with other teachers to talk about my work or lack of it. I notice the chair to the side and think maybe he did not want to risk me flashing him again.
Do I make you nervous, sir?

Then I realise he had closed the door behind me. That is odd. Teachers never close the door! I wonder why maybe he is going to yell at me. I don't want him to yell.
Please don't shout at me.

He shows me my academic record, informing me I'm not doing well. (Yeah, well, duh!) Warns me that I could face failing if I got suspended now. It being so close to exams. He tells me he does not want to do that, but I need to be punished for what occurred in his class.

He asks me if he should call the Headmaster or should we work this out. The thought of the Headmaster starts me crying again. The Headmaster is scary, swoops about the halls in that silly robe like he is Snape.

"Sorry sir, please sir don't…" Tears flowing freely now.

"Please, sir, I will do anything, sir, don't let my mother know. She will send me away!" I beg him not to call the Headmaster or my parents, my eyes pleading as the tears roll down my cheeks. *No one can resist the power of the puppy eyes, mwahahaha!*

I look down, so Mr Wyles can't see the small smile as I realise suddenly that he has no intention of calling my mother or the Headmaster. He would have done so already. He must have something else in mind.

Maybe he wants to see my panties again. I bet he has been looking at that picture all day.
So, I say, not looking up.

"I will do whatever sir says, whatever sir wants, just don't call the Headmaster, please, sir."
Anything.

He calls me Rebecca.
My heart is racing. He called me Rebecca. I liked that, enjoy hearing him call me by my name, so much nicer than when he calls me Miss Lawson.

He is telling me he is old-fashioned and believes that if someone is naughty, they should be punished. My heart skips. He was going to spank me, just like the dream I had. I think I soaked my panties at that thought.

He is talking about his school days and that they used to cane the students. But he can't cane me as he does not have one. I am kind of relieved, his hand on my bottom I think I would like but the cane!! That has to really, really hurt. I don't want the cane, do I?
No, I want to feel your hand's sir.

Then he picks up an old-looking ruler and tells me that this will have to do today. I look at the ruler. It is quite long, longer than the one I use in school, and it looks like it is made from wood, not plastic.

He asks me if I am sure that I would not rather be suspended. The ruler is scaring me a little, but I wanted sir attention and I have it now. I knew he likes kinky stuff from his profile. He even has a dungeon and I know that means he must like hitting girls. Just like that Christian guy to Anna something, the whiney girl in the movies.

I wanted this; I realised I really did want this to happen. The ruler was not what I had imagined, but maybe he would use his hands another way or another day. If I do this, I was sure he would find reasons to do it again. Or I would find a way to be sent to his office again if he did not.

"Yes sir, I mean no sir, I will take my punishment, sir," I said, trying to keep any excitement out of my voice.
Yes, punish me, then fuck me over your desk with your big fat cock, sir.

Sure, that Mr Wyles wanted me to feel like I am being punished even if I wanted this. I faked a few tears by thinking about my dog, which always teared me up.

This trick got me out of trouble often. Well, with anyone but mum.

He tells me to bend over the desk as he comes around behind me. God, I wanted to feel him press against me, feel his cock slide in my tight little cunny. I was so wet right now. I bet even if he is huge, it would slide in. Like, mum's big black dildo that I borrowed the other night. That was hard to get in at first but felt so good when it finally slipped into me.

He calls me Rebecca. (My heart flutters hearing that name from his lips).

He asks me to lift up my skirt; I do as he tells me, exposing my bottom. I hope he likes it. There's no fat on my ass I keep fit and my bottom is small, firm and round.

He talks about removing my panties!
Please, sir, remove my panties is going through my head, but he does not, as the thong is buried between my cheeks, and he does not need to.
Damn it.

Six strokes he tells me, but he calls me by my name again. If he keeps doing that, he can hit me as much as he wants. Just keep calling me Rebeca and I will do anything! Anything?
Yes, anything.

I really like it when he calls me Rebecca.
He tells me to call him Sir and then tells me to say it again, properly.

So, I the emphasize the Sir this time. In my head though I am saying, Sir, yes Sir spank me, Sir, fuck me, Sir, can I suck your cock please Sir?

I feel the rule hit me for the first time; It hurt more than I thought it would, but sir calls me Rebecca again, well after he called me miss Lawson, but maybe that is because I moved. I promise myself I won't move again when the ruler hits me again.
Ouch, that really did hurt!

Five more times he hits my bottom, moving the ruler so he is not hitting the same spot each time. Then he swaps to the other side. He calls me a good girl though, and that puts a smile on my face, even though I am crying a little.

The last one hurt the most, but as he left the ruler in place, I realised no more were to come.
He moved behind the desk. But when I looked up, I could see him. I could see his cock. He was hard, and he was not hiding it. I could clearly see the outline of his cock through his trousers. I had done that. I had made Mr Wyles hard.

I wanted to feel that cock, wanted him to bend me over the desk again and take me…
He calls me Rebecca again. But now all I am thinking about is his cock, how big it looks and how hard it looks. The trousers are barely containing it. He might break his zip, it looks so hard…

"You wanted me to notice you, I have..."

"Yes sir, I wanted that Sir."
Then he tells me to remove my panties and hand them to him…

I turn and slip them off, pretending to be shy, when in reality, I wanted him to tell me to strip everything off. Mr Wyles would

then see that I am a beautiful woman, and I was his if he wanted me.
Please want me.

When I hand them to him, I notice they are very wet. I am such a dirty girl. Being punished turned me on more than I ever thought it would.

I hand them over. He then tells me to lift my skirt and show him what my panties were hiding…

He does want me; he must want me if he wants to see my special place.

I lift my skirt, not shy now. Why be shy? This is what I wanted. I wanted his attention. My plan worked. Now he wanted to see my little pussy. And I wanted him to see it too.

I watched him looking, the smile on his face as he looked at the little stipe of hair and could see that I had a nice, neat vagina, though it was also a very wet one. I could feel myself getting wetter as he watched. Do you like it, Sir, you can eat it if you want?
Hmmm, oh yes, please lick me!

Then he took out a camera and took some photos. I did not mind; it means he liked what he saw. He likes me.

He tells me to lower my skirt and tells me that I must not misbehave in class again. No more flashing panties or breasts…

I knew it. He had noticed me. I thought happily.
He says that I have his attention and asks me if I know what that means? What could happen now?

I tell him I do, that I know what sir will do to me. Or should I say what I want sir to do to me…

240

Please do me…

Mr Wyles says this can't happen at school… I feel downhearted, thinking he is going to tell me it can't happen again. But then tells me that he will tutor me, and he will employ me to look after his dogs, Geri and Freki. Those must be the dogs on his profile. Tutor me!
I want your cock, not an education…

I write my number down as he tells me, and then he puts my hand on his cock. OMG, it feels so stiff and big in my hands. He tells me this will be my reward. I watch him sniff my panties; I hope he likes my smell; I am clean, always clean, and I'm sure they don't smell bad.

He explains about punishing and rewarding me. I don't care as long as he calls me Rebecca and looks at me like he is now. I would do anything. I squeeze his cock, imagining it deep within me as he talks, but then he tells me to go. I liked it when he sniffed my panties; he seemed to like the scent, my scent.
You will like the taste too, Sir.
I'm saddened I wanted to feel it properly, hold his cock, feel it in me. But maybe on Saturday, as he is right, we can't in school, someone might catch us, and I don't want that.

I headed home to explain to mum about Saturday. She will be happy I am getting extra help with my studies and even happier that it is not costing her anything. After dinner, I think I am going to have a very long and hot bath. Now, where did she hide it this time?
Aha, here you are.

Rebecca's Story.
Crush.

Chapter: 4 Tuition

Mr Wyles called me to his office once more in the week. He goes over the weekend plans and tells me he would send a text so I could show my mother that the offer was genuine.

He told me to wear something nice and white panties; it is going to be warm, so a summer dress, but nothing too revealing. We don't want to raise any suspicions from your mother. It disappointed me a little that he did not ask for another show, as I had not worn panties to his room; they were in my bag now.
Your loss Sir.

I kind of liked the feel and the naughtiness of not having panties on in school. Deciding that I might not wear them later on the bus and when I go to town. I always hitch up my skirt in town. All the girls do, to show off our legs, maybe someone will get lucky and see a bit more than a little leg and pantie flash.

Saturday came around, and I showered and made sure I was doubly clean in hopeful anticipation of Sir checking. I put on my last pair of white panties. I would have to get mum to buy more, I suppose if Sir likes me in them. I put on a little yellow summer dress, white ankle socks and sensible flat shoes so I could walk the dogs. I was excited to see the dogs as well. I missed having a dog and Mr Wyles dogs looked so cute.
Looking cute might fuck Sir later, IDK.

Mum gave me a lift to Mr Wyles's house. He lived in a nice part of town, right on the outskirts near the woods. It was a nice house in a dead-end cul-de-sac. It impressed mum and she made some comments about teachers' pay before she left.

My belly was flipping again. Nerves, I guess. I did not know what Mr Wyles planned, but I was willing to do whatever would make him happy, and that would make him happy with me especially. Anything to hear him speak my name.

I entered, and he greeted me. He was dressed smartly; I wondered if he always dressed like that or did he dress up for guests. Maybe he had worn the suit for me. That was a nice thought. Maybe he wants to impress me.
It's working.

He showed me into the living room, a room that he had set up with a school desk and wooden chair. The chair had two round holes in it. I wondered what they were for. Mr Wyles must have guessed what I was thinking and told me not to worry. Those were not for today. Mr Wyles then went over the plans today. I did have to wonder what could possibly go in those holes.

He also told me that he liked my dress and checked that I had worn white panties, so I showed him. He said he would buy me more, as he expected they would not last in his house; I wondered what he meant by that. But I was happy he liked my dress.

I watched as he went and sat in the window, looking directly at me. I realised he would be able to see up my little dress even if I did not hitch it up, but then again, I wanted him to see me more than ever now.

So, I spread my legs wide. My panties were an old pair from two years ago. I had grown, and these were almost too small...
Perfect for today.

As I spread my legs, the material stretched tightly against my pussy. I liked the feel of them pressing in so tightly. I was wet already, and I was sure that could be seen by Mr Wyles. I hope so.

243

You make me wet with just your eyes. Imagine what your cock will do…

I looked up to make sure he was watching me, and every time I looked; he was. His eyes never seemed to leave the little wet spot in the crotch of my panties. I wondered how wet they were. Knowing that the material stretched as much as they were now and being wet, they would become almost transparent.
He wants me…

He could probably see the outline of my pussy clearly now. It was very distracting, but I knew it would disappoint him if I did not study, so tried to concentrate on the revision and then the test.

After I had completed the first test, he made me bring the paper to him. Holding it out with both hands, but he did not take it… Making me wait for a little.

He then told me to kneel! I knelt and held out the test paper again. He made me wait a little longer before taking it. I hate waiting, but somehow being on my knees before Mr Wyles felt right.

He called me Miss Lawson. My face may have dropped at that, then I realised it is because this is lesson time and I forgot about my disappointment at not being called Rebecca. I had gotten just two wrong, which I thought was pretty good for me. Mr Wyles even said it was quite good. I liked that. No one ever said I was good at anything these days.

He told me the punishment can wait until the next test as I had done so well. I was conflicted. I desperately wanted to feel his hand on my bottom. He had promised a bare bottom spanking for each wrong answer; I suppose I could have fluffed the test to earn more, but I really did want to make Mr Wyles happy with me.

Mr Wyles told me to hand him my panties; I realised that would mean he could see me without them while sitting here. I almost climaxed at that thought. I lifted my dress, no teasing this time, and slipped off the wet white panties and handed them to him before letting my dress drop. I watched as he sniffed them like he was smelling a sweetly scented flower.

My flower I like that name for my pussy. I hope he would like my flower too.
Flower, that is such a pretty name for my cunny.

He complimented me on my scent said it was very pleasant, which made me feel so happy. I am singing inside.

I returned to the desk and started the next session of revision, seeing that Sir was watching I spread my legs wide as I could and slipped a little down on the chair, thinking that would give Mr Wyles a good view, by spreading my legs my flower would open and Sir would see how pretty it was. I am yours Sir; my flower is yours; I am wet because you are looking at me, wet because I am thinking about you fucking me.
I am such a slut.

I looked up and saw him staring at me; I was sure that was raw passion, that he wanted me, he could have me if he wanted. I would do anything to make him happy, I realised. I noticed his eyes drop a little when I looked at him as if he was looking at something little below my pussy. Then I realised with my legs spread and as low as I had slid in the chair, he could see my butt hole. Did he like that as well, I wondered?
Hmm bum Sex!

Anal is super popular nowadays. All the porn I see, they always seem to be fucking girls in the arse. I wonder if Mr Wyles wants that, too. Did I want it as well? I wondered as I felt a trickle of

cum dripping down my body and across my little rosebud.
Rosebud?
Yes, rosebud and flower.

At the end of the second test, I walked over again, remembering
to kneel this time. Once more, I held out the paper to Sir and
again he did not take it immediately but let me hold it for what
felt like ten minutes. My arms were shaking, but I did not let
them drop. I don't like this waiting lark, but if Sir wants me to
wait. Wait, I will.

He took the paper and marked I had not answered all the
questions; I had run out of time, and he told me I got another
five wrong, so that made seven minutes of spanking, he said.
Yay, spanking time.

But he also told me that I had done very well, and he wondered
why I did not do as well in class, telling me maybe I should sit at
the front from now on. I would like that, as Sir would be able to
see me every time he looked up. Though obviously, I could not
flash Mr Wyles again… But he would remember every time he
saw me, though, and that was enough.

"You have earned seven minutes of spanking Miss Lawson. You
have a choice, over the desk or over the knee. Choose now," said
Mr Wyles.
Knee obviously I want to be as close to you as possible.

I told him,
"Over knee please Sir," as I wanted to feel his hardness against
my body. I could see he was hard from where I was kneeling,
and I really wanted to feel that against me.

I laid across his lap. He lifted me up and adjusted me, balancing
my body across his knees. I could feel his hardness press against
my belly! I wished it was my face… My hand or better still, my

246

pussy, but I could feel how hard I had gotten him with my little show. And that made me very happy.

He lifted my dress, exposing me. I felt his hand cupping my bottom. Good, I hoped he liked what he felt. He gave me his watch and told me to press the timer when he started the spanking. He then pressed my damp panties into my mouth and told me not to spit them out.

I could taste myself on them, but I did not mind. I did wonder if other girl's pussy's taste so nice? Maybe I would find out one day. Maybe Lucy will let me taste her next time I stay over.

Then I felt his hand strike me. It stung. His hands were bigger than I realised and hurt more than the ruler!
Ouch!

He swapped from cheek to cheek, his strokes hurting and stinging each time, making me move a little. So, he used a hand to press me down, pressing me harder into his cock. I felt him stop now and then, feeling my bottom and occasionally slipping a finger between my legs. I liked that feeling. I wanted him to slip a finger in me.

But then he returned to the spanking. I looked at his watch and he had been hitting me for 5 minutes; I was enjoying it now, and it seemed he never tired of hitting my bottom. The stinging was still there, but it was pleasant now, the warming of my bottom somehow making it pleasurable. And when he paused the spanking to feel my bottom. I was almost praying that he would slide a finger down to slip it into my little flower.
Yes, finger fuck me, Sir.

Eventually, the seven minutes were up. He removed the panties and I realised I was crying! I don't recall that starting, but now he had stopped spanking me. I could feel the tears running down my cheeks. Mr Wyles used the damp panties to wipe away my

tears. I could see black stains; my mascara must have run as well.

Then Mr Wyles did something unexpected, but so lovely. I almost cried again. He hugged me, settling me down on his lap. *His arms feel so good.*

I wiggled, to get his hard cock in the best place possible, pressing along my pussy. It was such a nice feeling even though I longed to feel his flesh against mine, the press of his hard cock against my flower, the way it separated my vulva as he held me. My pussy was soaking and getting wetter all the time, but he did not seem to mind that I was making his trousers wet. I wondered if I should wiggle a little; I was sure he would like the feel of my little special place wiggling against his hard cock.

He told me how happy I made him, and that I could obviously feel how happy he was with me. But he said today was an introduction really and that he was going to train me in the way a submissive should behave. Or at least how he wants me to behave and promise of a treat later if I behave. I don't know what he had in mind, but I was going to be the bestest little girl for Mr Wyles, today that is for sure.

Rebecca's Story.
Crush.
Chapter: 5 His breath

Mr Wyles held me like that for what seemed an eternity. I really did not want him to ever let me go. His embrace felt so good, and so did my flower, pressing against his hard cock. I liked that I had made Mr Wyles, Sir as he wants me to call him, excited, hard and he was very hard.

I had to wonder why he did not just fuck me here on the sofa. Most boys say if they get hard, they have to cum, as it hurts them. Usually, that means I have to have sex with them or give them a blowie. But Mr Wyles has been hard for some time and was hard in his office and he never made me make him cum. Though I would have, I would like to suck Mr Wyles cock. If I can fit it into my mouth, that is.

He tells me I am a good girl once again and then shows me about the house. I can't wait to meet the dogs. I see the bedrooms and the bathrooms. His bedroom is wonderful, looks old-fashioned but in a posh way, enormous bed and dark wood panelling...

But he tells me I won't be sleeping here unless he invites me. I feel a little down about that. I was hoping he would throw me on the bed now and take me finally. But he is showing me more. He takes me up to the loft room and oh my god; it is beautiful, and I am excited to see lots of rope and a massive four-poster bed.

The bed has metal rings on the posts with scarves tied to them. I can guess what those are for. As I imagine myself being tied up while wearing my uniform spread wide on the bed.

Mr Wyles could do what he wanted to me, tied like that! That was a happy thought, though, and I could feel myself tingling down below again. My panties would be soaking...
If I was wearing any, lol.

He shows me the dog cage; I had wondered if they slept up here but seems he likes to make girls sleep in the cage! I did not like the sound of that... I wanted to be wrapped in his arms at night, not stuck in a cold metal cage.
Then something he called a Spaniard donkey that looked very uncomfortable. I would not like to sit on that!
That would hurt my flower...

He shows me the ropes. He seems excited when talking about rope like it is a big passion. Sir tells me he might tie with me a little later. I am dancing inside. I am so excited.
Yes, rope! Tie me up. Please.

I let it slip that I had seen his rope; he looks at me oddly and I explained that I looked at his FB and IG accounts and found some images of him and the girl. I thought he might be annoyed or angry, but he seemed relieved for some reason. So glad I have that off my chest, I felt so guilty for snooping.

He took me out to what he called a veranda. I have never seen anything like this before and the view was beautiful. He said he sits up here naked sometimes during the warm summer evenings. I think I would like that.

Mr Wyles says the best is yet to come. I can't imagine what room is better than the loft. That was heaven. I can't wait to be tied and hung from Mr Wyles rope or tied to that bed. I would let him do anything he wanted. Not that I could stop him if I was tied, I suppose. A very naughty thought, but a happy one.

We enter the kitchen. I'm confused still. This is not the best room, this is a kitchen, I want to go back to the loft again, be

tied, and hang from one of those poles. Then Sir pulls out this cupboard and there is a stairway hidden behind!
That is so cool…

Mr Wyles takes my hand and leads me down the stairs. It's his dungeon! He shows me about the room, explaining about all the toys and benches. Letting me touch the straps, floggers, and canes, he tells me I am not ready for the cane yet. I am relieved, but I pouted a little, so he thinks I want it. I don't think I do…
Do I?

He shows me a cabinet that he calls a grope box. I got the idea of the box straight away. I have played a game like this at friends' houses where we go in the closet with a boy and let them touch us. I go inside and see a hole at waist level; I stick my tongue out, guessing that is what it is for. I have seen glory hole videos on Pornhub and know that some guys like to stick their cocks in them and get them sucked. I kinda hope that Mr Wyles was going to put his cock in the hole, but he didn't.
Sulk face.

Then Sir told me he wanted me to see what I was going to be expected to do, and he led me over to what he called a horse. Pushed me over it and told me to watch a video as he strapped me in…
Yes, push me down, tie me, fuck me, Sir.

He walked away, leaving me there, telling me to watch and see what he expects from his submissive's. I watch as he leads a woman to the cross thingy and hits her with various toys. He seems to be building up as each one seems to be more hurt than the other. I watch as he swings the floggers; he demoed them to me earlier and they do look cool.
Sir is so cool. She is lucky. I want to be her!

Then he used various paddles and straps. At last, it seems it is time for the canes. The woman cried out a lot and looks like she

wants to run at one point, but Mr Wyles just waits, and she returns to the position again, allowing him to use the cane on her bottom. Wow, she must really like the pain. I think I would have run out of the room.

I was right. I don't think I would like the cane; it leaves nasty marks on her, and I can hear her cry out after each strike.
Ohh god, that looks painful.

Mr Wyles drops the cane, and the woman turns to him. He hugs her for a little, then says something I can't hear, and she gets on her knees, and he pulls out his cock. It looks big! As big as I had imagined it being, and she puts it in her mouth. He takes hold of her head and starts pushing it in really fast like he is fucking her face. I never like it when boys try that... But she seems to like it. Maybe I have been doing it wrong. Maybe Sir Will teach me how?

She is choking a little and drooling a lot, but she has it all in, and I hear Mr Wyles call her a good girl as he holds her head to his waist. His cock must be all the way in her mouth now.
Good girl! I can be a good girl, too.

He then grabs her hair and pushes her to the ground. I watch as he guides his saliva covered cock into her. I think it was her arse. Mr Wyles is not being gentle, and I can hear her cry out as he thrusts his cock into her. That is so hot. He just takes her like she is his.
I want to be his.

I have tried this, but it hurt, and I stopped the boy. I had to suck him off to make it up to him, which was ok as I like the way they cry out as I suck them off, making them cum on my face. It's like I have a superpower when I use my mouth. The boys will agree to anything.

He is being very rough, but she is enjoying it. He is calling her names but now and then he calls her a good girl and she calls him daddy? Something like is daddy really happy with me, and sir replied with yes princess. I would love to be Sir's princess.

I think I would love being called a princess by Mr Wyles.
I feel something on my pussy; I was soaked and tingly there, and now something blew across my moist flower.

It's Sir!
My heart is going to explode!

I hear Mr Wyles,
"You can say no, by calling red at any time, please confirm you understand this."

I understand this. I have heard it before; he is telling me I don't have to do anything I don't want or like.
But I know I do want this. I want him to touch me. I want to feel him in me, his kisses, his hands on me, even what he did to that woman, if that is what it takes to hear him call me a good girl again… Or better still Princess.

"Yes, Sir, I can call red to stop anything I don't like."

He calls me a good girl; I am so happy…

I feel his lips kiss my flower! I have never been kissed there before. Ohh it feels so nice. His lips kiss my pussy, sucking on my clit. I feel his tongue exploring, sliding between my legs, and then his tongue is on my rosebud! My arsehole, he is licking it! and now his tongue is in my bum…
OMG OMG OMG.

It feels so nice. Why has no one ever told me this is so good… I want to feel it, and he pulls away. I try to press it in again, I

don't want it to stop! He presses in again and I cum... I am shaking so much now it feels so good.
Please, Sir, don't stop...

The video had ended. I heard Mr Wyles as he cried out. He made quite a noise, sounding almost like a wild animal... Now she licks his cock again even though it was just buried deep in her arse! That's kind of nasty! But if she is sucking him after it has been in there; I suppose she prepped herself. I have heard that they do that on porn. I will make sure to prep from now on.

Mr Wyles stops licking and kissing me in that special place; my rosebud and my flower are both tingling and wet. I wish he would just fuck me, fuck me like he did that woman. I would not even mind sucking his cock after he had been in me. I just want Mr Wyles to take me, to fuck me like he did that woman, to make me his slut...

He unstraps me and then tells me about what he has in mind for me, that it is not all sex.
But I want that!

He tells me about rope, assuring me that there will be a lot of rope. This makes me happy as his rope looked so pretty and I am sure I will look very pretty tied up and helpless.
Then he talks about wax and UV (I'm not sure what UV is, but it does sound fun).

Bath and showers also sound fun. I love the idea of being bathed by Mr Wyles.
Then he mentions dressing up, this is so cool. Lots of costumes to dress up in and he says he will buy them for me, so I can look pretty for him. I will love dressing for Mr Wyles, I just know it...
A rubber dress, please let there be rubber.

Mr Wyles tells me about the sex stuff he wants.

Cock worship.
Well, I already do worship your cock, Sir.

Anal, well I guess I will have to learn how to take a cock. It will hurt, but if Mr Wyles wants my arse, I will let him have it even if it makes me cry. Anyway, the girls on the videos like it well enough and they take some very large cocks. I am sure I can learn to take Sirs.

Orgasm denial sounds hard. I don't know how I will ever manage to hold that back! Is it even possible? Now he is talking about punishments and something he called funishments, and he explains about calling red once again, explaining what it means.

I do understand and I like that I can say no, even if I think I would never say that to Mr Wyles.
I trust you, Sir.

I tell Mr Wyles that I understand about negotiating and it is nice that I can ask for things I like as well.
Please, Sir, lick my pussy again.

Mr Wyles takes me up to the kitchen again and hides the dungeon entrance… That is so bloody cool. He orders me to stand in the corner and wait for him! I hate being put in the corner, but I do as I am told. I'm a good girl, me. I hope that he tells me that again soon.

Rebecca's Story.
Crush.

Chapter 6: A walk in the woods.

Sir was gone for ages, it seemed, but I don't move. When he returned, I hear him coming down the stairs and tried to look like I had not been bored, stood here all this time. Maybe he will call me a good girl again.

He orders me to follow, but he is smiling, which makes me happy even if he did not call me a good girl. Maybe it takes more than just doing what I am told to be called a good girl.

He takes me out to meet the dogs and I fall in love with them straight away. They are so lovely and well behaved. I recalled their names and repeated them to Sir. He smiles happily again. I like it when he smiles at me. I tell Mr Wyles about my dog and how much I miss him. He is smiling at us as I play with the doggos for a little while, then he leads me and the dogs down the garden to a gate.

The dogs are so cute.

He lets me take one of the dogs on a leash and we walk across the field towards some woodlands. We get to a path in the woods, and he tells me to let off Freki, and he lets Geri go and they both run off into the woods, obviously enjoying their freedom.

I want to run with them too.

Sir is talking, telling me about himself and the sort of things he does at clubs. Some of it sounds exciting and I guess he is letting me know the sort of stuff we could be getting up to eventually. I like the sound of the clubs and especially naked Sub Day. Being led around on a lead, like a dog, naked so everyone can see how

pretty I am. I would have to learn my place as they held competitions and tested subs for their obedience. I would like that and would never let Sir down, I am sure. I would be like a well-trained dog, walking at his heel.

We reached a spot in the wood Sir stopped and indicated we would stop here. It was a pretty spot, with flowers, a low bank and a shallow stream. Mr Wyles said he would like to take some photos of me paddling into the water. He told me I would look like a beautiful wood nympho or something. I really liked being called beautiful, especially by Sir.

I said I would love to pose and went and danced happily in the water before removing my dress and playing in the waters again. It was so freeing being naked in the woods. I know we were deep in the woods, but someone could still come along and see me... I think I liked the idea of being caught as well; it felt kind of bad but exciting too. I do like being watched. Maybe Sir will like that too.

He asked me to play in some flowers and took some more photos. I bet they were pretty pictures of my naked body lying in a bed of flowers. Now I think that would be art. No one ever made me feel a beautiful as Mr Wyles was making me feel right now. I was striking poses. I was not really sure what I was doing, but Mr Wyles guided me and was calling me beautiful, sexy and a good girl when I got the pose right.
I love you...

Then he took the rope out of his pack. I think I wet myself when I saw it, or came, maybe both, I was so excited about being tied up by Sir.

It is hard to explain the feeling of being tied, but I will try.

Mr Wyles ran the rope across my skin, my neck, and my arms. It was a bit scratchy and not like the rope in his room, but it still

257

felt nice. He even rubbed it against my nipples, which were still a little puffy, even though I had a good C cup these days. That was a lovely, nice feeling, though. But then my mind drifted to the thought of Sir's lips on my nipples. If I were wearing panties, they would be dripping right now.

He took my hands behind my back and tied them both together, then wound the rope about me. He was so close, though, I could feel his breath on my neck as he tied. My knees nearly buckled a few times. He then ran the rope below my breasts, cupping each as he passed the rope under them. I felt him squeeze each breast. As he squeezed, I heard a murmur from him in my ear, as if he liked the feel.

This made me so happy, Mr Wyles liking my body the way he did. He had mentioned how lovely and long my legs were, how pretty he thought my flower was. He also said I tasted like candy, and he said he enjoyed tasting me earlier.
You can lick me anytime Sir, my flower is yours.

He told me he knew I liked it as I had climaxed on his tongue, and he had drunk me all up. I had a very silly smile on my face as he spoke. I could not believe he thought I tasted like candy.
I can't wait to taste Sir on my lips.

He told me that I had pleased him today and that if I wanted and with some training, I could be his submissive. He explained a lot about what this meant; I did not understand it all, but he said it will take time (I did not really think so, I would say yes now if he asked). He insisted that it will take time and it will have to wait until after I finished school. He was going to help me with the exams, as he wanted me to do well.

This was so odd. No one ever cared before how I did. All assumed I would get pregnant and have someone look after me like mum did. He said he will teach me and if I do well, I could be his submissive if I wanted to.

258

I said, "I honestly do want to Sir, I want to learn and be a good submissive for Sir, I want to be Sir's..." I assured him. I hoped he could see how much in my eyes. Looking down from Sir's eyes, I could see how much he wanted me to.

His cock wants me...

Mr Wyles then undid his trousers and pulled out his cock. It was as big as it seemed when I saw it on the video earlier. Not massive, though, which was good. Not sure I would be able to handle something too big.

He told me this was my reward for being so good today. If that is my reward for being good, I will always be good for Sir.

Then he pressed his cock to my lips. He told me I had to make him cum, and that I was not to spit. Mr Wyles did not know I guess, I never spit, though it was a kind of nasty, at times. I liked it; it made me feel like I was a good girl. Just like the girls in the video, I would swallow the cum if they got it in my mouth. Some boys shot it over my face, messy, and it made me feel very naughty. I loved that feeling.

Mr Wyles told me to show him what I know, how I suck cock. I wanted him to love me, and I knew if I did well that he might want me to do it again and again. He told me I was good, but then he took hold of my head and pulled it down hard.

Gack!

I could feel his cock at the back of my throat. I wanted to take it, but I choked, and he let up. I felt bad for not being able to take his cock the way the girl did in the video, so tried and tried again. I just could not do it; his cock was so big that it would not go down before I choked each time. But I tried, and he was smiling when I looked up at him.

I like that I make you smile.

I hear him growling and he shaking as I felt his cock jerk in my mouth and then my mouth filled with his cum; I remembered not to spit and not to swallow, as he had directed me.
Tastes a little icky. Don't spit. Don't swallow. Wait.

He told me I was a good girl.
So happy.

He went over to get his camera. He wanted a photo of his cum in my mouth; it was getting cool and starting to taste funny, but I did as I was told. When he returned, I stuck out my tongue a little to show I still had his offering in my mouth, and he took some photos before I was allowed to swallow. At last, that was getting to be horrible. But I was a good girl, though, and did as he told me.

He told me I had done well but I could do better; He wanted me to practice and had a gift to help me back at the house. I had an idea what it was. My own dildo, I won't have to steal mums anymore. But as I did not do well enough, a lesson had to be taught. I had to learn that if I did not try hard enough or please Sir, I would get a punishment.
But I made you cum, Sir! I will do better next time, I promise.

I hoped it was another spanking. My butt still felt a little sore from the one earlier, but I loved Mr Wyles' hands on my bum. But he told me to hug the tree. I was disappointed but went over to the tree and wrapped my arms around it. The bark was rough against my tits and belly, but I did as he told me. Then I felt the coarse rope on my back as he hit me like he did the girl with the floggers in the video. That hurt a little, but not as much as spanking.

On the way back to Mr Wyles's house I took over walking both dogs and even managed to control them while Sir walked on ahead. Mr Wyles was very happy with me for controlling them so well and was happy that the dogs seemed to like me.

I think I danced all the way back to the house; I was so happy. Rope, praise pretty photos and the look on Mr Wyles's face as I made him explode in my mouth... I could see it in his eyes. Mr Wyles was never going to ignore me again after today. He is going to love me. He just does not know it yet.

Later that night, I took out Mr Wyles's gift. Mum was out, so I went into her room and used her big mirror on the door to her wardrobe to attach the suction dildo. I watched a training video on how to deep throat and started practising. I promised myself that the next time I will take all of Sir's cock in my mouth...

It was a lot harder to get it to the back of my throat. The dildo was about 7 inches long and maybe as fat as Mr Wyles's cock. The girl in the video said it takes a while to get past the gag reflex and not to worry if you can't do it straight away. I kept trying, though, and I did get it all in but nearly threw up. So, I stopped pushing so hard.

After I cleaned the mirror and the drool that was running down to the floor now. Mr Wyles said I need to learn not to drool so much as he does not like sloppy blowjobs. I promised myself that I would practice every night.

I was naughty in the night. Sir had said not to use this for anything but practice, but I wanted to feel it in me. It was about the size of Mr Wyles's cock, and I could not help imagining it was him as I slid it in and out of my flower until I climaxed. I then l put it in my mouth imaging myself cleaning Sirs' cock after he had fucked me, just like a good slut should. Sir was right. I do taste sweet. I very much like the taste of my pussy. I hope someday soon I can taste another girl's pussy.
Must call Lucy.

Rebecca's Story.
Crush.
Chapter 7 Suspended.

At school the next week, I made sure to sit at the front of the class but not in front of Mr Wyles's desk. My friends teased me a little, but I told them I just needed to study for my exams, and I had been told that I should sit in the front so I could see and hear better, which was true, Sir had said he thought I would do better sat there...

I realised after a few days I found that I could follow the classes better. Mr Wyles walked past me in the hall one morning and smiled at me and said, good morning, Rebecca, no one was near so only I heard him, but it made me so happy.
He loves me, I just know it.

On Friday, he asked me to stay behind after the lesson; I was worried for a bit, thinking I had done something wrong in class. But he told me he was pleasantly surprised with my work this week and then in a lower voice as the door was open that I should wear normal clothes this weekend as although the dress was beautiful, he felt that it might be suspicious if I dressed like that all the time to go to his.

My friends were waiting, so he sent me on my way. I had to think about what he said about my clothes. I had planned to wear another summer dress this weekend but what he said made sense I guess, and there was mum. She had been asking questions about his house. So, I decided to wear jeans and a T-shirt. I enjoy wearing jeans as they show off my legs and bum.

I was practising every night, but I still could not get the dildo all the way in without throwing up a little, but I was controlling the drool more. I hope Mr Wyles checks to see how much I have learned this weekend. I love the way he smiles and the joy on his

face as he looks at me while I held his cock in my mouth. I love his eyes when he looks down at me. It feels so right being on my knees looking up at Sir.

On Saturday, I was excited. I think mum was wondering why I was excited, but I told her it was because I was seeing the doggos today, not the tutoring. She would have thought it odd that I have started to enjoy learning, but I think I actually was, for the first time in a long time. I showered, and I shaved all my hair from my flower.
I adore that name from my special place.

I wanted Mr Wyles to see how pretty it looked all smooth and exposed, and maybe he would lick me again like he did the other week.
That felt so good.

When I entered the house, he told me to strip and waited while I did this. He looked me up and down and smiled when he noticed I had shaved. Telling me it made him happy, and it was very pretty. He told me to wait, but as he went, I could see him looking back at me, smiling. I liked the way he looked at me. Like he was going to eat me.
Hopefully.

He came back later with some clothes, underwear and makeup and told me to get dressed in it. I have never worn anything like this. Not even mum has sexy underwear like this set. It was silky smooth and a bit retro, I think, something you see on old fashion films from the fifties or sixties. The Makeup was from Kat Von D. How Sir knew I would like her stuff I don't know but I loved him for knowing.
He is so clever, and this outfit, swoon.

I looked so grown up and felt so sexy in this set. I had put on deep red lipstick and tried my best to be creative with the eyeliner. I hope he liked it. I was worried that I did not do it

right, that Sir would think I was silly, but his smile when he saw me told me I had done well.

He had his camera out, and I did several poses and again he was guiding me and telling me how pretty I was, how hot I looked in the outfit and I was dancing about after a while as he took photos. He told me I was learning fast and a natural in front of the camera.

He is so nice to me.

Mr Wyles said he would get me some other outfits to wear soon. I was looking forward to trying them on for him and he again called me beautiful. My heart aches every time he says that.

When I went to sit on the chair for today's lesson, I saw a vibrator of some sort in one of the holes. Mr Wyles told me to sit with my legs on either side, so it kisses my pussy. I will have to tell him to call it my flower.

Apparently today I would have to endure the vibrator as I learned and if I got any questions wrong, he would turn it up and make me sit for another 10 minutes. I don't know how I will be able to study with the vibrator against my little clit, but if Mr Wyles tells me I have to, I will.

Mr Wyles also set up a video camera, telling me he would watch it when I was not there, as he enjoyed seeing me like this. I think I blushed a little. Even though the vibrator was set at the lowest setting, I still found it very difficult to concentrate. Seeing Sir watching me like that, and the constant vibrations, made me cum so like I have never cum before. I thought I was going to faint the second time. I am sure I messed up the test, I just hoped it was not too bad.

I need one of these, oh my goddess.

I got five wrong! I was going to have to revise again and sit here for another fifty minutes! Fifty Minutes with the Vibrator set

even higher. And Sir said there will be another punishment if I get any wrong after that.
Gulp, fifty minutes!

Mr Wyles turned up the vibrator. Oh, my goddess, that felt so intense and so good, but how was I ever going to be able to concentrate on the book, feeling like this?
OMG, that feels amazing.

Mr Wyles left the room, which was a relief as I could squirm about on the chair a little, though the camera was still going so I did not dare move away from the vibrator. I came several times; the seat was wet, but I kept trying to read the study book.

But then I felt a massive climax building inside me. I held on to the desk, shaking as I think I wet myself. I was scared Sir was going to be angry, but then I had another climax and it happened again! My panties are soaked, my legs are dripping.
What did I do?

My body shook for several minutes after. I was sweating and tears were rolling down my cheeks as I tried to think about what had happened? I cheated and moved away from the vibrator so I could think straight and stop shaking for a minute or two.

I thought about the porn I had seen; I had seen women pee during sex before, and the men were never unhappy. There was a name for it, I think. Gushing that what they called it gushing. Had I just gushed? I did not know I could do that. I hoped Mr Wyles would be happy about it even if I had made the floor wet. I looked around the desk and there was a huge puddle.

Mr Wyles was not unhappy though; he was ecstatic even kissed me on the lips. Our first kiss. Yes, yes, yes, kiss me.

He removed my wet panties and after fitting a collar and lead on me like a dog one. He then placed the soaking wet panties in my mouth. They are soaking wet and smell a little of my flower.

He then put a new pair on me. I watched as he lifted them up, his face so close to my flower, I really wanted him to run his tongue through my petals again. But he did not even shake his head. I think he wanted to, but it was not the time.

Lick me, Sir, lick me like you did last time, tell me how nice I taste. Please…

He then led me out into the garden. I could see he had a new cage built, that was quick as there were only two last week.

He put me in one, attaching the lead to a hook and pointing out the cameras that were watching the cages. Sir told me I had to stay here for an hour.

An hour!

An hour, In the cage like a dog. Well, at least the dogs were happy to see me.

I said hello to the doggies, drank from the bowl, looked back at the camera to show Sir I was being a good little girl and eating the food (it was a breakfast cereal, not dog food) and drinking my water as instructed. The dogs kept me company, and I talked to them about Mr Wyles, sharing secrets as I knew they would never tell on me.

The hour was not too bad as it was sunny, and the dogs were there. When Mr Wyles came out to get me and the dogs, he told me to put on a coverall and change my shoes for now. When we reached the woods, though, I was allowed to remove the coverall and walk in the lingerie set he had given me. I feel so sexy and so bad right now.

266

Once again, Mr Wyles led me through the woods. While the dogs run off and played, I was dressed in a black underwear set, bra, waspie cincher, a suspender set and matching panties, so clever of Sir to have ordered a spare pair...
Maybe he knew I would do that.

I think I looked incredibly hot, and secretly hoped that someone might see me; I liked the idea of being seen, and I was planning to go to the park tomorrow wearing something short so they could see my panties. Maybe I would flash mum's boyfriend, totally by accident, of course.
Wink, wink, evil grin.

We reached a spot by the river again and Sir told me to play with the dogs while he prepared. I watch him as he set up a strap and ring on the big tree. It looked a bit like his loft room set up and I knew he was going to suspend me; he had promised, and I think Sir likes to keep his promises. I like that, people always say things they don't mean. Like dad.
Loser.

Then Mr Wyles stood me in front of him and tied a harness about me. Something dragon, he told me. I liked how it felt against my body; I loved how close he was, how his hands touched me as he tied me. I wanted to be naked, so I could feel his rope against my flesh, feel his hands touch my breasts as he tied the surrounding rope. Maybe I could ask. He did tell me I could ask him anything. Part of negotiating play meant that I could ask for stuff as well. Maybe next time I will ask to be tied naked. I loved being naked around Sir.

He fixed a rope about my legs, his hand touching my special place now and then as he ran the rope through my legs. I wondered if he could feel me getting damp again. Then suddenly I was off my feet and flying.

He tied my feet and told me to move about while he took photos; the rope was a little tight, but it felt so good too; I was able to move about a bit and pull my legs in and straighten them out if I wanted. He adjusted the tie a few times, allowing me to move about like a model posing for her photographer. I felt so special, like a bird or something. Sir kept checking I was ok too. I loved that he cared so much about me, that he was always thinking about me, even when he was taking pictures. I feel safe with him. He would not hurt me. OK well yes, he will (remembering spanking) but not by accident.

Then he untied me, lowering me down to the ground where he was waiting for me. He caught me in his arms as he released the rope and cradled me there while I came down from my rope high.

Hold me, forever.

On the way back to Sir's house, I thought about the rope and the BJ I had given him. He said I had done so much better this week and he looked so happy again as I held his cock in my mouth after he had cum, making sure I got every little of his cum. I showed him again, and he called me a good girl and then I swallowed it and showed him my empty mouth.

I enjoyed making him smile like that. I was walking alone with the dogs, in my heels and sexy underwear, really hoping some old man would come along and catch me. Bet that would make his year seeing a cute eighteen-year-old girl in sexy sixties underwear. It would probably give them a hard-on or maybe a heart attack lol. I was so going to the park tomorrow, sitting on the swigs and letting the old pervs have a treat.

I waited for Sir at the edge of the woods; he was packing the rope stuff away, so would not be too long, I am sure. The dogs were happy, and I loved being with them.

When I got to the house, I cleaned up, and we talked about next weekend. He was going away and needed me to watch the dogs. He thought, and I agreed that my mother would probably want to check out the house. I had told him she was asking a lot of questions about him. Worried that he might be taking advantage of me. I had laughed, thinking if she only knew what we got up to. The house to myself. I am so going to be naked all day.

Mr Wyles said it was ok though, and he expected this. He would make sure the house was safe for her to look around. She would not find the dungeon, and he would lock the loft room.

The next week, we did some revision, and though Sir watched me as usual. I had dressed in trousers and blouse, and he did not make me strip or play with me! He never spanked me for the questions I got wrong. Instead, he went over the errors and looked at why I had gotten them wrong.

He was teaching me and told me that I was actually doing well and if I studied hard for the next few weeks, I could pass my exams with good enough grades. I might even get into a college. Maybe clearing, but still, he thought I could go to college. No one had ever said that before. Sir actually cares about me, not just my body, but my mind.
I love him.

He left me with the dogs, some money to buy a pizza, and I sat with the dogs all night, watching videos and movies. I slept in the guest room, as he told me to. I wanted to sneak into his room, but he would know, I am sure. The dogs slept with me, though. They weren't supposed to, but I missed having a dog in my bed at home, so I let them this time.

Mum, when she picked me up, had a little nosey about the house.
She is so embarrassing.

She saw my room (Ok the guest room) and checked out Mr Wyles's, admiring the ensuite bathroom. We only have one and Sir's bedroom is as big as mine and mum's rooms together. She asked about his family with kids; I said I had not asked, as I was busy studying. But I made a note to let Sir know what she had said. Maybe he could think of something to put her mind at rest. I introduced her to the dog's mum was taken with them as well. She may be a bit of an embarrassment, but she does love dogs.

Rebecca's Story.
Crush.

Chapter 8 Show and tell.

The next few weeks are full of study and no play. Mr Wyles tells me it will be worthwhile, and that he is very happy with me. I keep doing well in the tests he sets, which make him smile at me... I love it when he smiles at me. But I love the smile he gives me when I suck his cock more.

At home each night, I study and practice with the dildo when I can, using the mirror in mum's room when she is out. I also started using her sex toys while I'm practising. It feels so naughty to have one in my pussy while I am trying to deep throat the other.
I am a slut! Giggles.

I told Mr Wyles about this, and he smiled and told me he was not surprised and maybe one day he will arrange for me to have two cocks at the same time! Maybe if I ask right, more than two. But he says that is something for the future and he will not make me do something like that unless I ask. More than two!
Could I do that?

I got bored with the park, teasing the dirty old men and dads that would watch me play on the swings. So last Sunday I went to town in only my little summer dress. No panties or bra. I rode up the escalator many times at the mall. I bet some people got a good look at my bottom and even a glimpse or two of my pussy.

I really like being seen; Sir has told me he thinks I am an exhibitionist. I think he is right. He has promised that he will show me off lots once I have finished school. I am looking forward to that. I told him I would like to go to one of those naked subs nights. being naked in front of dozens of men. The

thought alone makes my panties damp or would if I was wearing any.
Tee hee.

I think it is nice that I can tell Mr Wyles about these things, and he is not judging me. Mum would have a fit if she knew what I had done at the mall. Though I think she knows I have been borrowing her dildo. It was missing from where she usually kept it, and I could not find it anywhere.
Sulk.

Sir just has told me he is going away for a weekend.
Sad girl.

But he told me to go to the loft room, there was a surprise and oh my, was there. I squealed when I saw what Mr Wyles had laid out on the bed for me. He is so good to me.

A dress not just a dress but several outfits, a Lolita dress that I was admiring in the mirror when Sir made it up to the room. It was beautiful. I loved it, but Sir had said I could not try it on today.

Then I see a black shiny rubber dress, lots of buckles on the waist, so it is a bit like a corset, it is beautiful.
Yay Rubber dress. So happy.

Then I spot the catsuit, black rubber again, with a corset waist cincher. This must be why Mr Wyles measured me a few weeks ago to get my size. I better not overindulge. I think this is going to be a tight fit.
I love it...

Sir says this is for our first club night. I almost faint the excitement is too much! Outfits and a club visit! He says after the exam's sweetie; He calls me that now and then when I am being a bit silly or giddy and I am feeling very giddy now. But I

secretly love him calling me that. Although Princess and good girl are better.

There are masks and more sexy underwear, and a net dress Sir says I can wear with or without underwear. It is almost transparent. That would be amazing to be out like that. Dressed but not dressed. He shows me a mask collection and I agree that I should wear one when out with him. I don't want him to get into trouble and dating a student is frowned upon.
Silly rules.

When he drops me off, he comes in to talk with mum, and he is charming her, I can see. I don't like it, but I know he is just trying to make friends with her. He checks that it is ok to have me stay over for two nights next weekend as he is away.

Mum is ok with it. Means she can have her boyfriend over and not have me in the way. Sir has told me he has sanitised the house and loft room. Mum had tried the door last time and I know she wondered what was up there.
Nosy bitch.

Sir said he will put out some pictures that should put her mind at rest for now. Though she will eventually work out something is going on after I finish school and continue my tuition. He said we will have to deal with that when the time comes.

I go to my room and open his new gift; he gave it to me on the way over; He said I need to practice with this as he will want to be able to fuck my bottom soon. I wish he would fuck me now, but he is making me wait until after exams are over with.

I think to myself I wonder if I can use all three together, but maybe I should start small and do as Sir has asked. I have never done anal, not even a finger. Just Mr Wyles's tongue. Such a fun memory. I wish he would do that again and soon. I am excited by the very thought of Sir's tongue in my arse.

273

So naughty, but felt so good. Is it hot in here?

I have been getting really good with the other dildo, though. I have not told Sir, but I managed to get it down my throat with ease the other week and I had been practising on mum's dildo until this week. I intend (when I find it) to be able to take all of it by the weekend; it is as thick as mine but longer, it will be hard, but I am sure I can deep throat it now. Mr Wyles will be so happy when he sees me swallow his cock.
I bet his eyes will be really wide and his smile wider hehe.

The dildo Sir got me is an odd shape, about the same length but tapered to a smaller head.

I suppose that is to make it easier to get in. There is lube in the box, so I used a little and try it in the bathroom.

It hurt a bit, but soon I relaxed and got most of it in my bum. It was an odd feeling, but I started to fuck my little rosebud like it was my pussy. I needed to use some more lube, but I got a good rhythm with it and thought this is quite pleasant. I tried the bigger dildo, but that hurt still, so I will do as Sir suggested and use this for a little each night until I can take the bigger one.
He is always right...

As we suspected, when Mum dropped me off, she had a good look around again. This time she checked the loft, loving the room. I told her it's the room he uses in the summer. The wardrobe was locked, but she did not try to look inside, anyway.
Imagine her face if it was not locked, lol.

She loved the veranda, saying this would be a lovely house to live in, so big perfect for raising a family. "It is a shame about his wife."
Back off, bitch, he is mine.

274

This threw me for a second, but then I remembered the faked photo he had put out and the cover story about his wife passing away a few years ago. So, mum thought he was a widower that was just not ready to marry again. I hope she did not think she could swoop in and get his interest. I had to laugh when she warned me not to ruin this arrangement by inviting boys over. Like I wanted a boy. When I had Mr Wyles...

After mum left, I did the revision Sir had left out for me. I find I am enjoying the material now, even understanding it, which never really happened before. Mr Wyles thinks I will get Cs and maybe Bs in the test and that will be enough to get me into a college somewhere.
College! Me!

I go and shower, using Sir's bathroom. His shower is so much nicer than the guest one. I shave and cleanings myself ready for tonight. I have something special planned and want to send a thank you to Sir.
I walk about the house naked, been so long since I have been able to do that, it has been study, study, study these last few weeks, but I understand what Sir is doing. He wants me to succeed, pass my exam and go to college. Have a chance at a career.
But I do love being naked.

I head up to the loft room, carrying the laptop and cam equipment. I video myself dancing around naked. I think Mr Wyles will like that when he finds it on his laptop. But I have something more special in mind as a thank you.
I must stop grinning.

I go over to the wardrobe and use the key that is hidden under the bed on a little hook to unlock it. I pull out the catsuit and blindfold masque that goes with it and slip it on. Well, slip it on is a simplification. I pull and tug it on. Rubber is hard work, but once I have it on and buckled up, I look bloody amazing. I get

the bottle of shine out and polish up the suit. I worked up a sweat getting that on, but so worth the effort.

I set up the camera, pointing at the large mirrors that are on the wall, check the positioning on the laptop screen, make adjustments until I am happy. I decide that tonight I am going to show Mr Wyles that my exams are not all I have studied for. *He is going to love this…*

I unzip the back-access zip (they think of everything these designers) Add a little lube to my rosebud, pick up the scarf I am using to tie my hands and then the dildo I brought up from the dungeon. This one is big much bigger than mine, longer than mum's even. But I am determined that I will do this. *No, I am not nervous. Shut up.*

I stuck the dildo onto the mirror at head height, turn to face the camera, unzipped my back zipper, and slid the anal toy all the way into the base and then zipped up. Then I lowered my blindfold and wrap my wrists behind my back using the scarf. I then try to find the dildo with my mouth missing and getting poked in the side of the face. I laugh a little at that. Using my tongue, I find the end of the dildo and run my tongue up and down it, slowly licking the rubber cock, imagining it was Sir's cock. He is not as big and really, I would not want to have someone this big as fuck me. But playing with it like this was hot.

I slowly worked the dildo, unable to see how much I was getting in my mouth, but I intended to get all 11 or twelve inches in! I had managed mums' dildo the other week and that is ten inches! My throat was sore for a day…
So worth it, though.

I slide up and down my spit lubrication on the dildo and allow me to get past the first obstacle, my gag spot. I had learned to control this now, though sometimes it still made me choke a

little. But once passed there, it was easy going. I slid down a little more each time, thinking how hot Sir will find this video later. Ok, a little gagging, still I am getting there.
Gack…

I felt it as I reached the end. My throat was full now. I don't think I could take any more, but my lips pressed up against the base. I pulled all the way out and turned to where the camera should be and smiled a very dribbly smile. (My hands were tied so I could not wipe the drool away.)

Then I swallowed it whole, my tongue out so it could lick the base of the dildo and the mirror if I was lucky. I proceeded to throat fuck myself on the rubber cock for a few minutes. My throat was a little sore, but I was taking at least four inches down my throat.

That was hot. I want to do that for real.
I edited the video then sent it to Sir later that night.

Sir sent a message back later with a photo of his hand. I could see it was covered in cum. He told me he had to wank watching that video. Said I was so sexy and looked amazing in that catsuit. He told me he was very impressed with my skills and could not wait to feel my mouth wrapped around his cock. I wish I was there to lick that off his hand, I bet he would like that.

Sir tells me it is time to think of a kink name, but I have already found one. I had been thinking about this for a few weeks and found one in an old book I was reading. Yes, I am actually reading for fun now! How things have changed these last few months.
I is becoming smart lol.

The following weeks are all exams, I don't get to see sir even on the weekend (I did message him but as per our rules I kept it

polite and clean) telling him that I had felt ok in the exams and even felt that I knew the answers. I said I missed the doggos. Sir knew that meant him as well. And I will still be able to look after them for him if he wants. Cover story, of course. I love the dogs, but it is Sir I want to see.

I finished school soon after I completed the last exam. It was rather an emotional day saying goodbye to so many friends. I was also hoping to get to see Mr Wyles soon; it had been two weeks since our last tutorial and I was missing him.

I was almost 19 now, my birthday coming up soon in a few weeks, and I did not have to tell mum where I was staying if I stayed out. She had told me this. Just stay safe and let me know you are ok in the morning. I was planning on staying at Lucy's. Maybe we could kiss. I had mentioned it to her, and she was kind of up for it.

But then she surprised me with a holiday treat for my birthday… 2 weeks in Greece! I wanted to cry… I had not seen Mr Wyles in a month and now I was going away for 2 more weeks when I could stay over if I wanted, and I knew Lucy would cover for me.

I called Mr Wyles, but he told me not to worry, he will be here, and the extra two weeks will not hurt. It will give him time to get something special for our big graduation day. He would not tell me what he had in mind. I knew this was to be the day he took me as his submissive if I still wanted (I did, and I told him so). But he insisted that I spend the next two weeks having fun and think about what he has said about becoming his submissive.
How can anything be fun without Sir?

He loved me! I knew and wanted me to say yes; I was sure, but he wanted me to be certain I wanted this. He was much older than me. His position at the school meant that we had to keep

this undercover for a few years. I did not care; I could wear the masques and nothing else no one would know. It was me, not even mum, well maybe mum would, but no one else would know.

I promised him I would have fun while away; he told me what happens while away stays there; I owe him no explanations for having fun.

"Love you, Rebecca," he said as he ended the call.

I just sat in the park with a silly smile on my face.
He said he loved me…………… Oh wow.
Swoons.

I had a bit of an audience, and I was in such a good mood that I decided to treat them. Looking around to make sure no mums were watching; I slipped my panties off. The four older men that were watching seemed to appreciate this. I lifted my skirt a little and spread my legs as I had for Mr Wyles; I showed them my special place, my flower. I slipped my finger in and then lifted it to my lips, sucked on it a little, teasing. I don't think they could believe their eyes. When I left, I left my panties there.
I am a cock tease, mum's right. Giggles.

The men did not follow me, they never did, but I wonder which one of them would be the lucky one and get to take my panties home with them. I hope they liked the scent of my flower. Mr Wyles is right. I am an exhibitionist and mum is right. I am a cock tease. But not Sir, I will never tease Sir. I am going to be the best submissive he ever had…

End.
TBC in Rebecca's Submission.

If you enjoyed this read, please see my other stories, and please leave a review (thanks).

Printed in Great Britain
by Amazon